2/9/02

Red
Whiskey
Blues

For Tamara,

" And all will be well
and all will be well."
St. Julian of Norwich

With my abiding
affection,

Denise

Also by Denise Gess
Good Deeds

Red
Whiskey
Blues

Denise Gess

CROWN PUBLISHERS, INC.
NEW YORK

Excerpts from "The Lady with the Dog" by Anton Chekhov. Translated from the Russian by Constance Garnett. Copyright 1917 by Macmillan Publishing Company, copyright renewed 1945 by Constance Garnett. Used by permission of Macmillan Publishing Company.

Excerpts from "The Five Stages of Grief" from *The Five Stages of Grief* by Linda Pastan, copyright © 1978 by Linda Pastan. Used by permission of W.W. Norton & Company, Inc.

Published by Crown Publishers, Inc., 225 Park Avenue South, New York, New York 10003

CROWN is a trademark of Crown Publishers, Inc.

Manufactured in the United States of America

Library of Congress Cataloging-in-Publication Data

Gess, Denise.
   Red whiskey blues : a novel / by Denise Gess.
      p.   cm.
   I. Title.
PS3557.E82R4   1989
813'.54—dc19   88-30158
                                                                       CIP

ISBN 0-517-55990-0

10   9   8   7   6   5   4   3   2   1

First Edition

For Michael O'Dwyer,
1959–1987,
With much love always

The night I lost you
someone pointed me towards
the Five Stages of Grief.
Go that way, they said,
it's easy, like learning to climb
stairs after the amputation.

Linda Pastan
"The Five Stages of Grief"

PART ONE

ONE

Emily recognized the woman's brocade purse before she recognized her face. She knew this wasn't much of an accomplishment; the owner of the purse was her mother, Francine. They had decided long ago without ceremony or handshakes that they could only stand to be in each other's company not more than twice a year. So, quite by accident or quite on purpose, their visits with each other had become notoriously seasonal—just before the start of summer and at Christmas—leaving spring and fall to those other kinds of mothers and daughters.

Francine's purse was a black envelope bag with blue, reddish orange, and gold threads woven through it. She was wearing a white silk suit with creamy colored hose, pumps with heels too high and narrow for early afternoon, and a cotton paisley scarf at her throat that was too casual for the suit. Her sandy brown hair was drawn back from her face and wound in a full knot at the back of her head, and as she strode through the restaurant where Emily had been waiting for twenty minutes, Emily was struck by how right her mother looked despite her battling pieces of clothing. It was one of Francine's peculiar talents: to make clothes behave on her body.

When she was just a breath away from Emily, Emily leaned forward to give or receive a kiss, but Francine slipped into the chair opposite her. "You're wearing black, Em'ly." Francine reached for the mauve napkin, flicked it open, and was busy laying it across her lap. "This is not the Middle Ages. I don't think you're required to wear black. Have you been wearing black every day?"

As a matter of fact she had been.

"Only for formal occasions like this."

Francine shook her head. "This is not a good thing. Not good at all."

"Well, Mother, no one taught me how to be a widow. I wasn't expecting it for about thirty more years."

"And why should anyone want to learn? I'll tell you one thing— not that you'll listen—color has absolutely nothing to do with it."

"You almost sound as if you know what you're talking about, Mother."

"And don't I?"

Emily expected this fleeting reference to her father. The night he left her and Francine it was snowing. There had not been a snowfall as memorable, as deep and powdery, in south Jersey in over ten years. It was the stuff of five-foot drifts. They lived then in a place called Haddonfield, a town with its nose in the air and its heart just slightly askew. Emily's father had never let on that he was planning such a disappearing act. For instance, he never said any of the usual things she associated with impending departure such as, "If things don't change around here, I'm going to beat it," or, "I hate this place." He didn't even offer something as clichéd as, "I'm going out for cigarettes, ladies, it may take a while. Don't wait up." What he did manage to do was to pen a brief note that he left on the dining room table. It read, in his exquisite hand: "Dear Francine and Emily, I can't. Forgive me. Love, Tom/Daddy." It was the slash between his name and Daddy that had offended Emily the most. Which one of them could have mistaken him for any other Tom or Daddy? But she knew her father was one who could leave no stone unturned, let no dog lie. He'd wake a sleeping Doberman.

"Well," Emily said, finally, "Daddy may still be alive for all we know. It's been eighteen years."

4/

Francine hated to be outsmarted. She shot right back, "You don't know how many times I've wanted to hear that your father is dead. There's nothing worse in this world than not knowing for sure."

"You don't mean that."

"Oh, but, Em'ly, I do."

Because she was craning her neck, looking for their waitress while she spoke, it was difficult for Emily to judge the sincerity of her mother's last remark. You had to catch her eyes straight on to be sure she wasn't being flip for flippancy's sake. Before Emily could say anything, however, Francine succeeded in flagging down the waitress, who wanted to know if they'd like to begin with cocktails.

"I'll have a Perrier with a twist of lime, please," Francine said. Then she patted her misshapen purse. "I only carry it with me for old times' sake," she whispered to Emily. During the old times all she ever carried in the purse was a handkerchief and a miniature bottle of Johnnie Walker Red—the size airlines served—just in case any trip away from home was too much to bear unintoxicated. And even now that she was the founder and leader of SPSC, Support for Parents of Special Children, a counseling center for parents of the severely retarded and disabled, she clung to that brocade relic of her past.

Emily ordered coffee, black. "Might as well be consistent," she told her mother, and she pointed to her black linen shirt. And safe, she thought. One of the benefits of having grown up with an alcoholic parent was that she'd learned to steer clear of liquor anytime she was feeling badly. Emily's best friend, Barbara, told her she was a statistical oddity. "According to psychological findings," Barbara had said, "you're destined for addiction."

"Maybe I'll be addicted to something else," Emily said.

As the waitress left their table, Francine smiled. Emily knew the smile well and had always thought of it as her mother's disingenuous smile. She'd learned to read it ages ago. It was the smile that said: Tell me what I want to hear, Em'ly. What she wanted to hear amounted to three things, Emily knew. First, she wanted Emily to tell her that she was working on a new Flora Flamingo book, which would be the ninth in a series of children's books about a blue flamingo. Second, she wanted Emily to tell her that she was, at last, moving to New York where she believed all writers of children's books should live. And last, she wanted Emily to tell her that she was happy or at least all right. Emily told the truth.

"I'm renting out the second-floor apartment of the house this summer."

The house had been passed from Francine's mother, Nana Irene, on to Francine and Tom Perone, and finally to Emily and her husband, Peter. Built in the early 1900s when Ocean Gate was still just a seven-mile stretch of beach and marsh, it had been the original lifeguard station, storage for rescue boats, intended as shelter for the coast guard, whose focal point was the ocean and external distress. In a burst of eccentricity uncommon to them, Emily's grandparents had bought it before it could be demolished, but it had always resisted Nana's, Francine's, and Emily's taming of it. Despite intricate landscaping, the planting of marigolds and shrubs, the building of a front, wraparound porch and a screen-enclosed side porch, it was the lookout tower (a twelve-by-eight-foot construction of wood and glass rising from the right side of the red tile rooftop) that drew the eyes and heart away from the domestic bowels of the first two floors to the uncertain world above and beyond. It was a house that expanded and contracted with the periods of contentment and sadness of three generations. It could never be an ordinary place. A standout on the block and in the town, as a family they felt obliged to live up to its reputation. Now, with Peter dead, Emily only felt obliged to stay sane.

Francine put her hand over her heart, one of her many dramatic gestures. "Are you up to this?"

"I could use the money." It was a lie. Peter's pension more than covered her and Lizzie's expenses, and she had money from the Flora books because to everyone's surprise they had sold well.

"I could give you money."

"You could give me company too, but you won't."

Emily heard the petulance in her own voice, but Francine was staring at her with that self-satisfied look of the reformed. Alcoholics, recovered ones, Emily had learned, could be as righteous as any converts. Having found sobriety or religion, they could be doubly hard on anyone who showed the slightest sign of weakness.

"You don't need my company, Em'ly. You've got your friends."

"*Had* my friends, you mean. Past tense."

Francine was perusing the menu and she looked up, surprised.

"I told you," Emily said. "Barbara and Fred have left. Company transfer to Bangor, Maine. I told you all of this on the phone when you called to make this date."

"You're angry that I'm going to the mountains for a month? I don't deserve a vacation?"

Emily shook her head, bit back the words. She was angry that her mother saw her desire to have her stay at the house, even for a season, as a weakness. Francine, Emily, and Emily's own daughter, Lizzie, were all that remained of the Perone/Hansen families. As only children of only children, Emily and Peter had often joked that their family relationships were sorely limited; there weren't enough of them to make even a fifteen-minute situation comedy and/or drama—no eccentric aunts, no rebellious cousins, no cantankerous uncles to contend with. After Peter's parents passed away in the mid-seventies all they were left with was Francine, whom Peter referred to as "the invisible mother-in-law."

"I'm not coming there," Francine said suddenly. "And if you're upset about Barbara's leaving it's partly your own fault. You get yourself all attached to one person, and then when the person is gone you're miserable. Been doing it since you were a child. You need to learn to embrace the world a little more," she said, closing her menu. "I'm not changing my plans."

"No one asked you to. I'm renting. It's rented."

At that moment the waitress returned with the coffee and Perrier. As she placed the glass down before Francine, Emily thought her mother seemed amazed that she could be sitting in a restaurant drinking something benign. Francine lifted the glass and held it up ceremoniously. Exhibit A. "It took a long time to come to this."

"I know."

She sipped some and then put the glass down. "Well, my point is made."

The waitress was on standby, smiling politely during this display. "We'll order," Emily said. They both ordered the spinach salad, and after the waitress left the table, both wished they'd ordered the tempura sampler.

"A college student as usual?" Francine asked.

"Who?"

"The boarder."

Emily looked away from her. "No, Gene Lisicky. Remember he stayed with his wife and little boy, Christopher, about, uh, I think it was three summers ago? The playwright. With Barbara gone and you so determined not to spend time with me or your granddaughter, I figured why not? They seemed nice enough."

"I'm not coming to stay with you."

Emily was sure then that her mother believed she had invented this tale of the playwright boarder in a last-ditch attempt to change her life and beg her back to the house she'd not been in since the day of Peter's funeral, and before that day, only on the occasion of Lizzie's christening and a few scattered Christmases here and there. Even the day of the funeral, when she was supposed to be a comfort, she had walked through the house clicking her tongue and letting out little moans. "This place is filled with ghosts, filled with them," she'd said as she helped Emily dress in the black wool suit.

The house rattled Francine to the core. And while this season Emily wanted her mother to be occupying that upstairs apartment, as she studied her that afternoon across the table, she believed that Francine was just as much, if not more, a stranger than Gene.

Emily sipped her coffee, fussed with her napkin, looked around the room trying to avoid the dead-ahead gaze into her mother's eyes, a gaze that would have been filled with more expectations than her mother could fulfill.

"My birthday is in two days," Francine said. It was June 2, 1982, and Emily thought her mother seemed very comfortable with the fact that she would be sixty years old.

"Would you like your gift?"

Francine extended her hands. "Useless and pretty, I hope."

Emily had hidden the box under her chair and she reached down for it, brought it up quickly, and handed her mother the peach-ribboned, silver-papered box. Francine took it from her enthusiastically; she shook the package. "It doesn't jingle," she said, "and it's too odd sized a box to be a blouse." She made a production of opening the gift, careful not to tear the paper or twist the ribbon. When she finally lifted the lid, she just as slowly folded back the leaves of tissue, and when she saw it, her face was empty of all expression. "It's truly lovely, Em'ly," she said, pulling the brocade purse from the box.

"It's vintage thirties. I know it's all wrong—the minute I saw you walk in with the purse. I can return it."

Francine ran her hand over the purse. She played with the silver latch, opening and closing the purse several times before she said, "I think in a while I will love this."

"I'll return it."

"No. You will not. I will love this in a while, Em'ly," she said, touching the purse uncertainly.

There was a time Francine would not have been so tentative, when she would have known exactly what she loved and wanted. When she was very young, for instance, what she wanted more than anything was to grow up and marry a musician (preferably a black musician), definitely a saxophone player because she believed the saxophone was just about the most blatantly sensual instrument in the universe. Even better would have been marrying a fat, black sax player who perspired with great abandon and laughed, a little on the evil side, from deep down in his belly.

She was to have no such luck.

Francine Riley met Tom Perone at the Bueler Athletic Arena in the winter of 1941. It was a blustery December night, and she and her friends were amusing themselves on the ice when a young man in a second-rate sweater (by their definition, not cashmere) glided toward her. "He moved only from the hips," she told Emily. "Something young ladies were not supposed to notice. He was like Fred Astaire on blades."

When he asked her to skate the pairs number, she pretended not to hear him at first. She averted her eyes and tilted her chin, but Tom Perone was not easily daunted. He asked her again, but this time he also took her hand in his solidly, and before she could protest, he had her in a tight hold against his hard hip. They skated to the then recently released rendition of Harry James's "You Made Me Love You." As the trumpet blared and reverberated, he held her, cocksure and silent. Midway through the number he lied to her and told her he was descended from a long line of Milanese figure skaters, and Francine smiled in spite of herself. When the pairs number was over and the singles flocked back to the ice, he asked her if she wanted to join him for a cup of hot chocolate. They sat in the bleachers together, warming their hands on their heavy paper cups, and it was then that she confessed her girlhood dream to marry a musician. "I thought it would discourage him," Francine had told Emily, "especially the interracial part." Instead Tom Perone told another lie and explained that he had played in various hard-to-pin-down New York clubs.

It wasn't a complete invention. Tom Perone played the clarinet, and while no club in New York, Chicago, or any other major city would have hired him, he persisted in his love for the instrument until the time he left Francine and Emily.

Hearing that he was a musician of sorts led Francine to tell him the Katharine Hepburn story that finally became part of the Perone family folklore. According to Francine, Katharine Hepburn had visited the Bryn Mawr campus when Francine was still a senior there. As Miss Hepburn approached the podium to give her talk to the girls of Bryn Mawr, she dropped her scarf, and Francine, sitting in the front row of the auditorium, retrieved it for her. Emily and her father had always believed this part of the story, but it was the other part, in which Miss Hepburn supposedly said, "Oh, am I looking into a mirror?" that they had grave doubts about. Still, the first time Tom Perone heard the story he was charmed by Francine's immodesty. And once he even told Emily, "You know, she really does look like Katharine Hepburn, but don't let on I ever told you."

Emily was the vessel of their secrets, big and small. If it had been up to her, she would have ended their story there with herself as the nonjudgmental child still, there before the heroine's fall from grace, there before the hero's flight. The final shot would have looked like a photograph taken of them at the ice rink in the winter of '49: Francine, in a long wool skirt and sweater, fur earmuffs, and fur-trimmed gloves, standing at the edge of the rink with Emily in a snowsuit in her arms; Tom, in baggy pants and a first-rate sweater—at last cashmere—standing on the ice itself, his arm around them.

Emily was picking at her salad while Francine ate her own heartily, pausing now and then to look at her purse, which she kept on the edge of the table.

"You're not eating, Em'ly."

"I haven't been very hungry lately."

Suddenly Francine put her fork down, reached over, and picked up Emily's fork, then stabbed into Emily's salad with it. "Eat, you'll feel better."

"That's easy."

"It's all mothers are good for. Eat, you'll feel better; sleep, you'll feel better; take some castor oil, you'll feel better. I wish there were more."

Francine was straining forward in her seat, her forearms pressed against the table, her hands open and full of questions.

"What? Too many bacon bits?"

Emily laughed.

"See?" Francine said. "Smiling helps, doesn't it?"

"No, Mother, it doesn't—but it doesn't hurt either."

★　　★　　★

When they finished with lunch they decided to sidestep dessert, opted for one last cup of coffee, and seemed by that time, sipping quietly, to have come to that always awkward moment when they knew they'd be parting again.

"I think I'm going to die," Emily blurted.

Francine raised one eyebrow and returned her cup to its saucer; she did not seem to Emily to be the least bit shocked by the announcement.

"You, Em'ly, are not going to die. And I'm going to the ladies' room. I'll be less than ten minutes."

While Francine dashed off, Emily paid the bill and then waited for her mother in the glass foyer under the hanging ferns. In nine minutes exactly, Emily saw Francine weaving her way through the obstacle course of lacquered chairs and tables, and Emily noticed how everyone's eyes followed her mother's stately walk before she noticed that her mother was carrying the new purse under her arm and the gift box in her free hand.

"Let's go," Francine said.

Outside under the glare of the hot sun she handed Emily the box. "Take it with you," she urged, as if the old purse were a talisman.

Emily took the box from her and lowered her eyes. "It's so hard, Mother."

"I'm sure that it is."

Emily looked up at her then, into that face she'd always thought of as hard and beautiful. "Don't you have any sympathy at all?"

Francine reached for Emily's shoulders, held her just slightly longer than usual, then pulled away.

"Em'ly, I have so much sympathy I could drown us in it."

"Then help me."

"My baby," she said, "I am."

12 /

TWO

Ocean Gate was a small town; rumors flew quicker than sparrows. Everyone had known the story of Peter's illness, and when the students at Ocean Gate High School, where he'd been the assistant principal, had grown bored with their ailing leader, they embellished, adding a few gory details of their own. There was the rumor, once the radiation treatments had made Peter too sick to go to school, that his hair had fallen out, that Mr. Hansen was a bald recluse in a wheelchair and that at night people could see his head from the tower of the house. And there was the rumor that the disease had made him fat and bluish, rendering him a plump recluse, visible once again from the windows of the tower. Emily was astonished that there'd been no rumor of the bald, fat, blue Mr. Hansen driving off into the night to meet Margot Compton, the woman he had had an affair with. She finally sent him back to Emily, for good but not for long.

The night of Peter's funeral, after everyone had gone home, Emily went into her bedroom and drew back the closet doors. She counted Peter's shoes lined up on the floor, fingered each of his ties, tugged at the inanimate shirtsleeves that hung according to color and design: whites, beiges, grays, blues, stripes, plaids, denims, flannels. She wandered from there to the kitchen, where she opened the cabinets and stared at the boxes of crackers lined up on the

/13

shelf. Wheat Thins and Ritz for Peter; graham crackers and melba toast for her and Lizzie. On the lower shelf was Peter's carton of cigarettes, half empty. He'd begun smoking almost as soon as he found out he had Hodgkin's, as if he were intent on sabotaging any slim chance of recovery.

Emily took a pack from the carton, unwrapped the cellophane on the stubby red box, and pulled out one cigarette. She took it and a pack of matches out to the yard where she stood in the dark, wearing only her bathrobe, learning how to smoke. It was well past midnight, bitterly cold, a moonless, starless night in Ocean Gate.

When she was finished smoking she felt light-headed, but she tossed the cigarette to the ground, bent down, and grabbed for a small rock at the edge of the walk. With the rock, she beat out the smoldering embers, thinking that this addiction of his, begun in a fit of recklessness or resignation—she could never decide which—was just another part of him she would never know.

She waited there in that crouched position for several minutes before she stood up, put the crushed butt in her pocket, and walked back into the house. About two months after his death Emily got wind of the rumor that the Widow Hansen smoked marijuana in public at night on her lawn.

A week after Gene moved in upstairs, Emily had not yet heard any rumors, but she was certain that they were simmering and percolating in the watchful minds and eyes of the neighbors because he arrived without Carlotta and Christopher in tow. His only belongings now were an old duffel bag, a typewriter, and a record player, and before settling in upstairs he said he wanted to settle the matter of rent. "Might as well have things squared away," he said as he leaned against her kitchen counter and withdrew three months' rent in crisp bills from his back pocket, then laid them out. "Are there any new rules?"

"You remember the old ones?"

He smiled for the first time since his arrival. "No wild parties, no drugs, no banging around in the middle of the night, no water balloons thrown from the second floor, and so forth."

14 /

"Well, I see success hasn't distorted your memory."

"No."

"Just keep the noise down at night—because of Lizzie."

He turned to face her, folding his arms across his chest.

"Without my wife—estranged wife—and Christopher, there'll be no noise."

"I'm sorry. She seemed very nice."

"She is very nice," he said, raking his fingers through his thick dark hair, which, Emily noticed, had turned considerably grayer. "A distortion of success."

Emily turned away and took his set of keys off the hook on the kitchen bulletin board. She dropped them into his waiting palm. "Is Christopher with her?"

Gene snatched the keys in his fist. "Yep. I've been working on something new for nearly a year now. I thought if I got away, somewhere familiar but not too familiar, I might finally get the damn thing off the ground." Suddenly, he tossed the keys in the air, caught them again in his fist. "How about you? What's your blue bird up to now?"

Emily pressed out a smile. "When she lets me know, I'll let you know."

He reached over and picked up his bag. "Enough said. Well, let me get out of your way here. I'll see you around."

Emily walked ahead of him and opened the back screen door. On his way out he turned around halfway. "Is there still a key to the tower on this ring?" She remembered then how much he and his wife had liked having access to the tower; she and Peter had joked about it after Gene left because they knew he and his wife had used the glass-enclosed room for midnight rendezvous. It was a perfect hideout for a couple with a young child, and their Christopher was six years old the last time he rented the apartment, the same age Lizzie was now.

"It's all yours," she said, holding the door wide, waiting for him to pass through.

At the end of Gene's first week at the beach, Emily found a note taped to the back screen door. Since the day she showed him to his apartment he had made himself scarce. She'd not heard any typewriter or record player in the middle of the night or during daytime working hours, and if not for his bathing suit and towels drying on the clothesline in the late afternoons, she would have thought him a figment of her fertile imagination. The message that he left for her proved him to be alive and thinking. Scrawled on the back of an envelope he'd written: "Is the bird Fanny or Flora?"

The Peter Joseph Hansen Memorial Tennis Courts were to be dedicated at 9:00 on a Monday morning, the twenty-eighth of June. Emily had fought the Board of Education and the school principal on this for months. They had begun bombarding her with their plans in late February and by April, out of sheer exhaustion, she'd given in. Their arguments, she thought, were far from flashy: he was the tennis coach; he was the assistant principal.

"There have been other assistant principals," she reminded Wayne Lithcomb, the principal.

"But they've left," he'd answered feebly.

"So has Peter."

They were talking by phone and Wayne Lithcomb cleared his throat and asked her to excuse him while he took another call. Emily didn't believe there was another call and when he returned to the line he said, "Mrs. Hansen, Emily, we regarded Peter very highly. Yes, there have been other tennis coaches, but he was the best. And yes, there have been other assistant principals, but he was the finest. And"—he cleared his throat again—"and he didn't leave, he died. We don't want to forget him. We want future students to know who he was."

Emily was sitting at the desk in her office. She'd deliberately chosen the dimmest room in the house for her writing space, a small room at the back of the house. Her logic was that the dark room would be a metaphor for the embryonic state of any Flora book; the story, once it began to take shape, would be the light. She was the first to admit that it was corny, but it was necessary. Outside her window that day, the birds were chirping wildly while buzz saws whined at the construction site of new beachfront condos a block away. She wanted to march over to Lithcomb's office and slam her fist on the desk. She wanted to shout, "I don't want this! I don't want to remember!" Instead she said, "Mr. Lithcomb, I'll have to get back to you. I can't talk about this."

"Mrs. Hansen—"

"If I don't give permission, can you people go ahead?"

"No."

"Then good-bye, Mr. Lithcomb."

That very same evening, Wayne Lithcomb appeared on her doorstep. In his hands he held a white bakery box, its sides taped down. Lithcomb was a portly man, a *hungry* portly man Emily assumed, one who could not discuss business without jelly doughnuts or crullers. She waved him in and he pushed the box into her hands.

"Would you like some tea or coffee?"

"Coffee," he said, "if that wouldn't be too much trouble."

He'd shown himself into the living room, but once there, Emily thought he seemed nervous, unsure of himself.

"I find it interesting," she said, "that you don't want me to go to the trouble of making coffee, yet you people insist on badgering me about tennis courts."

It was dark in the living room because she hadn't bothered to turn on any lights. She was only vaguely aware of the time of day, always lagging behind. She turned on lights now only when she caught herself squinting to see or if she bumped into a piece of furniture. Lithcomb was standing, wiping his forehead with a hanky he'd pulled from his pants pocket. "Is there an electrical problem?"

Emily pointed to the table lamp. "Just reach under the shade. Make yourself comfortable. I'll bring these to the kitchen."

She wasn't sure why she expected him to heel like an obedient dog when her feelings in a matter much more important were being disregarded. He followed her to where there was bright light and life (the dinner dishes were still on the counter), proof that func-

/17

tioning people still inhabited the rambling old house. While she started the coffee, he sat in a chair at the table.

"I hope you and Elizabeth—"

"Lizzie. We always call her Lizzie."

"I hope you and Lizzie like powdered doughnuts."

The bakery box was on the table and Lithcomb placed his chubby hands on it. Emily thought the gesture made him look as if he were praying over it. She dropped the coffeepot lid then, and both of them reached for it. Emily found herself staring eye to eye with him, and suddenly she was telling him to please go home.

"Emily, Emily," he said, "wouldn't he have been proud? Wouldn't Peter have felt honored?"

Emily looked away from him, from his well-meaning eyes. She didn't know Wayne Lithcomb very well so she knew she couldn't say, "You know, Wayne, you live with someone for thirteen years and what do you know? You know his habits, you know the movies he'll never agree to see, sometimes you can finish the person's sentences, but now there are days that I have so many questions I think I'll burst, and there's no way for me to get an answer. It's all guesswork." She couldn't say any of that to Wayne Lithcomb.

"Do it," she heard herself say instead. "He would have loved it."

Lithcomb grinned and said he'd changed his mind about the coffee, that it was a little too warm for coffee after all. He patted the box on the table. "Enjoy them, Emily. I'll be in touch."

She walked him to the front door, ushered him out into the spring night, and then returned to the kitchen where she sat down at the table. She opened the box. A dozen puffy, white doughnuts stared back at her. She reached in, pulled one out, and ate it, then she threw the rest in the trash.

On the twenty-eighth of June, Emily dressed Lizzie in white eyelet and she chose a black dress. They arrived at the high school at 8:45, the sheen of perspiration on their bare arms, and walked directly toward the new clay courts, which were located behind the high school to the left of the football field. The courts were protected by a high chain-link fence, and as they approached them, Wayne Lithcomb, the secretarial staff, about one hundred students, and all of the faculty were gathering in rows two and three deep along the perimeter outside of the fence. At the gate there was a large green ribbon that Emily would be asked to cut, and welded to the fence was the metal plaque that read: IN MEMORY OF PETER JOSEPH HANSEN, A LEADER IN EDUCATION AND SPORTS, with the dates of his birth and death inscribed below.

The crowd began to applaud, softly at first; then the applause grew more hearty as Emily and Lizzie, hand in hand, neared the podium Lithcomb had set up. The faces were a blur and at any minute Emily expected to hear the soundtrack from a made-for-television movie. She didn't know why they were clapping. Joy? Out of approval and encouragement for the young widow and her child? she wondered. In their lightweight seersucker and cotton duck, Emily thought they looked like a convention of summer faith healers.

"Mommy," Lizzie whispered, "I think they like us."

Emily looked down and Lizzie was smiling, baring all of her teeth, her dimple showing. Lithcomb rushed toward them, extending his hand. Emily offered him her hand and he shook her arm. He was perspiring profusely. "Emily, Lizzie, isn't it wonderful?"

Emily looked over at the crowd. "It's an impressive turnout." But it's nowhere near wonderful, she thought. Wonderful would have been Peter smashing a lob over the net.

"I told you he was highly regarded. Well, shall we begin?"

Lithcomb took the microphone first and gave a short speech, thanking everyone for taking time out of their busy days to attend. Then he followed his thanks with a eulogy befitting the king of some tame and perfect country. As he spoke, a sharp breeze kicked up, and Emily wished she could be carried away on it, lifted out of her black pumps and swooped up into the clouds. It was difficult for her to concentrate on the words because one eulogy for Peter had been more than enough.

Lithcomb was suddenly turning toward her and asking her to say a few words before she snipped the ribbon. Emily took her place at the microphone, and in a voice that seemed wholly unknown to her, she said, "My daughter and I are deeply touched by both the courts and the turnout here today. Peter would have counted this as one of the top moments in his life, I'm sure. Now whenever we pass the courts, and when Lizzie is old enough to attend Ocean Gate, she'll be able to point proudly to that plaque. Thank you, all of you."

The applause started up again, this time accompanied by cheers from the students. Emily held her breath, felt her heart banging against her chest, believing that Peter would have found all of this silly, believing that she'd done the wrong thing in giving Lithcomb the go-ahead. She'd betrayed her husband, she thought, who had detested a lot of fuss, shunned the giant celebration. In a flash she remembered him pacing in front of the television set, year after year, as the Macy's Thanksgiving Day Parade spilled out onto the screen. "I can't figure out what the big deal is," he used to say. "What do these Donald Duck balloons have to do with Thanksgiving?"

"It's American."

"Should be pilgrims."

Wayne Lithcomb handed the scissors to Emily and led her to the gate. She cut the ribbon quickly, smiled for the camera, and let Lizzie open the gate to the courts. The crowd kept clapping and Wayne Lithcomb said, "Now, aren't you glad I talked you into this?"

Following the dedication a reception was held on the new courts, but Emily drank little of the sugary punch and didn't even consider eating a cookie. Margot Compton, a guidance counselor at the school, was present, lingering on the sidelines, her long angular hands curled around a small glass of punch. She was talking to two other teachers and was too engrossed to look Emily's way, but Emily couldn't take her eyes off of Margot. Their physical similarities aside—both of them were tall, slender, dark haired—Emily wondered, as she had all too often in the past, what Peter had needed from that woman. When Margot tossed her head back and laughed, the sound lilted in the air. When she brushed the hair back from her face, the gesture was unfettered, natural. Although Emily hated to admit it, she thought Margot looked like someone who could slip into any situation easily, the kind of woman who could walk away from a car wreck claiming it was only a "little accident" while she delicately mopped the blood from her brow.

As if someone had tapped Margot's shoulder to let her know Emily was watching, Margot glanced in Emily's direction. The breeze kicked up again, blowing a strand of hair across Emily's face, but even as she pushed it aside, Emily continued to stare back until Margot, either in deference or embarrassment, turned away. Emily watched as Margot left her punch glass in the keeping of one of the other teachers and began making her way toward her.

Emily didn't wait. When Margot was about a yard away, Emily withdrew her sunglasses from the brocade purse, which she'd been carrying ever since Francine turned it over to her, and she eased the glasses on. "Lizzie!" she called out. "It's time to go."

They walked home slowly in the escalating heat, people whizzing by them on bicycles, passing them on foot on their way to the beach, while Emily kept her eyes fixed on the house at the corner, her house. As she and Lizzie neared it, Emily noticed that the yard was shabby and run amok; she knew it would have hurt Peter to see it that way. She had married a man who could landscape. Walls could have cracked, electrical wires might have blown, the roof could have caved in, but judging from the outside, no one would have known. Emily found it a small and unusual comfort to live with a man who knew the difference between ginkgos and weeping willows, who understood intuitively the exact second an azalea should be planted, someone who could smell the need for peat moss the minute he stepped into the yard. Peter had never been able to make a decent cup of coffee, but he could frighten crabgrass away in a blink.

"Come on, Liz, hurry!"

"What for?"

"We've got to mow the lawn," Emily said. "Look at the lawn." They were standing just on the other side of the street and Emily pointed straight ahead.

Lizzie complied quietly, her small feet running double time to keep up with Emily. Once they were in the yard, Emily headed for the garage, possessed by the spirit of landscaping. In the throes of such mindless momentum, she forgot that she was wearing a dress and heels. It was Lizzie who stopped dead in her tracks in the center of the yard and said, "Aren't we going to change?"

"I'm not. You go in and put on shorts and a shirt."

Lizzie didn't move, however, and when Emily's hand was on the garage door latch, she felt Lizzie's eyes on her. "What? What is it, Liz?"

"The back door is locked."

Emily took the keys out of her purse. "Come on, I'll open it for you."

Lizzie hurried to the back door. "Go on in," Emily said. "I'll be right here when you're changed." Lizzie scooted in past Emily, and Emily tossed the purse on the back step, then returned to the garage with renewed enthusiasm.

The door creaked when it opened; inside it was cool and dark, just a sliver of sunlight streaming in from the one slim window at the end of the garage. Emily slipped off her shoes and pulled the mower into the yard. With her hands on the handle, barefoot, and dressed in black, she surveyed the yard, wondering where to begin, deciding to start at the side of the house and work her way to the middle in long symmetrical rows, the way she'd seen Peter do it hundreds of times.

The lawn mower had a mind of its own. When she reached down to pull the cord, the machine sputtered, then went silent. She tried several more times, frantically, in the same way one guns a flooded car engine, but the mower sat stubborn and mute. Sweat was running down her face and formed a damp V on the bodice of her dress. Emily pushed the mower as if that would start it. She never heard Gene come into the yard.

"Need help?"

"I didn't hear you come out."

Because she saw him so infrequently, his appearance always caught her off guard. She found it difficult to reconcile the image of this aging but still darkly handsome man, alone, his patient eyes saddened, with the first image of him on that hot June afternoon three years before. The white compact had pulled up to the curb with a screech and he had bounded out of the driver's side, already deeply tanned, wearing a bright green knit polo shirt. His wife, a woman as tall as he was but more graceful, emerged slowly from the car with Christopher, a miniature version of Gene, following behind her. Emily had watched them from the living room window as they made their way up the front walk, and she had already opened the door just as Gene was about to knock. On the porch he'd slung his arm around the shoulders of the big, tawny woman whose eyes were so green Emily was certain she was wearing fashion contacts.

"Is the vacancy still vacant?" he'd asked, and Emily had wondered how he made the words come out so distinctly when it seemed he'd barely moved his lips.

"Yes," she said.

He'd smiled broadly. "Then we'd like to change that."

Now, standing in her yard, he seemed wary, picking at some nonexistent lint or string on his blue work shirt, avoiding her eyes. Then he gave her a bold once-over, head to toe, said nothing, and knelt down.

"Let me have a look at this."

Emily stepped back as he turned the mower on its side and examined the blade as if it were a rare artifact.

"Unless you're a magician, I don't think you're going to have much luck."

He mumbled, "We'll see."

"Of course, there was never a problem with it when Peter mowed the lawn." She had not mentioned Peter's death to Gene, partly because she'd had to tell so many people over the past six months that she'd stopped counting those who did and didn't know, and partly because with someone like Gene, to whom she and Peter had no real connection, she believed she would have to adopt a sort of fecklessness in announcing it; the news always made people so uncomfortable. Gene hadn't asked, so she decided to let him think what he would.

"You just didn't have to think about it."

"That's right. And I prefer not to think about it now."

The underside of the mower was greasy and loaded with clumps of grass and moss left over from Peter's last gardening days. When Gene tried to spin the blade it barely budged, so he began pulling out the clumps of grass, turning the blade as he pulled until at last the paralytic blade was rotating smoothly in his hands. He looked up at Emily, shielding his eyes from the strong sun with his hand.

"Let's try it now."

He turned it upright, stood up, leaned over, and pulled the cord. Once again the mower made no reply. Gene then took a loose cigarette from his shirt pocket and lit up, studying the mower while he inhaled. With the cigarette between the fingers of his left hand, he reached for the cord with his right and yanked it. The machine roared and while the noise continued between them he shouted, "I can do it for you."

She waved her hands at him. "I can handle it now."

He dragged on the cigarette and pointed at her feet. "Not like that, I hope. You're going to lose a few toes."

Emily looked down at her bare feet; she felt soggy and disheveled. At that moment, Lizzie came out the front door and into the yard.

"I wouldn't mind," Gene yelled.

"I'll pay you then," Emily yelled back.

He scowled at her, threw the cigarette on the ground, and crushed it under his sneaker. "Don't insult me!" he hollered. "Don't be ridiculous!"

"Why are you shouting?" Lizzie screamed, running toward them.

Emily then motioned for him to go ahead. He nodded, the shadow of a scowl still on his face, and took control of the mower, turning his back to her, pushing the mower toward the fence.

"All right, all right, now glide. Gliiide. You are a gazelle, aren't you? Right? A gazelle?"

Her father's blades barely touched the ice, and Emily was too young to know what a gazelle was. To her the word sounded like *angel,* so she thrust her arms out as wide as she could stretch them in the bulky snowsuit while her father floated figure eights around her. "Your feet. Move them," came his voice in breaths as blue and icy as the rink beneath him.

Emily moved one foot on the double-blade skates and promptly fell on her rear. Tom Perone dive-bombed toward her in the camel position, sweeping her off the ice, righting her, and laughing. "I suppose you're still my stuffed parakeet, huh?" He circled her, his legs apart and stiff, his gray pants flapping against his hard calves, his feet splayed in opposite directions in a strong spread eagle. He leaned in and made patterns around Emily, and he flew away from her, his hands clasped behind his back. She was content, in a snowsuit and extra scarves, just to watch him.

At adult time on the rink, Tom led Emily to the first row of bleachers where she could see him. His legs moved in the pumping crossover. Right over left, right over left, cutting the ice, sending up flashes of white in his wake before he dragged his right leg wide and pulled it in quickly for the spin. He began the spin upright, the colors of his clothes colliding, then he moved to the sit, still spinning, and up again. He was more beautiful to her than the dancer in her jewelry box as he disappeared into the loudspeaker rendition of "Sheherazade." With every jump and turn and whirl, he dissolved into the music.

THREE

A few days after the tennis court dedication, Emily was distracted by what she saw outside her kitchen window. It was close to dinnertime and the heavy air had become slightly less so; with the shift in tide came a shift in the salty breezes. The sky, what she could see from the window, was like a primitive, two-dimensional oil—dashes of orange, pale and brilliant yellows, shades of purple, all melting together against blue and white. Everything settled. The traffic out on Atlantic Avenue was intermittent; fewer people walked the streets so it was easy to hear the rubber ripple of a bicycle tire or the grating whir of a skateboard on a driveway. It was the cooldown time of day, pretwilight, orchestrated to the thwacking of screen doors opening and closing, the din of distant voices, the sudden rush of an outdoor spigot being turned on, the flapping of wet clothes on the clotheslines in a row down the block. It was the most rhythmic part of any summer shore day, as expected as a heartbeat.

That evening she had forced herself to stay in and cook a sensible dinner instead of dragging Lizzie out to the Shore Mall where they'd stop at a fast-food place for hot dogs and french fries just so she could avoid being home where she would never hear the sound of Peter coming in from work again. As she stood at the sink, shaving carrots for a salad, she noticed Gene in the backyard. He was hanging his bathing suit and towels on the line next to hers and Lizzie's, and Lizzie had wandered out into the yard to talk to him.

Wearing a white playsuit, her hair still wet from her shower, Lizzie stood before him while he fastened his towel to the line. She was talking and gesturing, one foot jutted out in front of her. Because his back was to the window, Emily had no way of knowing whether or not he was being bothered by Lizzie, but as soon as he secured his towel to the line, he reached for Lizzie's hand and encouraged her to sit down. He sat down himself first and patted the grass beside him, then Lizzie collapsed to the ground, sitting Indian-style.

While watching them, both of them picking at the grass as they spoke, Emily dropped the carrot in the sink, and as she grabbed for it, it slipped out of her hand and down the garbage disposal. They leaned in toward each other, their heads bobbing.

From her position at the window, Emily could only hear the mumbling of voices, so she walked to the screen door, which was more in line with where they were sitting. Although she couldn't hear every word, she heard "Alaska" and "Hospitality Story." She moved close to the screen. Gene was telling her he knew a story she might like, that he used to tell it to his son, Chris. "You met Chris once. Do you remember him? We stayed here three summers ago when you were just three." Lizzie shook her head no and Gene smiled. "Well, he always liked this Alaskan story."

"Was it cold?" Lizzie asked, faking a shiver.

"Not cold."

"Hot then?"

"No, no," Gene said, shaking his head. "You've held an ice cube, right?"

Lizzie nodded. She shifted sideways and Emily could see her rolling her eyes. "Oh, an ice cube is very cold," she told him seriously.

"An ice cube is freezing," Gene said. "Right?"

"It's too cold to hold," Lizzie said.

"Well, that's what the weather is like in Alaska—too cold to hold, all the time."

"All year?"

"Forever," Gene said. "So, do you want to know what the people do to take their minds off the cold?"

Lizzie's eyes were saucer large; she nodded yes.

"They tell each other stories," he was saying.

"The hosipitality one?"

Gene threw his head back and laughed at her mispronunciation. "You're a good listener for such a pint-sized girl."

"Tell it now," she demanded.

Gene took a deep breath, as if he were preparing, Emily thought, to blow the story out like a wind god. "All right, I'll tell it," he said. "But first you should know that the Alaskan Indians have a name I bet you've never heard of. They're called Eskimos."

Lizzie reached up and pushed her index finger on the end of his nose. "They rub noses," she said. "We learned it at school."

"Well, there were two very special Eskimos whose names were Cara, that's the girl, and Carl, that's the boy. According to the old story, Cara and her husband, Rorck, invited Carl to visit them in their igloo."

"What's that?"

Gene tapped Lizzie's wrist. "That's an Eskimo house. It's made of ice."

Lizzie hugged herself. "Too cold to hold."

"Exactly."

"What happened?"

It was Emily's favorite question, and she imagined it must have been Gene's favorite question as well. The storyteller had every opportunity to change the sequence of events, to follow the telling of the tale as it had been told before or reinvent it as he or she wished. A rapt and curious listener like Lizzie posed the greatest challenge to the storyteller's seductive powers. Emily often thought her daughter was even sharper than her editor, Jill.

"When Carl came to visit," Gene began, "the three of them sat around a very wild and colorful fire, so strong it could have burned for days, and they shared a large dinner of whale meat— "

"Blah."

"You mean your mother doesn't cook whale meat for you?"

Lizzie covered her face and giggled. "That's stupid. No." Then in a more meaningful tone she added, "Mommy doesn't cook."

Emily suppressed a groan, not wanting to disturb them; she hoped he didn't believe Lizzie even though, except for that night, what Lizzie had confessed to him was true.

"Okay," he said, "but these people ate whale meat and they drank wine, but they called it mead in those days. All through this delicious dinner, even though Carl and Cara had not spoken one word directly to each other, they were falling in love, just like that, just like the Prince knows the very second he sees Cinderella walk into the palace."

"Mommy tells me that story," Lizzie said, "and 'Sleeping Beauty' too."

Gene eased back on his elbows and stretched out his legs, crossing them at the ankles. Lizzie imitated his every move.

"Rorck knew then, even though no one said a word, that Cara and Carl were in love."

"Was he mad?"

"What do you think?"

She answered without hesitation. "Yes."

"Not at Cara," Gene said, "but he was mad at Carl. He was angry that his guest was even thinking of taking something or someone that wasn't his. So, when Carl left and went back out to the tundra where it's all ice and snow for miles and miles, Rorck followed after him and—he killed him. But that wasn't the worst of it."

"It wasn't?"

Gene shook his head. Emily's palms were sweating now. What was worse than killing the poor guy? she wondered. Although she'd not seen any of his plays, she'd read the reviews, particularly of the last play, *Thetis Island*, set in Alaska, which the critics called an "earthy, violent drama."

"After he killed Carl, Rorck gathered his huskies, his sled dogs, together and sent them out after the body. When they came to the spot where Carl lay, Rorck commanded the dogs to tear off—"

At that second Emily pushed the screen door open with such force it slammed against the back of the house. Lizzie flinched and Gene looked as if someone had just hit him in the chest with a hardball.

"Lizzie, go inside right now."

"But Mom, I—"

Emily pointed to the door. "Don't argue with me. Now, go now."

Lizzie stood there digging her sandaled foot in the dirt. In the meantime, Gene stood up and was dusting off the seat of his shorts. Emily stared hard at Lizzie until she ran past and on into the house.

"I'm sorry," Gene said, although it was clear to Emily he had no idea what he was apologizing for. Emily could feel the heat rising in her throat as she walked over to him.

"For crying out loud, Gene. What kind of story is that to tell to a little girl?"

He stared at her, not looking quite as upset as she thought he should have. He wasn't smiling, but his head was cocked so arrogantly, it made her want to slap him.

"That child has been through enough."

Gene seemed confused, but more than that he seemed angry, and when Emily couldn't look at him anymore she turned away. "Her father just died. A story like that . . ."

"I didn't know," Emily heard him say. "When I didn't see him around I assumed you two were divorced."

Emily turned back to look at him.

"I guess there was no real reason for you to know. I stopped announcing it months ago, and people don't know everything about their landlords. It's one house, separate lives—"

He put his hand up then, stopping her onslaught of words. "I get your point. Forgive me. I'm very sorry, for both of you."

The edge of pity in his voice angered Emily all over again. "I'm trying to make this time as easy as possible for her."

"Please," he said, with such emphasis that Emily realized she was embarrassing him.

There was a long pause between them as they each tried to get gracefully out of the ungraceful moment. Finally Gene said, "I'd better go in too," and he strode past her, his arm just brushing hers, and on up the back staircase.

Emily knew she had offended Lizzie in the worst way by coming to her rescue when there'd been no need. Lizzie was proud and stubborn, and she was also unwilling to accept Emily's apology at dinner. She sat at the table mashing her peas with the prongs of her fork, staring woefully at the mound of whipped potatoes, which must have grown unappealingly cold.

"Liz, aren't you ever going to speak to me again?"

Lizzie blinked her dark eyes and said nothing.

"Listen, I know you're lonely and I know it's hard not having your friends around this summer, but it's not easy for me either. I didn't think the ending of the story was something that you should hear."

Still Lizzie said nothing, but at least she looked up at Emily. After a minute or so her lips parted and she said, "Why don't you like him?"

"I like him."

"No you don't. You yelled at him the other day and you yelled at him today. I like him."

"He likes you too, I think."

"Then why were you mad?"

"I was mad because the story was—well, it seemed scary and I thought it would give you nightmares."

" 'Sleeping Beauty' gives me nightmares and so does 'Snow

White.' Even the Flora book where she gets lost in the forest gives me nightmares."

Emily was flabbergasted. It was the first she'd heard of her own work giving Lizzie nightmares.

"Well, then, isn't it good that Mommy stopped writing? Just think, I won't be giving kids nightmares."

Lizzie pushed the food around on her plate, then dropped the fork onto it. "He's a fun man, Mom."

"He's also a tenant here, and you really shouldn't bother him."

"May I be excused?"

Emily looked at the plate: a pile of untouched potatoes, a half-eaten pork chop, mushy peas. "Yes, Lizzie."

When she got up from her place, she surprised Emily with a kiss on the cheek.

"Does this mean we're friends again?"

But Lizzie shrugged. "I'm going out on the porch, Mom, okay?"

"Okay."

After Lizzie was asleep, Emily washed two loads of clothes to keep busy. Then she decided to scrub the kitchen floor, which was already clean; she'd scrubbed it just two days before. By the time she was finished it was eleven thirty and still she wasn't tired, so she drifted off to the family room where she flipped through all the television channels and settled on the cable news show. She was appalled at the list of local crimes, delivered, she thought, with an air of barely suppressed glee by the local anchorperson, Bill Hanks. Hanks seemed to take particular pleasure in telling the story of the woman who was admitted to Shore Memorial Hospital after her husband cut up her pet iguana and forced her to eat it uncooked. "How's that for strange, folks?" Hanks asked. Then there was the story of the woman who had strangled to death that afternoon while washing her second-floor window. The woman's family, a husband and a college-age son, were off at the casinos in Atlantic City when the tragedy occurred. Apparently, no one else on the block had heard the woman gasping for help when the window crashed down on her neck.

Disgusted, Emily turned off the set and went out to the front yard. The night was dazzlingly clear, and up the street she could make out the figure of someone rocking in a chair on their porch. Most likely the person was a stranger in town; all of the houses on her block were summer rentals save for the Zeidmans' three doors down and, of course, Barbara and Fred's. The rental properties, once privately owned and lived in year-round, were now distinguished by the Vacancy and No Vacancy signs out front. The rental units were large clapboard two-stories with white trim on the shutters and doorframes, an odd collection of mismatched lawn chairs, and white wrought-iron furniture on the porches, perhaps a green-and-white awning here and there. Only her own house, Barbara's, and the Zeidmans' had the feel of permanency about them— lawns and fences, shrubs and flowers instead of the expedient pebbled front yards. Emily figured it would only be a matter of time before one of the many developers who had descended upon Ocean Gate in recent years would buy up Barbara and Fred's property, strip it of its Victorian trim, whitewash its deep blue exterior, and replace its old four-pane windows with something sleek and modern, something in keeping with the new condos rather than the interesting mix of Colonial and Victorian homes Ocean Gate was once noted for. The Zeidmans had already begun upgrading, and when they were finished installing their Andersen windows only Emily's house would be a reminder of the Ocean Gate nights when the neighbors collected on each other's porches with their children, sipped iced tea, argued endlessly about the blue laws that prohibited Sunday shopping and kept the town dry, made plans for the sand castle competition in late July and Holiday Night in early August.

Whoever had been rocking in the chair got up and went inside, the screen door squeaking behind him. The street was eerily quiet. Within the hour people would begin coming off the boardwalk, having had their fill of junk food and amusement rides. Often

Emily used to sit with Barbara and they would watch the people passing by, make up stories about their lives, try to discover everything about a family by the way a father held a child's hand or walked behind or ahead of his wife. A few times Emily tried to amuse herself this way alone, but her mind drifted and the sight of those intact families made her throat feel sore and pinched. Now with everyone gone she felt her loss was solitary confinement. It was a runaway road or a patch of ice on a dry, smooth highway. It was the Great Wall of China. There'd been no way to stop it and there was no way around it, and although she tried not to dwell on it, memory followed her like a shadow.

She had her cigarettes with her, stashed in her shirt pocket. She took one out, struck a match, and inhaled. It never occurred to her that Gene was watching from his front bedroom window, his own cigarette burning, sending up trails of blue smoke that meshed with hers while the flies batted blindly against the screen.

FOUR

July 8, 1982

Dear Barbara,

Got your package yesterday. I think I've had my fill of Kübler-Ross for now, but the Irish folktales looks interesting. I assume it's no accident that all of the women in the tales are alone with children and not the proverbial frail, pale things of most fairy tales? Well, at least as long as you send me packages of books I'll have an excuse to sit down and write you thank-you notes, since I haven't been able to write much else of late. At least you write me letters, which is more than I can say for my mother.

She's been sending me postcards, you know. One every three or four days, from ten different mountain resorts. Ten, imagine! She said she would be staying at the Split Rock Lodge in the Poconos, but I think she likes to create the impression that she's on the road. I imagine the variety of postcards must give her a sense of an itinerary. Maybe she thinks she's the Katharine Hepburn of *Holiday*, unbound and free spirited, huh? Name one mother in America who cannot find the time to visit her widowed daughter for even a lousy week. She sends these ridiculous messages, designed, no doubt, to inspire me, usually one or two lines noting the bigness of the mountains and the general insignificance of the smaller problems of mankind. She says, and you'll love this, "A purple sunset, Emily, is grander by far than our passion, though we like to think we equal it," and this ditty, "The mountain air, so cool and so clean, so good, is a constant reassurance." I take it she was reading *A Farewell to Arms* when she dashed that one off. Anyway, she's not coming home in July as she promised, which infuriates me. The awful thing is, if Peter were here, we'd joke about these notes, you know. He'd do his Francine imitation, which could always make me laugh. Remember the time he did her stopping by at Christmas? He had that dish towel wrapped around his head like one of her scarves and he swooshed into the room, took one look at the Christmas tree, and said, "These lights are all wrong, but absolutely"? Well. God. By the way, that reminds me, tell Fred that I solved the Mystery of the Disappearing Tennis Racket. It was lying under a fifty-pound bag of fertilizer in the garage. I came across it when I tried to mow the lawn last week. I say tried because the damn mower was corroded with gunk from last season. Actually, I ended up doing nothing. Remember that family who rented the apartment a few summers ago? The playwright? Well, he's renting this summer, but he appeared without that pretty, large woman and without his little boy. Seems they're separated. He mowed my lawn. I didn't ask; he offered, loudly I might add, over the roar of the motor. Lizzie has a crush on him and I think he on her. As for me, well, I haven't managed to work up to being very cordial, and I admit it bugs me a little to know that another writer is writing in my house when I can't.

Well, I'm going to say good-bye for now. Should I read the Kübler-Ross, I'll let you know what I think. Give my love to Fred and tell him I'll mail his racket, and kiss the boys for me and Lizzie. I would have called, but we can begin bad habits talking long distance from Jersey to Maine. Never mind, I will call. You call too.

My love,
Emily

Emily folded the letter, sealed it in its envelope, and sat back in her chair, thinking about what she had not included. How she hadn't told Barbara about the smoking or the fact that she never slept in her bedroom but instead camped out on the sofa like an overnight guest in her own living room. She always woke before Lizzie in the morning and rushed to hide the sheet and the pillows. Emily knew her daughter would think sleeping in the living room was "neat," an adventure, and she would be hard-pressed to explain why she was doing it. She had read somewhere that it wasn't unusual for women alone to sleep in the room closest to the front door. Something primitive and protective worked in these women, the article had said. What could she say to Lizzie? "I'm a lioness guarding my lair"? "I plan to attack, to be alert for the intrusion, stare down the barrel of a shotgun, fend off the blade of knife with my bare hands for you, kid"? She felt Lizzie had enough of her own normal childhood fears to deal with; there was no need to add the possibility of robbers, ax murderers, and mad dogs to those.

Emily very deftly left out of her letters to Barbara the fact that she was wearing black still, despite her mother's frequent postscripts on her cards advising: "Wear yellow today" or "Wear green—it's hopeful." Black was easy; it felt right. She steered herself away from mirrors. Seeing herself as less than attractive, forcing herself to assess the damage, would mean that she would have to take action: she'd have to go out to Hoy's five-and-dime and invest in new Maybelline blushers; she'd have to investigate a new way to contour her high cheekbones or experiment with tea bags for the puffiness under her eyes, or try a new mousse for her lifeless hair. If she accomplished any of these quick pick-me-up tricks, she knew she would still be confronted, albeit more beautifully, with the truth: she wanted not a stunning face but Peter.

So she banked instead on the unqualified love of her child, her precocious girl, who said, "You can't see you, Mom, but I can see you. You're gorgeous." Emily grabbed her and kissed her so hard her lips made violent sucking sounds against Lizzie's cheek, and because kisses like those came out of her so rarely now, Lizzie would burrow into her and beg for more, but Emily found, much as she wanted to respond, that she had only one or two more kisses like them in her, some tickling maybe, before Lizzie's need for her devotion left Emily feeling listless. Her nipples ached, the way they had when she was nursing Lizzie, and the ache was confusing, desire run wild, and how she missed Peter, his mouth on her, the demand of it and the love.

She didn't tell Barbara either how aimless her days had become, how each morning after driving Lizzie off to the day camp, where she would spend the morning in swimming lessons and making baskets from popsickle sticks, ashtrays from modeling clay, and footprints on long white sheets of paper, she would drive back home, make coffee, go into her office, and never pull up the shade. There she would stand, cup in hand, staring at her eight-foot-long flea-market-find desk, above which, on a large wide piece of corkboard, hung the phases of her life. A snapshot of her in her early twenties looking slightly more bosomy in a white knit turtleneck, proudly holding up her first advance check for a mere two thousand dollars. And much later, a photograph taken of her and Peter, dressed to the nines at Jill's house in New York, on the occasion of the publication of the fifth Flora book. Peter was wearing a tux and she was wearing the navy taffeta, simple, strapless. They were holding martinis and had turned toward the camera together looking solicitous. Care for a drink? their stunned expressions seemed to say. There was a picture of the two of them holding Lizzie on the day she was born, a wedding snapshot, a blurred action shot of Peter on the courts. But more prominent than any of the other photographs was the large color print of herself that Peter had taken the previous spring. He'd found her kneeling by the broad up-turned section of earth along the side porch. He'd planned to do something striking with this trench, but after many days spent pondering it, he still hadn't thought of a flower or a bush that suited his tastes. Emily had been kneeling before it, imagining all sorts of possibilities at first, but they knew about the Hodgkin's then and the dug-out section of the yard seemed menacing. "Look up, Em," he'd called out, and when she did he clicked the shutter, freezing forever the shock in her eyes.

Emily had never liked the picture, but Peter thought it was wonderful and had gone to great lengths to have it matted just right and framed in a thin band of curved rosewood. After he hung it in her office she asked him, "Don't you think it should go in your office? Wouldn't that make more sense?"

He slung his arm around her shoulder and stared at his master-piece. "You got you, babe," he said, trying to make a joke about the Sonny and Cher song of their high school days.

Between the photographs were the framed covers of the Flora series and letters from children and friends, all protected in plastic and strung up together like the unfolded guts of a wallet. There was a calendar, the kind with large blocks in which she used to mark off a day's work with ease, but the month of July was blank so far, as were June, May, April, March, and so forth. The desk itself was littered with plot outlines, some handwritten, most typed, books to be read and reviewed, correspondence to be answered, and Emily stood before all of it, one hand on her lower back, drinking coffee. At one time she had known how to sit down and work, but that morning she took the letter she'd written and walked away from it, thinking that food shopping was something she could do until it was time to pick up Lizzie.

Walking through the Foodtown at the Shore Mall, she looked for signs of widowhood the way she used to look for other pregnant women when she was carrying Lizzie, but the emblems of widowhood were secret.

She plodded up and down the aisles not paying particular attention to what she was putting in the cart, and then when the cart seemed sufficiently full, she headed for the checkout line. As the other women unloaded their purchases onto the conveyor belt, Emily looked at the racks of magazines geared to the women of the nation: *Self, Working Woman, Mademoiselle, Vogue, Savvy, Glamour, Bazaar.* Where, she wondered, is the magazine for me? She could see the cover copy now: "Famous Widows Recount the Long Road to Recovery. Jackie says, 'I've had to endure it twice.' Betty White Shares Her Sorrow." There would be how-to articles: "How to Wear Your Grief and Not Offend Others." In the back of the magazine there would be ads for widows' retreats, widows' support groups, Widows Anonymous.

At that moment she glanced into her cart and stared at the lamb chops. Only Peter had eaten them because Emily thought they had a strange taste and Lizzie thought they were too greasy. And there were the frozen pizzas with sausage that he liked. And the dried papayas. How had they gotten in there? Emily wouldn't eat or use half of what she'd picked from the shelves, so she excused herself to the old woman standing behind her as she tried to angle her cart out of the way.

"Forget your wallet?"

The woman's eyes were knowing and kind, but Emily snapped at her.

"No. I forgot my husband is dead."

The woman gasped and, clutching her shirt at the lapel, made soft beating motions against her chest. "Well, I beg your pardon," she said as Emily stalked off, pushing the cart.

Emily's heart was racing, her sneakers squeaked on the linoleum floor as she steered the cart down the aisle. When no one was looking she abandoned the cart. As she drove out of the parking lot she could feel the tears welling up behind her eyes, but she wouldn't permit them to fall. She'd stood woodenly through the wake, stoically through the funeral mass and at the cemetery, and while other people may have mistaken her control for coldness, only she knew the truth: if she had shed one tear she would have shed a million; she might never have stopped crying for all she knew. Driving back into town, she despised herself for being so nasty to that woman, but she suspected she might be just as nasty again if anyone caught her at the wrong moment.

That afternoon when she picked up Lizzie from camp, she stayed inside the car even though it was terribly humid and uncomfortable. She wanted to avoid Madge Perkins and Linda Robb, Betty Miller, and especially Vanessa Thornton, who in her thickest southern drawl would have told Emily that she looked washed out and would have added, "And, honey, that's no way to look with or without a man around." Usually she was tan by May, and with her olive coloring a good tan never took more than a few days to accomplish. Emily stared at her arms, which were pale, especially against her black shirt and shorts; she decided that she would walk down to the beach with Lizzie when they got home.

In the house, delighted that they were going to the beach, Lizzie rushed off to get into her bathing suit, peeling off clothes as she headed for her room. In her own bedroom, Emily pulled on a royal blue one-piece suit. She had a good body still. The first time she and Peter ever made love he had commented on the tightness of her belly. "It's practically concave," he'd said.

"Get me a ruler and I'll show you a trick," she said. He was visibly alarmed, an emotion in Peter that registered in short intakes of breath, until he saw her place the ruler on her hipbones and slide her hand under it without touching it.

"Jesus Christ, Em. I thought you were going to insert that somewhere."

Emily pulled on a sweatshirt, flicked a comb through her long hair, and in the mirror she swore she could see Peter standing behind her. She even put her fingers to the mirror to touch the face and blinked incredulously when the smudges evaporated on the glass. The tricks of denial were strong and short-lived. "Son of a bitch," she murmured.

She and Lizzie stayed on the beach far too long that day and by eight in the evening neither one of them had the energy for a trip to the boardwalk. Instead they walked across the street for ice cream cones and returned to the front porch, where they rocked together on the glider. Lizzie was halfway through eating her black-and-white cone when she said, "I think Daddy will be home tonight."

Emily had a glob of ice cream in her mouth and forced it down quickly. "What are you talking about?"

She kept licking as she spoke. "Sometimes I think he didn't die and that he's away. In my mind I think of that and I see him, in my mind, coming home."

"And what does he look like, in your mind?"

She licked more ice cream, her eyes focused on a rivulet of melted chocolate running down the side of the cone. "He's wearing pajamas and black shoes."

Emily put her arm around Lizzie's shoulder and pulled her close. "You know that's only a wish, don't you, angel doll?"

"Uh-huh. My mind knows it," she said. Lizzie ate two more mouthfuls of her ice cream, then passed it to Emily. "I don't want any more, Mom."

"Are you okay?"

She rubbed her stomach. "My belly aches, just a little."

Suddenly Emily couldn't finish her ice cream either, and she threw the unfinished cones away in the trash can at the side of the house. When she came back to the porch, Lizzie was lying on the glider, eyes open, staring out at the yard. She is perfect, Emily thought, and so smart, and she knew that if Lizzie had said what she just said about someone *else's* death, if Peter were here to share it with, they would have told the story over and over, they would have written it down so years later they could point out one of the many brilliant things their baby had said.

Emily stepped up onto the porch and lifted Lizzie's head gently, letting it rest on her lap.

"When I was little, but not as little as you, I used to tell Grandmom the very same thing. I used to say, 'Mother, I think Dad might be home tonight.' "

"Did Grandpop die?"

"I don't even know, Liz. He left me and Grandmom and we've never heard from him since. We don't know if he's alive or not."

"Were you sad, Mom?"

"Very." Emily paused and began twirling a strand of Lizzie's hair around her finger. "Are you sad, Lizzie?"

"Only when my mind can't see him in the pajamas."

At that moment, had Peter appeared on the front walk, Emily would have run to him; she would have yelled, "Where have you been and why are you dressed that way? Don't you know we've been waiting for you? Don't you know we need you here with us?"

Lizzie was quiet, her eyes were closed, but Emily could tell by her breathing, which was steady and loud, that she was still awake. "Do you want to go to sleep?"

"Tell me a story."

"Any story?"

"Uh-huh."

And so Emily began the story that she'd read in the folktale collection Barbara had sent.

"Once upon a time—"

"What time?" Lizzie asked, eyes still closed, voice dreamy.

"Once upon a very long time ago—"

"Did you have me yet?"

"No. It was a very long time ago in a faraway place and a woman had a child, and the woman and the child lived alone."

"Where was the daddy?"

"I don't know. It never said in the story. Anyway, the woman has to work in the fields to make money to buy food for herself and

44 /

her child. Every day when she goes to work in the fields, she has to take the baby with her."

"You don't have to take me to work."

"No."

"Because you work at home."

"Yes."

Lizzie brought her narrow index finger up to her nostril. "Don't pick your nose, Liz."

"I was just touching it, Mom."

"You were going to pick it."

"No. I was just touching it."

"Do you really want to hear this story?"

"No. Read me *The Cat in the Hat*."

Emily went in and brought out the tried and true Dr. Seuss, and before she was halfway through it, Lizzie was in a sound sleep. Emily slid out from under the weight of her head and carried her into her room.

Two months before he died, Peter had bought one of those Plexiglas cubes for pictures, and he'd spent a day selecting photographs of himself and the three of them to fill it with. Lizzie kept it on her nightstand. After Emily covered her with the sheet, she picked up the cube and held it up to the light from the window. There was one shot of Peter and Lizzie sitting on the sofa. He was wearing pajamas and she was nestled in his arms.

Emily put the cube back in its place, kissed Lizzie's cheek, and returned to the porch where she saw Gene at the foot of the walk, coming into the yard. In the dusky light he appeared pale and compelling. She had not seen him since the day she reprimanded him for telling Lizzie that story, and seeing him so starkly untanned in a town filled with sunburned faces, she assumed he must have been holed up in his apartment these past several days. She didn't know from where he was returning, only that the air of having gone somewhere important was all around him. He waved to her first.

Emily nodded in the direction of the beach. "Were you on the boards?"

He shrugged his shoulders, looking around him as if he wasn't sure she was talking to him. She sat in the glider, pushed off with her feet, setting it in motion. By this time he'd planted one sneakered foot on the porch step. "Don't you have to yell at me for something?"

He wasn't smiling. She said no very quietly and then, "You must think I'm a madwoman. First you find me out here barefoot as Isadora, then the other day I practically shout your head off."

"I don't think you're a madwoman," he said, but he seemed to carefully refrain from saying what he did think. He came onto the porch and half sat on the railing in front of her. She had to look up to him to speak, and although standing they were nearly the same height, the present disparity in their positions made her feel contrary again. "Why are you here, anyway?"

He raised an eyebrow.

"What I mean is, why not an expensive condo on the beach? Why not New York? Surely you have theater friends in Montauk or something."

He looked sideways toward the yard and Emily saw him bite down on his lower lip. He was balancing himself against the railing, the muscles in his arms straining to support him. "You are . . . never mind," he said. "Listen, would it be better for you if I left? Maybe this isn't working out for you," he said, turning back to look at her.

Emily thought of the old woman in the supermarket, how she'd attacked her. "I'm sorry," she said, throwing up her hands, "I never even thanked you for the lawn. It looks very nice. I appreciate it. I do."

"You're not going to offer to pay me again, are you?"

"No."

Gene cocked his head toward the wicker chair. "Could I sit there?"

"Sure."

As soon as he sat down he pulled a pack of cigarettes from his shirt pocket, tapped the pack against his fingers, and held one out to her. It was a gesture that, whenever her mother had seen it done in the movies, could make her swoon. Now, the gesture only made Emily nervous.

"I don't smoke."

His eyes held her steadily; she knew he'd seen her at night. "I don't smoke," she repeated, so he withdrew one for himself, put the pack away, and lit up.

"Once," he said, "when I was in Alaska, I stayed out on the barge all night. To this day I can't remember what it was I was trying to escape inside—endless talk, cabin fever, I don't know. I just stayed out there, freezing my ass off. Almost lost a finger, lost some sensation in my nose, but in the morning I felt better."

He seemed to be making the point, rather abstrusely, Emily thought, that he understood her need to stand in that yard night after night.

"You really were in Alaska?"

"For four years on the pipeline. I'd written four plays by then. Two produced," he said, holding up two fingers, "two unproduced and unpublished. I was out of money, unmarried, and I'd already done the teaching stints for lousy pay. I was thirty-eight years old. A friend of mine offered me a job painting boats on Martha's Vineyard for the winter. It was a choice between that and Alaska. I took Alaska. I had nothing to lose."

"What happened after that?"

His eyes cut to her, but she couldn't be sure he was really looking at her; he seemed settled on some private distance beyond her.

"Well," he said lazily, "after that I had money. I moved back to New York, wrote *Thetis Island,* suffered a kidney stone attack midway through the writing, and that's how I met Lottie. She was my nurse. By the time I finished the play, we were married. It wasn't a commercial success—"

"The marriage?"

Gene smiled. "No, the play. But it was a critical success, which in this business means a theater company might just want to attach itself to you. It's different from what you do. I can't write and mail, you know? A playwright needs the whole group—directors, producers, the actors. Anyway, now I'm here. That's it."

He tossed the smoked-down butt onto the ground and was lighting another when he said, "I was shocked to hear about your husband. Was it an accident?"

Emily stopped the motion of the glider with her foot. "I think I'll go in now."

"No. I mean, don't, please," he said. "I'm sorry. We can talk about something else. This is nice—the hot night, the crickets, conversation. After a day of silence."

Emily began rocking again.

"It wasn't an accident," she said suddenly. "Oh, I guess disease is accidental in a way because it's random. Who knows who's going to get cancer or leukemia? Peter had Hodgkin's disease; unfortunately, by the time we caught it, it was in the third stage, which is rarely curable."

Gene nodded knowingly.

"Well, of course, I suppose you know a lot about medicine by proxy."

"Yes."

They said nothing for a while and the silence between them was not awkward. Emily was remembering the spring day a year ago when she found out. They were riding their imported Italian cycles, hers red and Peter's the golden shade of hot mustard. She had Lizzie strapped to the kiddie seat on the back of her bike, and as they pedaled around town, she found it hard to keep up with Peter, who was moving furiously fast ahead of her. Just as she began to pick up speed, she saw Peter's feet miss the pedals. His legs went slack, and by the time she called out to him, he was on the ground.

He lay sprawled in the middle of the street, so she skidded to a stop, almost toppling her own bike, and rushed to him with Lizzie propped on her hip even though she was perfectly capable of walking herself. His right leg was cut just above the knee, a gritty abrasion filled with specks of asphalt, and there was a gash, like a four-inch lipstick streak, along his cheek. She knelt down to give him a hand. "Come on, Peter. God, what happened?"

She expected that he would have been angry for falling in public. She expected that he would mumble that everything was okay and for her not to fuss. She expected that he would get up or at least make a move toward getting up, but he lay there, moaning a little, holding his leg. And then he looked up at her, the breeze lifting the strands of hair off his forehead, and he said the words she never thought she'd hear him say, not until he was ninety or a hundred years old.

"Emily, I'm dying."

A chill as cold as the day was hot worked its way from the center of her heart to the tips of her fingers.

"Bad joke, Peter. Daddy's making a bad joke, teasing Mommy again, Liz." But Peter shook his head no, no joke.

As she told Gene about that day, he listened intently, and although he hadn't finished his second cigarette, he shot it out on the walk where it flickered and burned beside the other.

"I remember a very healthy, tall guy," Gene said.

"Me too. It wasn't as hard in the winter, in January after he died. I don't know, maybe I was still in shock, which is strange because I knew it was coming."

Gene nodded and leaned forward in his seat, his hands folded, hanging between his knees. "Are you . . . are you writing?"

She shook her head.

"You might break some ground with a book for children about the death of a parent. It might be worth thinking about."

"Not now."

"Just a thought, Emily."

He stood up then, eased his arms into a long stretch. "Yard needs water. You've got a sprinkler?"

"Two sprinklers," she said.

He put his hands on his hips and said, "Well, you show me where and tomorrow night we'll put the sprinklers on." To convince her that this was necessary he walked to the lawn, knelt down, and plucked out a handful of grass. "Burned to a crisp, you see? Might as well be in Algeria."

"Sure. Okay, all right. You want to play caretaker, be my guest."

He was picking up the cigarette butts that he'd thrown on the walk. His gray hair shone in the moonlight; his face seemed featureless except for those eyes, wide set and dark, in the shadows powerful. "I am your guest," he said, "and I'll be the caretaker too."

Every day, Emily woke believing that the passage of another twenty-four hours would have moved her closer to lightness—lightheartedness, light-headedness, just the absence, finally, of the nameless weight that pressed in on her skin. On first opening her eyes, she would often mistake the sunlight for a tunnel of benevolent yellow she could float through. She never imagined more than this ephemeral travel through light, however, before she blinked herself fully awake, stood up, and began folding the sheets.

But this morning was different. There was no sunlight, for one thing, just a hot gray mist rolling inland from the ocean that wouldn't burn off until ten, maybe even noon. And despite the humidity, which made her sinuses throb, she didn't feel the paralysis, the inertia that accompanied the start of each day. Above her, Gene paced the floor, then a burst of syncopated typing would break through the quiet before he began pacing again. She sat on the sofa, wearing her clothes from the day before, listening to the sounds as if they were an old song that had suddenly come on the radio, at once familiar. When she looked at her watch she saw that it wasn't even six thirty, yet the rhythm of his movement seemed to suggest that he'd been working for some time. Lizzie would sleep for at least another half-hour, which gave Emily time to hide the sheets and pillow, shower, and change.

It was in the shower, under the tepid spray of water, that she remembered today was the day she was to go to the high school and clean out Peter's desk, sweep all remains of him from the administrative office to make way for the incoming assistant principal. Lithcomb had been after her to do it sooner, and she always managed to make a passable excuse, but after the dedication ceremony he'd made it clear to her that it had to be now. "We can do it for you," he'd said, "but I think it's something you might want to do yourself." She agreed that it was. Surely if she didn't find the strength to face his office, Margot Compton would.

As Emily stepped out of the shower onto the cold tile, she heard Lizzie moving about in her room and Gene's typing, now furious and fast, above her. Keep it up, she thought, toweling dry the ends of her long hair. You keep typing and I'll keep going.

Emily dropped Lizzie off at the day camp by nine. Usually she walked with Lizzie beyond the fence to the picnic area where the children kept their knapsacks for the day. The camp was built on what used to be an overgrown vacant lot; now the thick green brush had been cleared away, making room for jungle gyms and slides, a sandbox, lunch tables, and, facing the ocean, a gate that led to the beach where the children swam in the early morning. Today Emily pulled up to the curb and told Lizzie to go on alone, that she would watch until she was safely inside the fence. When she could barely make out the outline of Lizzie's bright yellow knapsack in the distance, Emily made a K-turn and pulled out onto Ocean Avenue.

There were stoplights at every corner, but they weren't timed lights and Emily found herself waiting through one red light after another. Although the clouds had not lifted, many people were already on their way to the beach, lugging oversize beach bags, thermoses, and sand chairs. Suddenly, her long cotton skirt felt cumbersome and she wished she'd worn a simple sleeveless blouse instead of the long-sleeved linen that she had rolled up over her forearms. The light changed to green and the car lurched forward. Well, I look the way they'll expect me to look, she thought.

At the high school Emily drove the Toyota into Peter's assigned spot. There were several other cars in the lot, one she recognized as Lithcomb's. Emily hoped she wouldn't have to talk with anyone.

The stretch of asphalt between the lot and the high school felt hot even through her sandals, so Emily walked quickly to the glass double doors, a blast of stale air-conditioned air greeting her when she stepped inside. She stood for a minute just inside the school and stared down the long barren hallway at the end of which gray light streamed through a tall window. She fixed her eyes on the endless display of skinny metal lockers lining the glazed brick walls and was surprised to feel her stomach dip, the pulse in her neck jump, just the way it would have had she been a freshman on the first day of school. It had happened every time she'd come to the high school, as if she expected a nun smelling of incense to materialize before her with a demerit card and with a face as hardened and clean as marble, to admonish her for lateness, for not working up to her potential, for not sitting at her desk with her feet planted "firmly on the floor." Emily had gone through four years of high school feeling that her shame was as visible as the gold-and-blue emblem on her uniform blazer, and she had felt a strange relief when, in junior year, she read *The Scarlet Letter* and learned that Hester Prynne, too, was marked. Of course, it wasn't the same, but to her her mother's drinking and her father's abandoning them felt as terrible as adultery; she felt as if she, not they, had done something wrong. Then she reminded herself that this was not her high school, that there were no nuns here in this public institution.

She took a deep breath then and smoothed her hair back from her face, tucking the wavy strands that curved along her cheekbones behind her ears. Off to her right were the offices, and as she walked in that direction she could hear the whining and thumping of the Xerox machine as it dashed off copies, the insistent ring of telephones, and the low murmur of voices. She would have to pass five or six glass-doored offices before arriving at Peter's office, which meant that five or six people, maybe more, would rise from behind their desks to greet her, to ask her how she was. She decided then and there that she would say: "I'm feeling just great, really."

Fortunately, Judy Clayton, Peter's secretary, was taking a vacation day, so Emily didn't have to deal with her. Wayne Lithcomb practically knocked her down on his way out of his office, then, recovering himself, smiled broadly and told her how good it was to see her again. "You have the key?"

"Right here," she said, dangling it between them.

"Do you want me to come with you or—"

"I think I can take care of everything, Wayne, thanks. I'll just need some boxes."

He clapped his hands together. "Not to worry, Emily. I've already stacked some right outside the door there. Now," he said, placing his hand lightly on her shoulder, "when you're all finished, you give a yell and I'll have one of the students here for summer classes help you load them into the car. Don't you do it all yourself, you hear? Nothing heavier than packed books. Myself, I'd rather move furniture. Okay?"

Emily nodded. "Sure. I'll just give a yell."

He patted her shoulder once more. "Good. Well, I'm late for a meeting." And he fled down the cool corridor, his arms swinging.

Emily stood before Peter's office and found she couldn't make herself go in. It was quiet in the hall and she tiptoed several feet ahead to the last string of offices where she knew the counseling staff reigned. On one of the three doors was Margot Compton's name, stenciled there with four others. Emily stood staring at the black letters as if they might speak to her before walking back up the hall. She counted the number of paces between Peter's and Margot's offices; every day they had been only fifteen steps away from each other. Although their affair had been brief, or so he said, and had been over nearly a year before he'd found out that he was sick, Emily wondered how they kept themselves from taking fifteen short, quick steps to steal a kiss or just a look. She was shivering now in the air-conditioning that had been such a relief when she first entered the school, the muscles in her neck growing more rigid with rage by the second; but this rage always complicated her grief and she struggled to push it away. Anger made her feel ugly inside and out. And, she thought, it takes me nowhere.

There had been remarkably little to pack up in Peter's office; he'd taken a lot of books home with him in small cartons over the last months of his administration, and Emily discovered that he had neatly and precisely organized the materials the new assistant principal might need. Other than a few odds and ends, a few photographs of herself and Lizzie that he kept on his desk, all that was left for her to rummage through was his middle desk drawer, a thin compartment of gunmetal gray that was kept locked.

Emily sank into the swivel chair, unlocked the drawer, and pulled it out slowly over her lap, hoping that she would not find love notes from Margot, or worse, pictures. Without really looking she slid her hands in over the papers and manila folders first, fishing for anything small and scattered like a picture or some trinket of affection. Satisfied that she would find neither, she looked down into the drawer finally. There were smaller compartments in the front part of the drawer—one for rubber bands, one for pencils, another for paper clips, another for stamps, and not one object was mixed in with the others; everything was exactly where it belonged and for some reason this made her eyes sting. Like his closet in their bedroom, like his garage, this drawer, its organization, was so like him that Emily dug her hands in, pulling up a pile of rubber bands, squeezing them tight into her fists. She held on to them until she felt her fingernails jabbing the fleshy part of her palms, until holding them hurt too much and she had to let them go.

Oh, she thought, I remember this. Does nothing ever change? She was thinking then not only of Peter but of the night her father left, how her mother had looked reading his short note.

Francine had taken that note he'd written and turned it over in her hand as if she were turning to the B side of a popular record, that oh-let's-see-what-he's-up-to-this-time look in her eyes. The other side of the paper was blank, but Emily thought her mother looked at it as if it contained pertinent information. "He took his Tums, his briefcase, his overcoat, his ice skates, his clarinet, and that car," she'd said. "He did not, however, take his bathrobe."

Emily didn't know what this meant or what her mother thought it meant. "So?"

"Come with me, Em'ly."

She rushed away to the front hall and walked determinedly on up the large staircase. Emily followed her, keeping her eyes on the back of her mother's pumps as they hit the carpeted stairs. She went with her mother into the bedroom where Francine headed for the wide closet at the south end of the room. Francine opened the door, letting it fly, the glass knob making a dull thud against the wall. The hangers screeched along the metal rod as she whipped through the clothes and found his bathrobe.

"See?" she said. She held the bathrobe out, shaking it a little. It was a long gray-and-cranberry plaid with a thin line of the palest green running through it. "A man does not leave for good without his bathrobe."

Because she was only fourteen at the time and because she had not known many men except for her grandfather (by then dead), her own father, and the priests at school, she believed her mother; she assumed her mother knew what she was talking about.

"I'm sleeping with this," Francine said quietly. "I'm just going to sleep with this." And she pulled the bathrobe to her chest. "Go, Em'ly, go to bed."

Emily knew then that her mother could no longer stand to have her around, that what she wanted most was a drink. Emily asked if she could sleep with the note.

"Whatever for?"

"Please?"

On her way up the stairs Francine had stuffed it into her skirt pocket, and when she gave it to Emily, Emily smoothed it out against her palm, noting the creases and the smudges in the words. In her own room, Emily dared not turn on the light. She let the shade up on the window near her bed and climbed in fully clothed, rereading the note by the light of the streetlamp. After a while, when she began to cry, she slipped the note under her pillow, the way she used to hide a lost tooth, but with full knowledge that there was no fairy who was good for more than quarters in the middle of the night.

Emily flipped through a few of the folders in the drawer, looked over some papers, and decided that there was nothing she needed to take with her. She slammed the drawer shut, but within seconds opened it again, then reached for her purse, which was lying on the desk. She opened the purse and scooped all of the rubber bands and paper clips into it, leaving just the stamps and pencils behind. Wayne Lithcomb appeared in the open doorway just as she snapped her purse shut. She smiled brightly at him. "I'm finished now," she said. "I have everything I need."

Around dinnertime, just as she was setting the table, Gene tapped on the back door. "I'm not coming in," he began, even though she had not asked him. "I just wanted to remind you that we have a date tonight."

Emily wiped her hands on her apron. "A date."

"The lawn, remember? We're going to water the lawn. Were you planning to stand me up?"

The words *date* and *stand me up* had such a quaint, old-fashioned feel to them that, had she been the sort to blush, she would have.

"Is there a special time for this?"

Gene glanced at his watch. "How about seven thirty?"

Emily was standing close to the screen door now. The clouds and mist had never burned off that day. "It'll probably rain tonight, don't you think?" she asked, pointing out to the sky.

"No."

"You're sure about that."

"Yes," he said, smiling.

"Okay. I'll tell Lizzie then."

When he walked away Emily went to the kitchen window and watched as his shadow moved across the backyard. He was not returning to his apartment; he was leaving the yard and Emily could hear him whistling "You Gotta Have Heart." She couldn't remember what musical the song was from. Since it was only a little after five, she wondered what he was going to do with himself until seven thirty. She hated how slowly the hours seemed to drag by, but Gene seemed content.

At seven twenty-nine she called out front for Lizzie, but her answer came from the backyard where Emily saw her and Gene headed for the garage.

"You're almost late," Gene said when Emily joined them. He was wearing bathing trunks and a T-shirt for this sprinkling occasion, and Lizzie in a moment of abandon and silliness had pulled on a shower cap.

"This is really no big deal," Emily told them.

"It's a very big deal, Emily. Isn't it, Lizard?"

Lizzie shook her head and the cap slid down over her eyes. Gene waved at the garage door. "You're the gatekeeper."

As Emily walked past him she whispered, "Lizard?"

Gene shrugged. "Popped out. Well, what do we need?"

"Two hoses and the sprinklers are over there," Emily said, pointing to the left corner of the garage. Gene let out a slow, soft whistle.

"Your husband could have opened this place for business."

"The yard was his hobby."

"Then you'd better keep it up for him."

The remark, made casually while he was stooping over to pick up the sprinklers, hit Emily like an admonishment and she resented it. "I haven't even decided whether I'll keep the house," she said, which wasn't true. She couldn't imagine living anywhere else.

"Let's go," Lizzie said.

Gene hooked up the hoses while Lizzie and Emily attached them to the sprinklers and placed them strategically on the lawn. There were about half a dozen other houses on the block where neighbors were doing the same because it had not rained in weeks and the temperature continued to hit the mid-nineties every day.

"Okay, Lizard, you get the honor of turning on the spigots," Gene said.

As she got up to run toward him, she told Emily, "See, he's a fun man, Mom."

Lizzie stood in front of him, protected in the curve of his long muscular body as he leaned over her, his big hands covering hers as she turned the handle. Then they ran over to the other spigot and repeated the process. The water rumbled through the faded green hoses, then burst through the metal holes of the sprinklers, making high, wide arcs of rain over the lawn.

"All right. Now here's the good part," he explained to Lizzie. "Sprinkler tag. I'm it."

Emily had moved out of the line of water and she watched them running through it, Gene keeping a distance behind Lizzie, pretending to be out of breath, letting her elude his grasp when he could have caught her. Lizzie was giggling, pushing the shower cap up over her eyes. He caught her just as the sprinkler was making its return over them; they were drenched in its spray.

"Get Mommy!" Lizzie shouted. "We're it!"

The two of them turned toward Emily, hands out, fingers curled like claws.

"Not fair. You two are dressed for this." But they were coming toward her and there was nowhere for her to run but into the water.

"Better move it, Emily," Gene called, "we're gaining on you."

It was Lizzie who caught her, pulling at the hem of her shirt. She tagged Emily, threw her off balance, and sent her sliding onto the wet grass where the sprinklers met over her like huge, feathered fans. Lizzie pounced on her, pushing her down in the grass.

"We got her, Gene. We got her!"

He was laughing, now, pointing at Emily. "You're a sight."

"You should see yourself."

"We're all a mess," Lizzie shouted, delighted.

58 /

Had Emily rolled toward the house when she struggled to stand up rather than toward the fence, she wouldn't have seen the car, an ancient white LeMans convertible moving down the street as slowly as a cabin cruiser in the sea, dragging to a near standstill in front of the house. The driver was Margot Compton. Her dark hair was piled messily on top of her head, clipped into place with two big, pointed barrettes. She was wearing sunglasses. She held on to the steering wheel with one hand and kept her other arm outside the rolled-down driver's-side window, her fingers nervously drumming the top of the door.

Gene was watching Emily watch her, and when Emily looked at him under the arbor of water he mouthed the words, "Who's that?" Emily shook her head and walked to the front gate. Margot pulled her sunglasses down onto the bridge of her nose, surveyed Emily haughtily, tilting her head in Gene's direction before she gunned the engine and sped off down the street.

Gene was standing behind Emily and she spun around, her wet hair whipping her face.

"See what you've done now?"

"Me?" he cried. "Who the hell was that?"

"Never mind. Just stop. Just stop trying to fix everything. Don't you understand that nothing here can be fixed!"

The scowl had returned to his face. "Oh, for crying out loud, you are a madwoman," he shouted, and he stalked off, his sneakers squishing, his shirt plastered to his hard, wet back.

Emily was about to stalk off herself, but when she turned to go in she was confronted with Lizzie, looking confused and upset. Her shower cap was lopsided, her lips were turned down, and her arms hung loosely at her sides. Emily held her arms out to her. "Oh, Liz, I'm so sorry."

But Lizzie did not move a muscle; she did not blink an eye. Bravely, she reached up and adjusted her shower cap, threw her shoulders back, and said, "You need to go inside, Mommy."

★   ★   ★

"Who was that lady?" Lizzie asked. Emily was tucking her into bed and she lay down next to her.

"She is someone your father knew at school."

They were both lying on their backs on the narrow bed, staring into the darkness.

"She looked mean. Is she?"

Emily stroked Lizzie's arm. "I don't know, Liz. I don't know her very well."

Lizzie yawned. "Make her a mean queen in one of your books, Mom."

Emily was thinking that the characterization would be most appropriate. "All right," she said, "I'll think about that."

Emily got off the bed, then bent over to kiss Lizzie good-night. When she asked if Lizzie had forgiven her for ruining her fun, Lizzie said yes.

Emily was certain as she closed the door to Lizzie's room that getting Gene's forgiveness would not be as easy. She went into the bathroom to pull herself together, to practice the apology before the mirror. I'll do it tomorrow, she thought, but she was not going to be permitted to avoid him because she came out of the bathroom to the sound of a knock at the front door. She moved quickly down the dark center hall of the house and found Gene standing on the porch under the unflattering yellow light.

"Are you all right?"

Amazing, she thought, I snap at him for no good reason and here he is.

"I'm just very sorry," she said. "I don't expect you to understand, but I'm sorry. What you did tonight with Lizzie was wonderful for her."

Behind him on the lawn the sprinklers were still in motion.

"You want me to turn those off?"

"I'll help you," she said.

They each turned off a spigot, unplugged the hoses, and coiled them up again. Gene took everything around back and put them away. Emily was standing on the porch steps when he returned.

"Listen," he said, "if you want to talk about it . . ."

He was busy lighting a cigarette, waiting for her answer. No, she didn't want to talk about it, she realized, but she wanted comfort.

"There is something you can do for me."

He dragged on the cigarette, which made his cheeks look hollow. "Leave?"

"No. Could you . . . would you tell me the rest of that story? The one you were telling Lizzie?"

The request seemed to please him. He flicked his ashes and the smile he gave her was broad and open. "You want the kid's version or the real thing?"

"The real thing."

"Sit down."

Emily sat in the glider and he sat on the porch steps in profile to her, one leg up, his arm resting on it. "From the top?"

"From whatever part of the anatomy the huskies bit off."

"It wasn't his penis—it was a hand," he began. "As it turned out, Cara found a skeleton of a torn-off hand in the snow. She was deeply intuitive and she was also very smart. She knew that her husband's humorlessness had led to violent acts in the past. She didn't think twice when she found the bones. She knew it was Carl's severed hand. She dropped into the snow and wept, holding the bones in her own hands.

"She'd forgiven her husband before, but this was different, this hit too close to home—and too close to her heart," he said. Behind Emily's eyes, an image of Margot flashed, Margot missing one of her long, angular hands. "Anyway," Gene continued, "she made a promise to herself. And she planned. And then she did what all women who vow to carry out a promise do."

"Which is?"

"She waited. With a decision in mind she knew she could wait as long as she needed to. So, one night, after Rorck returned from the tundra very, very late, Cara was waiting for him, snuggled under the fur pelts. Once she pulled the pelts back to reveal herself to him by the firelight, he couldn't resist her. As the legend goes, they made love until he begged her to stop and then he fell into a deep sleep."

Gene took one last drag of his cigarette, blowing smoke rings in the air, then snuffed it out. "It was a dreamless sleep. It was a sleep deeper than any other because"—and he let his words hang in the air—"because she took his pearl-handled knife and stabbed him, several times, in the back. After that, she dressed in her pelts, and even though she was a small woman, she dragged him out in the snow.

"Then she called the huskies on him. She didn't shed one tear. Our Cara went back into the igloo, covered herself in the pelts, and drank the poison she'd prepared."

Despite the hot night, Emily shivered. "It's a ghastly story."

"There's more."

"No."

"The best part."

Emily let him continue. "According to the legend, whenever the aurora borealis is in view, two hands appear in the sky, formed by the stars."

"Why two?"

Gene smiled. "Because after drinking the poison, Cara cut off her own hand. Since their hands, Cara's and Carl's, had never touched in life, once dead, the hands are supposed to appear in the sky. Joined, you see, in love."

"It's very sad."

Gene shook his head. "It's the story the natives like to tell when a couple doesn't get together. I imagine the moral is that sometimes relationships that didn't happen are worse than the ones that did."

"Can that be? Can they be worse?"

Gene gave her his usual shrug, but he was thinking she could tell. "Well, I guess so, yes. I guess unconsummated love is worse than a relationship that begins, dies, and ends."

"Maybe."

He looked away from Emily when he said, "That woman tonight in the car . . ."

"She's a counselor at the high school where Peter was an administrator." Then Emily surprised herself when she admitted, "He had an affair with her."

"Bad news."

"Very."

"Was she with him, I mean, seeing him, when he died?"

"No. He'd given her up by then; after the affair we found out about the Hodgkin's."

"She thought I was the new lover," he said.

"Exactly."

He reached over and plucked a blade of grass, toyed with it between his fingers, kept his head down. "Then I do forgive you the outburst."

"Thank you."

For a while she just rocked in the glider and he sat twirling the blade of grass. She wanted a cigarette. If he had reached into his pocket for another, she would have asked for one, but he made no motion to smoke.

"I had to go to the high school today—to clean out Peter's office. Christ, I've been putting it off for so long. Do you know that their offices were fifteen steps apart?"

"You counted?"

"Yes. Is that silly?"

"No. I would have done the same."

"You would?"

"Sure."

This complicity made her feel sane, so much so that she found herself wanting to tell him about the rubber bands, how she'd held them so tightly, so fiercely, but she changed her mind. It was enough, the relief she'd gotten from talking, from the belief that he'd understood everything. Before she knew it, he was rising, dusting off the seat of his pants.

"I'm going for a walk," he said. "Will you be okay?"

She waved him on. "Go. Go. I'm fine."

As she watched him stroll toward the gate, a knot of air in her chest released itself. If grief needed an accomplice, she had found one.

/63

PART TWO

FIVE

"Mother? What is that racket? I hear voices. I hear glassware clinking, Mother."

"You galvanize me, Em'ly, but absolutely. I'm in a club. The supper club at Pocmount."

"You're in a bar?"

"The show starts at seven fifteen."

"What show?"

"Em'ly, shut up. If you'll just shut up a minute I'll tell you."

"I can barely hear you. This is a terrible connection."

"Never mind," Francine said. "Hang up and I'll call back. I'm going to find a quieter phone."

Francine slammed the phone down and caught the attention of a waitress who was breezing past. She asked where there might be a more *private* public phone, and the waitress stared at her as if she were making an extraordinary request. "Ladies' lounge," she said, "around the corner there." And she pointed to the right of the dining room.

The ladies' lounge was a big pale pink room with pale pink sofas and a wall-length vanity mirror. It was empty except for a large round-shouldered woman wearing a pink maid's uniform; she was picking out change from a glass ashtray on the vanity. Francine smiled at her as she moved toward the phone on the wall, but the woman didn't smile back. Francine dialed Emily again, and on the first ring Emily snatched up the phone.

"I thought you were staying at Split Rock, Mother."

"Tell me, is it my fault that you're such an exasperating woman? Tell me, Em'ly, did I raise you to be this way?"

Emily sighed into the receiver. "Yes, you did."

Well, I had that coming to me, Francine thought.

"Mother, what is going on? This is the first you've called in over a month. And, if I wrote out every word you've written on those postcards, it still wouldn't fill the page of a normal letter."

"What's this normal business?"

"I'm not fighting with you."

"Good. I don't have the time, Em'ly. The reason I called is to see how you're doing."

"Where are you this minute, Mother?"

Francine whispered. "I'm in the ladies' lounge and a very dear and very large lounge maid is now looking at me, piercing me with great concern in her eyes. Another woman can spot a mother and daughter fighting on the phone instantly. Gives off an odor, Em'ly."

"Why did you really call?"

Francine knew that Emily was probably thinking she'd taken off on a drinking binge, had gotten herself into some kind of trouble, had been beaten up maybe, or worse, raped, or robbed, that she was out of money and needed Emily to come rescue her. None of that could have been further from the truth, but Francine had abused her daughter's trust so many times in the past, she really couldn't blame her for having such thoughts.

"I really called to check up on you, my baby, and to tell you that I'm staying here longer. I'm having a wonderful time. I've even made a friend, a very nice woman, Eva Mina. Her cabin is two down from mine. We just thought we'd come to hear a different show tonight."

"Is there an AA nearby?"

"I don't need one, but yes there is. And there's an Overeaters

Anonymous, a Child Abusers Anonymous, and a Cocaine Abusers Anonymous. You don't have to worry."

"I worry."

Francine paused before she said, "Did I have a hand in your worrying too?"

"No," Emily said, and Francine sighed, grateful to Emily for not trying to get another lick in.

"Well . . . how is your summer going? How are your boarder and my granddaughter?"

"I've had better summers. We're, well, we're fine. We're okay. We'd love to see you, you know."

"You will."

"Christmas?"

"Before that, of course. Em'ly, I've got my new purse here with me. I have grown to love it."

"And I've got your old one."

"A fair exchange, wouldn't you say?"

"What are you up to? You sound funny."

"Rest, Em'ly," she said, almost reverently, "that's all. I just really needed a change of scene. Well, I've got to run. My friend is waiting for me. She doesn't like to sit at the table all alone. I'll write."

"A letter."

"I'll try, Em'ly. I will try."

Francine hung up and turned around to see the lounge maid staring at her. "Daughters," Francine said. "They can be difficult, don't you think?"

The woman shook her head and shrugged. "I wouldn't know about that, ma'am. All I've got is one son and he's a bum."

"I'm sorry."

"Me too," the woman said.

When the woman picked up her pile of fresh paper towels and carried them off to the bathroom sinks, Francine dipped into her purse quickly, pulled out a five-dollar bill, and slipped it under the ashtray.

By the time Francine returned to the supper club, the lights had gone down on the tables and a bright blue haze shone over the stage where the band members were taking their places. Francine spotted Eva, chin in hand, looking uncomfortable at a table in the back.

The two women had struck up a friendship quite easily because they seemed to be the only two people at Split Rock vacationing alone; this made them conspicuous to everyone else and to each other. As it happened, one day Francine was leaving her cabin at the same time Eva was leaving hers. Francine was dressed rather elegantly for the resort in a white swimsuit and hooded white cover-up, with matching sandals and just the dramatic touch that was her trademark: a white, silk scarf, a long billowy one wrapped about her hair and face in such a way that it provoked Eva's first words to her: "You look like something from the movies, from *The Philadelphia Story.*" It was all Francine needed to hear.

She never bothered to ask Eva whether she meant the original starring Katharine Hepburn or the remake starring Grace Kelly; she assumed she'd meant the original and wanted to hug Eva on the spot. Eva, who lived in the Roxborough section of Philadelphia, with her son Tony, his wife, and two children, was a dressmaker, had been all of her life, and she admitted that she had been secretly admiring Francine's clothes. They headed for the pool together, and it was under the mild mountain sun that Eva explained that her husband, Tony, had died a year ago, that this was her first vacation alone in her life.

"My daughter is a widow," Francine told her, "and I have been abandoned."

"Why aren't you with her?"

They had ordered tall glasses of iced tea and Francine sipped some of hers before answering. "I don't like her house."

Francine was being deliberately difficult, looking out for Eva's reaction. The other woman's lips parted slightly in surprise, but Eva made no excuse to leave. Francine decided this was a good sign. Over the years she'd lost the knack for making friends easily,

and she tended now to test new acquaintances for resilience. As ⊬
they sat by the pool exchanging snippets from their lives, Francine
felt herself relaxing and she stopped being flip with Eva.

"I'm trying to find her father," she said. "She wants me with (
her, but I think she'll be better off alone right now."

"I see," Eva said, nodding her head in a way that told Francine
she didn't see at all.

"First I'm going to check out all the mountain clubs. He used to
play the clarinet. I was thinking maybe he joined a band after he ran
away. I'm going to one tonight."

"To a bar? Alone?"

"Do you want to come along?"

Eva said she wasn't sure. She wasn't much of a drinker and she
hadn't brought nightclub clothes along.

"Eva, this is not Hollywood, and as far as the drinking goes,
don't worry. I'm an alcoholic—recovered," she had added quickly.
"I know all about bars."

"Well, that's done," Francine said now, sliding into a chair next
to Eva's. "Did you order us something?"

"How is she?"

"Angry with me. Did you order drinks?"

Eva nodded in the direction of the stage. "There's no clarinet
player. I wasn't sure you'd want to stay."

Francine looked up at the stage for the first time since she'd
reentered the room. She frowned. "How can they claim to do big
band without a clarinet?" She gathered her purse in her hands and
tapped Eva's arm. "You're right. Let's go. There's a place down
the road we can try."

Francine drove them to a small cocktail lounge that looked like
an abandoned barn. It was set back on one of the narrow mountain
roads, and if not for the army of cars in the dirt parking lot,
Francine would have thought the place was closed down or
condemned.

"I don't think we want to go in there," Eva said.

"We've got to go *every*where. Don't worry. We're in Pennsylvania. Nothing bad's going to happen to us in the Poconos. The place is probably crawling with honeymooners."

The lounge was crowded with young people: nineteen-year-old girls two years behind the current fashion and young men in denim shirts and jeans that were tight in the crotch. When Francine, wearing one of her suits, asked the bartender for a table in the back, he continued wiping a glass with a white towel and told her: "Lady, you can sit on the floor if that makes you happy. If you can find a table in the back, you can even take it home."

Francine narrowed her eyes at the man and leaned over the edge of the bar. "Don't make promises you can't keep, mister. When I carry my table out of here, don't you breathe a word." Then she steered herself and Eva to a table in the corner, leaving the bartender with a dropped jaw.

"Francine, you're going to get us in trouble. My son'll never let me go away alone again if he has to come bail me out of prison."

"Just sit, Eva. We're not going to prison."

They sat down at a shaky round table with a soiled red tablecloth that hung unevenly at the hem. The unevenness was pointed out by Eva. In the center of the table was a wrought-iron candle holder, a complicated black metal affair supposed to be an imitation of a medieval Spanish candelabra.

"This looks broken," Eva said when they first sat down.

"Just don't shake the table," Francine said. "That thing could kill us if it goes up in flames."

Francine requested her usual Perrier with twist when the waitress came to take their order.

"I don't think so," the waitress said.

"Well, then, how about club soda with a twist?"

"Twist of what?"

"Lime," Francine said, stretching her lips emphatically.

"Can do," the waitress said. "What about you?"

"I'd like a piña colada."

The waitress bobbed her head up and down. "You want that with an umbrella or without?"

Eva looked perplexed by the question and Francine said, "With. Preferably a pink one." The waitress closed her eyes but Francine knew that beneath those closed lids she was rolling them, thinking she and Eva were a couple of crackpots. By the time she returned with their drinks, the house lights dimmed and the band appeared on the cramped stage.

Although they'd been advertised as the "Band of All Sounds," Francine knew instantly that the only sound they'd be capable of was loud sound. This time there was a clarinet player, but he looked just barely twenty-one.

"Drink fast, Eva. We won't find him in this place either."

In the morning, Francine waited at a window table in the lodge dining room. She had already drunk two glasses of orange juice, was working on coffee, and had taken two vitamin C tablets. She figured she needed to keep her strength up if she was going to be spending nights traveling the mountain roads, tracking musicians in out-of-the-way clubs.

In the free space between her silverware on the table, she had laid out several photographs, mostly black-and-white ones with scalloped edges. Those were the oldest pictures, taken at the Ocean Gate house when she and Tom were first married. Lined up next to those were a few color prints, one of which had been taken at this very lodge in 1963. She lifted this one between her bony fingers, holding it at the white border so as not to smudge it. She held it away from her slightly, as if a few inches of distance might bring it more into focus.

She remembered the circumstances of the picture well. She and Tom had eaten breakfast, just as she was about to do now if Eva ever made it to the dining room before they stopped serving, and when they'd come out of the lodge, she had asked another guest who was going in to take the picture.

"I don't want a picture, Franny," Tom had whispered to her just before she caught the attention of the young man entering the lodge.

"Well, I don't see why not," she said. "Might as well have a picture of this part of our lives too."

"I never want to remember this part," he said.

But she had been insistent and the stranger was helplessly caught between them. Tom was in no mood to argue even if he'd been in less of a mood to please. She pulled him near the top step at the entrance and wrapped her arm around his slender waist, hooking her thumb through his belt loop. "This is fine," she told the stranger, who was holding the camera, waiting for his cue. "Shoot it—or whatever."

It was the only picture they'd taken on the trip. After the pictures were developed, Francine sent Tom to pick them up. At home in the dining room, she pulled the photos out of the yellow packet. The other photos on the roll were of their backyard, some of Emily, and then there was the one of her and Tom, he in lightweight slacks and a plaid short-sleeved shirt, facing the camera with his head tilted away from her. She had stared straight into the lens, her white shirtwaist dress fluttering at the hem, looking grim and lonely despite that arm around her husband.

"What's all this?" Eva was standing behind Francine, looking down on the pictures.

Francine quickly gathered them together. "I was beginning to think you overslept," she said, turning to look at Eva.

Eva came around to her side of the table, flopping heavily into her chair. "I'm not used to staying out so late." She was placing her napkin on her lap, but her light hazel eyes were fixed on Francine's pile of pictures.

"All right," Francine sighed. "You may see the pictures." Eva hesitated a moment before gathering them into her hands, and in the meantime, Francine withdrew a long list from her purse.

"This is you," Eva exclaimed.

Francine peered over her paper. "What do you think?"

"You two were a handsome couple."

Francine reached over and poked the '63 photo. "That's the last one I've got of Tom. I figure that's the one I should study. I don't think he'd have grown a beard. He didn't approve of facial hair. And his father was gray at sixty-five, so I'm assuming gray hair but not bald. Unless his metabolism changed drastically, I expect him to be thin still. I was figuring on jowls too."

Eva was staring thoughtfully at the picture, but when she looked up at Francine, her eyes had clouded over.

"No jowls?"

Eva tapped the picture. "It was taken here. I mean"—and she pointed out the window—"right there. On the steps. You both look miserable."

Francine, still holding the list in her hands, brought her wrists to rest on the table. "We were not on vacation. No. We came here to make a decision."

Eva straightened in her chair. "You're going to tell me something awful, aren't you?"

Now Francine let go of her list and Eva saw that there were at least fifteen names of clubs written down. Carefully and slowly, Francine folded her hands over the paper and leaned in toward Eva. "I suppose I can't expect you to come with me unless I tell you certain things, can I?"

Eva cleared her throat. "Anthony used to say that you don't have to know everything about a person—in time they show you everything without saying a word. It was easy for him to not know details."

"What about you?"

"I think I need more. Maybe not."

Looking away from Eva's round and trusting face, Francine said softly, "First of all, I had two daughters, Eva. And," she said, smoothing out the paper in front of her, "I don't think I deserved either one of them."

SIX

"It was winter," Francine told Eva. "Em'ly was four going on five. The day I went into labor with Maria, the three of us went over to the ice skating rink. We were living in New Jersey, in Haddonfield. Do you know the town?"

"I'm afraid I don't," Eva said. "Could you pass the cream, please?"

Francine slid the small glass container toward Eva.

"It's a beautiful town. Very old, with imposing fieldstone and Victorian houses, trees lining the wide winding streets, manicured—not just landscaped, but *manicured* lawns. Running through the center of town is Kings Highway. George Washington was supposed to have stayed in one of the houses on the highway. All the shops there are small—"

"And expensive," Eva said, smiling.

"Yes, expensive. Anyway, it is a lovely place. A place where you wouldn't expect inclement weather. Well, it had no ice skating rink, so we always drove over to Philly to ice skate. That was another of Tom's hobbies: skating and the clarinet."

"What did he do for a living?"

"Lawyer."

Eva nodded. "Why did I ask?"

Francine let the comment pass and continued. "I wasn't going to

/77

skate. I just went along because Tom didn't want to leave me home alone. I looked like an elephant that had been injected with helium. I was swollen beyond belief.

"Tom was off renting skates that day because his own were being fixed and I helped Em'ly get into hers. I don't know what made me look toward the entrance of the rink but I did, and when Tom saw me looking he waved at me as if he hadn't seen me in years. My arm shot up in the air, more a salute than a wave, and at the same time I felt this excruciating pain, not the crampy slow rumble I'd felt with Em'ly.

"Twenty hours of labor. Tom took Em'ly to his mother's and then he came back to the hospital and walked the halls, I suppose. I didn't wake up until the following morning and when I did I thought I was alone in the room. I'll never forget the weather—gray and slick, like the lining of a good coat. I had tubes in one arm and I rubbed my free hand over my stomach. It was still so swollen I thought the baby was still there. 'When's the labor over?' I said out loud, and then, as if he'd been blown in on a cloud, Tom said, 'Labor's over, Franny.'

"I wasn't alone. He'd been there the whole time waiting for me to wake up. I turned to his voice and saw him sitting in a chair, holding on to the bed rail. His knuckles were as white as flour. 'Why aren't you holding me? Where are the roses, Tom? You said there'd be yellow roses.'

" 'She has problems, Franny,' he said.

" 'A new girl? Is she pretty?'

"And he broke down. Mind you, Eva, I'd never seen him cry before. I found a way to sit up, and I reached for his head with the arm that was taped to the IV and the board. I could move my fingers just a little, and when he felt me he looked up, very quickly, and wiped his eyes. He took my arm and rested it beside me. 'Give me your other hand,' he said. So I did.

"Now I can run off the names of her disabilities like a pro, but that day he might as well have been speaking in tongues: unfused spine, cerebral palsy, profound retardation, seizures, deformed hands. He went on and on. Midway through his litany, I said, 'Blue eyes?'

" 'Franny . . . Francine, are you listening to me?'

" 'I've heard everything. Are her eyes blue? She does have eyes, right?"

"He took a deep breath. 'Her eyes are blue,' he said.

" 'How much does she weigh?'

" 'Eight ten.'

" 'How long?'

" 'Twenty inches.'

"But as soon as he said it he was out of his chair, pacing. 'Don't do this, Franny. Why are you asking such stupid questions? She's a mess.' He hollered it, and then realizing what he said, he covered his mouth. He looked so stricken. I must not have been in my right mind. Who would be? I was sitting straight up in bed and very calmly I told him, 'She's our baby. We'll name her Maria and get Father Ed to do the christening. I'm glad she's pretty like Em'ly. Now, Tom, let's have some flowers in this dreary room. Let's have red and yellow roses.' "

"You kept her," Eva said, her voice thick.

"Yes, we did. I wanted to. It was 1954 and we really had no one to turn to. The doctors put a shunt in Maria's head to drain off the water and keep it from getting bigger. They told us that there were newer and newer medications being discovered all the time to help with the seizures she would have. They said her heart wasn't properly formed and she would never chew food in her lifetime—it would have to be blended, like baby food. She wasn't going to be able to move around much, and if by some miracle she did, it would be crawling, animallike. She would grunt, they said, not talk. She would never stop wearing diapers. You can put her away, they told us. I couldn't.

"I planned a christening and invited relatives and friends. I dressed her in my christening gown; it was silk and Em'ly had worn it, but I had to take the matching hat apart and sew an extra panel in the back so it would fit her head. I pressed her into people's arms as if she were an angel and no one knew what to do. I told Em'ly, 'This is our real life now and we've got to take care of Maria.' I became obsessed with Maria's care. I even believed, Eva, that she would get better. I read everything I could find, which wasn't much, and I talked to doctors everywhere, hired quacks—of course, I didn't know they were quacks—who told me, promised me that they could make her better."

Eva looked away from Francine, out the window. Her chin was cupped in her hand and she was shaking her head. "I don't think I could have done it, Fran. How did you get through each day?" she asked, turning back to look at Francine.

Francine waved her hands. "Don't congratulate me yet, Eva. I made quite a mess of it. As she got older, the seizures were more frequent and she had to wear this leather contraption, like an old-time football helmet, because sometimes she'd bang her head on the floor after a seizure. The house was filled with special seats, boards, and tables, and by the time she was five, I couldn't take care of her alone anymore. Well, Tom couldn't stay at home with me all day and Em'ly was still a child herself. What could I expect from her? The poor kid never brought friends home. I had to do something, so I hired women to live in and help with Maria.

"None of them worked out for very long. They'd be fine for a few weeks, then I'd get a phone call and they'd make up some lie about needing to move to California to care for a sick aunt or something. Then, finally, I found Mabel Barley.

"I'll never forget the day she came to the house. She was a big black woman. I showed her into the living room and she walked right over to the feeding table. 'I thought I'd seen the last of one of these when I left Baltimore,' she said.

" 'You've worked with retarded children?'

" 'I'm the sister of one, Miss Perone.'

" 'My daughter's name is Maria.'

" 'How old?' she asked.

" 'She's five.'

"I was amazed at how comfortable she was in the room. She'd shown herself to the sofa, sat down, and crossed her legs at the ankles. She kept her purse in her lap and her white gloves on. I sat down myself and explained all of Maria's problems in detail, to which Mabel either sighed or hooted. Finally, she asked if she could see her. I'd just gotten her down for a nap, but I led Mabel up the stairs to her room.

"We kept the furnishings in Maria's room spare because if she got hold of anything she could hurt herself. Tom had built her a special crib as big as a child-sized bed but with high railings so she couldn't fall off at night. Well, Mabel crept right up to the crib and reached in, brushing back Maria's hair. I hung back by the door, holding my breath, marveling at this woman. Then she turned around.

" 'Does she bite?' she whispered.

" 'Yes.'

" 'Beat up on herself?'

"I swallowed hard, wanting to lie, but told her, 'Sometimes.'

" 'How many bowel movements per day?'

" 'Too many.'

"Mabel nodded toward the door and we went down the hallway, back to the living room. Mabel asked me then if I was taking vitamins. I thought the question was odd, and I didn't see what it had to do with Maria. I couldn't even answer at first.

" 'Well, are you or aren't you?'

" 'When I remember.'

"She opened her purse then and took out an amber bottle that she hook at me. 'These are vitamins with an iron supplement. We've got our work cut out for us, and I can't have you getting sick on me. Long as I work for you, Miss Perone, you take one of these per day. She's in sorrier shape than my brother ever was.'

"I wanted to hug her. I showed her through the rest of the house and for the first time in a year I felt a lightness in those walls, as if the house were expanding. In the kitchen, Mabel ran her gloved finger along the Formica countertop and I told her then that I had an older daughter too.

" 'Another one? Like Maria?'

" 'No.'

" 'How old?'

" 'Em'ly is nine now.'

"Mabel sniffed and her eyes darted around the kitchen. 'Well, I suppose she'll be needing vitamins too.' "

It was then that Francine became aware of the waitress standing by the table. "Yes, what is it?"

"I'm sorry, but we've got to set up for lunch, ladies."

"Lunch?"

Eva looked at her watch. "My God, Fran. We've been sitting here for close to two hours."

"Oh my," Francine said. "Well, let's have the check then," she told the waitress. The waitress laid the bill on the table, but Francine snatched it up. "I've got it, Eva, get your hands out of your purse. It's the least I can do. I've been gabbing away all this time."

When they left the lodge they were surprised to discover how hot it was, and how humid. The lodge was nestled among high green mountains, but when Francine looked up at those mountains she saw that the tops were obscured in a thick, wavering haze. "Would you just look at that," Francine said, pointing at the mountains. "I expected it to be cooler here, clearer."

"We could sit by the pool if you want."

"Good idea."

They had to cross a curvy road, thick with shrubbery and trees, to get to their cabins. "I used to spend all of my summers at the beach, in Ocean Gate where Em'ly lives now. That's a grand house, Eva. It belonged to my parents, then they passed it on to Tom and me, and I gave it to Em'ly when she was married."

"That's some wedding present."

"Well, she loved it there. It's a block away from the beach, a huge yellow clapboard house with red tile shingles on the roof. There's a wraparound porch in front and another little porch on the side, right off the kitchen. It's got big picture windows in front, and on the roof, just to the right side of the house, there's a . . . well, I guess you'd call it a captain's walk or—and isn't this ironic—a widow's walk. You know, one of those glass lookout towers, about the size of a roomy closet. There's a big backyard and a separate garage that was probably a carriage house at one time, and the front yard is a nice size, fenced in, flagstone walk up to the porch. Before Maria was born, I just loved spending the summer there. Em'ly and I would leave in June and stay till mid–September and Tom, because of his work, would stay on in Haddonfield and then come down to the shore on the weekends. Sometimes we'd have friends visit. At night we'd sit out on the porch and talk and laugh. You could hear the ocean thrashing in the distance; you could see the fireflies flickering in the yard. We'd get Tom to play his clarinet for us, then rib him if he made a mistake. They were wonderful times. . . ." she said, her voice trailing off.

"We went to Wildwood," Eva said. "Not as classy a place as your Ocean Gate, and we didn't own a house there. Usually we stayed at a hotel. We'd take Anthony with us and we'd take my mother or Tony's mother along too. We always wanted a beach house. Some nights we'd take a long drive through the other shore towns, you know? We'd go to Cape May and to Avalon and drive through the streets. I always wondered about the people like you, what it must have been like to be well off. I used to tell Tony, a little angrily even, that those people had everything."

"But we did," Francine said.

They were on the narrow dirt path now, twigs cracking beneath their feet. Eva stopped suddenly and turned toward Francine.

"What's wrong?" asked Francine.

"But you had problems too," Eva said.

"Look, don't start feeling guilty just because you thought of us as snobs, Eva. I *was* a snob. Still am," Francine said, raising her chin. Eva laughed.

When they reached their cabins they parted, agreeing to change and meet by the pool in half an hour. Francine arrived at the pool first and she got two lounge chairs, pulling them off to a more private corner of the tiled poolside; then she bought two large iced teas at the snack shop and was just heading back to the chairs when she saw Eva coming through the gate. Francine lifted one of the paper cups high in the air hoping that Eva would see her, but when Eva headed in the opposite direction, Francine had to shout, "Eva, over here!" to get her attention.

"God, this place is crawling with people," Eva said. She dropped her beach bag next to the chair and took her iced tea from Francine.

Francine was already sitting down, but she hadn't removed her cover-up yet. "Years ago when Tom and I were here you'd have thought the place was some kind of secret hideaway. Very few guests that summer."

"I don't understand," Eva said, sipping her tea, "why you came here when you had the summer house."

Francine put her cup down, then she leaned forward and peeled off the white voile cover-up, draping it over the back of her chair. Without saying a word she took her suntan lotion from her beach bag, squeezed some into the palm of her hand, and began rubbing it on her arms. She was well aware that Eva was staring at her, iced tea poised in her hands, waiting for an answer. She liked Eva; she hadn't found it this easy to talk to another woman in many years, particularly someone she barely knew. She liked that Eva saw her as strong and capable, even a little odd, but she wondered if she'd lose her new friend as quickly as she'd made her once she told Eva the rest of her story.

"Fran? Did I say something wrong?"

Francine began to put lotion on her legs. "No, no you didn't. I just don't know what you'll think once I tell you why we came here."

"Well, you said earlier it was to make a decision."

Francine offered Eva the suntan lotion, but Eva shook her head. "I never burn."

"Like Tom," Francine said, "that Italian skin. Em'ly's like him. She looks like an American Indian by the middle of June. Oh, well." She dropped the bottle of lotion into her bag, pulled her sunglasses down onto her face, and lay back in the lounge chair, her arms resting by her side.

"We don't have to talk anymore," Eva said. "Some things are too hard to talk about."

"I want to. I do, ah, now that I've started, I really do want to."

Francine could feel Eva moving in her chair, getting herself situated and comfortable, and as soon as Eva seemed to be at rest, Francine told her, "Everything got worse by the time Maria was nine. The strain of taking care of her, even with Mabel's help, was starting to get to me. Up at five every day—it took two hours just to bathe her because she didn't like water and she put up such a fight. And she was gangly, all arms and legs. By eight in the morning when Tom left for the office, I felt as if I'd been awake for a week. In the middle of all of it was Em'ly, quieter than death itself, looking on, staying out of the way. It was around that time that we started talking about a place for Maria."

"An institution?"

"Hell bins is how I thought of them. I didn't see how we could lock her away and go on living with any peace of mind, Eva. The doctor told us that everything would get worse. 'Puberty, you know,' he said, trying to be decorous. I had no idea a child like Maria would get her period. With everything else in her body lagging behind, you'd think God would have seen fit to stop her period. 'You must think of yourselves and your other child,' the doctor with normal children told us. 'Professionals will know what to do.' But would they love her, those professionals? I wondered. 'In their way,' the doctor said. Oh, Eva, when he said that I thought of my own love, which was half pity and half hate, and I almost thought their way might be best. Then everything," Francine said, her voice cracking, "began to fall apart.

"I can still remember the night. It was a golden rather than a dusky blue twilight, late spring, early evening. Maria could sit in a special chair at the table with us by this time. That evening she spat out most of her food, upset a bowl of gravy, and bit me when I tried to feed her some whipped potatoes. Tom tried to take over, but she kicked at him under the table. Suddenly he got up and stuffed his hands under her at the armpits, lifting her out of the chair. He said he was bringing her to the living room to cool down. Just a minute later, Em'ly and I heard the shattering of glass and Tom yelling, 'Franny! Come quick!'

"Em'ly and I rushed to the living room, where we found Maria sitting beneath the bay window in a sea of glass. Little bits of it glistened in her hair. She'd gotten away from Tom somehow and had punched the window. Oh, Eva, blood was oozing from her arm, and Tom was begging her to be still so he could lift her out of the glass, and then I shouted at him, 'What did you do to her?' Can you imagine the astonishment, the hurt in his eyes? He said, 'Get a towel, Franny.'

"We ran around each other like cartoon cops, clumsy, frantic, and in seconds we were leaving the house, hurrying down the long drive to the car. 'Emily, stay put,' Tom called back to her because she was following us. Maria's arm was wrapped in the towel and Tom held her against him so snugly. Em'ly told me later that she and Mabel cleaned up the mess, that Mabel said to her, 'That child's going to break every window in this house, if she don't break your Momma and Daddy first, Lady Jane. People have got to have some peace. They've got to.'

"Tom was saying pretty much the same thing to me while they stitched Maria up. 'It was only an accident, Tom. She needs a new medication,' I said. But he just bit down on his lower lip and turned away.

"When we came home, Tom carried Maria up to her room and I told Em'ly that everything was fine, just fine. She stared at me with those black eyes of hers and said not one word. She walked away, into the kitchen I thought. Tom was still upstairs. I was shaking from head to toe, so I went into the study—that's where we kept the liquor—and I made myself a quick one, whiskey neat, gulped it down in a flash. I stood there for some time, thinking that I was alone, but Em'ly was in the doorway, Eva, and she asked me what was going to happen. Know what I said to my thirteen-year-old girl? I said, 'Em'ly, my baby, we are going to be happy.' I was wrong, of course. I liked drinking and I wasn't very good at it, holding my liquor, and by the time summer rolled around, Maria had broken that window twice more. We didn't even consider going to the summer house."

Eva sighed. "So you came up here, just the two of you, to decide what to do?"

"Yes." Francine felt her throat swell, that tight suffocating feeling just before the start of tears; she swallowed, trying to keep her composure. She could almost feel the restlessness she'd felt that summer, the uneasiness, the strain of waiting for the next incident. She remembered the hot July afternoon, sitting in the kitchen while Mabel ironed shirts, sweat rolling off her forehead. Francine and Mabel each had a glass of lemonade, but unknown to Mabel, Francine's was laced with Johnnie Walker. It was her third glass in forty-five minutes. As Mabel worked the steaming iron over the shirts, she said, "If you don't lift up your eyelids soon and take a good look at what's happening, you won't be hearing my humming voice around here much longer."

"You have no right to threaten me that way," Francine said.

"That may be, Miss Franny, but I have a right to quit and quit is probably what I will do."

Francine looked up from her seat at the kitchen table. "Well, then unplug the cord on that iron and get out, you fat bitch."

Mabel then took the iron and laid it flat on the blouse she'd just begun ironing. It was linen, one of Francine's finest, and Mabel took her hands off the iron handle, put her hands on her hips, and stepped back, watching the steam surge up, smelling the burning cloth. "This time, Miss Franny, you've gone too far."

Emily had walked in the back door at that moment. She must have thought they were sending the house up in flames. "Now what? Now what next!" she shouted, pushing in front of Mabel, lifting the iron off the blouse. "Oh, God, look at this." She held the scorched blouse up, spun around, pushing it at Mabel's bosom. "She doesn't pay you to burn her clothes."

Francine didn't know what had come over her, but she was out of her chair, raising her hand to Emily's face. The blow landed like a weak karate chop against Emily's neck. Immediately after she hit her, Francine stood back, grasping the chair with her hands. "You shouldn't talk to Mabel that way."

But Mabel had moved up behind Emily. "It's all right, Lady Jane."

Emily stared at Francine. "You're disgusting," she said. "You're just plain disgusting." And she ran out of the kitchen.

Francine was livid, hollering after her, "Take that back! You take that back!"

Then she turned to Mabel. "Go get her, Mabel. Go after her and tell her she shouldn't talk that way to either one of us." But Mabel took Francine by the wrists, guiding her back to her chair. She smoothed Francine's hair, took the glass away from her.

"Why aren't you going after her? Why doesn't anyone here listen to me?"

Mabel stood at the sink, rinsing out the glass. "Nobody's going to pay mind to a woman who drinks in the middle of the day."

"I was drinking lemonade, same as you."

Mabel turned slowly from the sink. "Only thing worse than a lush is a lush who lies. From now on you pass these liquids under my nose, Miss Franny, otherwise you're going to be the downfall of this family here."

Francine was too hot and dizzy to argue. "The downfall of this family was born nine years ago," she mumbled.

Mabel rubbed Francine's damp back. "Miss Franny, you better hope the Lord is napping and didn't hear what you just said."

"Fran?" Francine felt Eva's hand on her arm. "Are you okay?"
Francine couldn't speak; she just nodded.
"I'm going to get us some more iced tea. I'll be right back."

Francine lay motionless in the lounge chair. "Good. Get extra lemon in mine, would you, Eva?"

As she listened to Eva walking away, she found that she couldn't open her eyes, that her lids felt weighted with memory. How clearly, with her eyes shut and the sun burning down on her, she could see Tom and her house, hear their voices, especially the night he came to her with Mabel's letter of resignation.

She had just finished the routine of combing Maria's hair and brushing her teeth, and she had rewarded herself with a glass of Scotch, was dipping her index finger into the glass when Tom found her outside on the patio, sitting in a white wrought-iron chair. He sat down in a chair, waving something back and forth to get her attention; she could see it out of the corner of her eye.

"Franny?"

She looked up and offered him her finger. "Want to taste?"

He shook his head and handed her the letter.

"What's this?"

"Read it."

She skimmed the letter, then pushed the paper across the glass-topped table. "For Pete's sake, Tom. She doesn't mean it. She threatens to leave every week. Gets her ideas from the movies."

Tom hung his head. "Where you get yours?"

"Oh, puuleeaase," she said, her teeth clenched, "do you know what I've just been through with Maria?"

"I don't think we can hold up much longer this way," he said.

"What are you suggesting, may I ask? It's something I'm not going to be able to do. I can feel it. I know it. Makes my knees ache."

Tom leaned forward so he could take her hands in his, and in that touch was the authority she'd felt years ago when he led her to the ice.

"Franny, my Franny, I think that we . . . I think we have to start looking for a place for Maria."

"A place," Francine said, still holding his hands, pretending not to know what he meant.

"Yes. There's no way to get relief, even with Mabel. And Emily, look what this is doing to her. She has no friends. Your drinking, Franny, it's worse every day."

She let her hands slide out of Tom's, pushed up from the chair, and walked to the edge of the patio, keeping her back to him. "I'll stop drinking. I'm not an alcoholic or anything. I'll chew gum instead. I'll take up needlepoint. You could teach me the clarinet. Yes! That's it. Tom. You teach me an instrument. It's only a matter of finding a more suitable hobby."

He hung his head.

"Don't ask me to put my baby away. She came out of me."

Suddenly his head shot up and he shouted, "Mere biology that she came out of you. She's mine too, Francine."

Francine laughed, a choked sound, that he should seem so jealous of her guilt and want it for himself.

She turned away from him again and announced to the blue-green yard, to the crickets clicking there, that she could not do this, could not even think about this yet.

"Till the end of the summer then," he said. "Either we get you help or we all find help, but by the end of this damn awful summer, Francine, we've got to begin saving what's left to be saved."

"Here we go. Extra lemon for you."

Francine opened her eyes, removed her glasses, and sat up. Eva was standing by the chair, the sun behind her, holding out the tall paper cup.

"Drink fast," Eva said, "the sun's already melting the ice. It's so hot, I can't believe it."

Francine sipped. "We should probably go back to the cabins soon."

Eva's eyes scanned the poolside. "Well, at least the crowd thinned out a little."

"Hmm."

90 /

"Fran, you came here to decide about the institutions, didn't you? There's one about fifty miles from here. I passed it on my way up."

"Yes. That's the one. I just got worse that summer. Tom and I, well, we weren't making love anymore. Mabel had left. Everything was a mess. He'd brought all of these brochures home. I hated it, Eva. Every good place seemed so far away. Then one night we were lying there in bed, waiting for her cry—she would do that, cry out sometimes—and I just got up and went to her room. I stood there at the end of the bed. Maria's face was pushed into the pillow and her breathing was, well, it was really strenuous. I waited. I waited, Eva, before I moved close to her and turned her head so she could breathe. I loved the sound of her life when she was asleep, and I reached through the rails to hold her before I felt her wriggling away. She rubbed her forehead with her fists, unaware of her own saliva. Her mouth was half open and swollen from where she'd punched herself earlier that day.

" 'You're going to have a whopper of a fat lip,' I said. She thrashed then, smacking her arm against mine. 'It's Mommy,' I said, kneeling down so I could put my face closer to hers, but as soon as I did, I pulled back at the smell of her breath, sour and rank. I thought, she won't miss me. Maybe she doesn't even know I'm her mother.

"So I got up and rearranged the sheets over her and went back to my room. After a long time I said, 'We'll go look at the institutions.' My head was throbbing with every syllable and I felt Tom's hand moving under the sheet until it found mine.

" 'When?'

" 'As soon as possible,' I said. 'Soon. Before I change my mind.'

"Tom made the reservations here the following day."

Eva was peering into her cup of tea. "What a horrible choice. I feel for you, Fran, I do. And you must question it every time you come to visit her."

"What?"

Eva looked up, shook the remaining ice in her cup. "When you visit Maria, you must feel awful all over again. You do visit her still, don't you?"

Francine searched Eva's eyes, hoping that Eva would make the connection, believing that Eva had understood.

"Why are you staring at me like that?"

Francine ran her fingers through her hair, then clasped them together tightly, making a fist that she thumped on Eva's knee.

"Eva, three months after we placed her in the institution—after I—*me*, Eva, I decided . . . Eva, she died. Maria is dead."

SEVEN

The news of Maria's death didn't sit too well with Eva, and exactly what Francine feared would happen between them happened. First, Eva claimed to be feeling ill. She began taking her meals in her cabin and refused to accompany Francine on any more nightclub searches. "I think I'm allergic to the smoke in those places," she told Francine.

"You never mentioned it before."

"Well, I think it's a sudden allergy. That can happen, you know. I read about it. A person can eat bananas for years and years, then just like that," she said, snapping her fingers, "he breaks out in a rash one morning after putting bananas on his cereal."

"You're angry with me, aren't you?"

"That's ridiculous, Francine."

"Oh, so it's Francine now. What happened to Fran?"

They were standing on either side of Eva's cabin doorway at dusk. Eva kept most of her body behind the opened door so that only her head, one shoulder, and one hand were visible, the way a woman might stand if a Jehovah's Witness were at her doorstep, selling her a religion she didn't want or need.

Francine noticed that Eva hung her head a little when she said, "I meant Fran."

Francine flicked her fingers over the lapels of her dress, tucked her purse under her arm. "All right. I just thought I'd ask if you want to come with me tonight, but if the smoke is going to bother you, I'll go alone."

Just as Francine turned to walk away she thought she saw Eva about to call her back, but on second glance she realized that Eva was simply parting her lips, perhaps in surprise that she would actually go on without her.

"See you," Francine said, not bothering to wave good-bye.

It was a fifteen-mile drive over curvy and poorly lit roads to Big Daddy's, which was one of the five remaining area clubs on Francine's long list. With Eva along, it had been easier to hide the frustration when, night after night, their search had left them empty-handed; now that she was hitting the clubs alone, she felt her spirits waning. She found herself thinking about a drink when she sat at the bar or at a table alone, watching groups of people ordering one round after another.

The interior of Big Daddy's wasn't much different from most of the clubs she and Eva had visited. The place was dark and cramped, smoke filled and loud, with low-slung ceilings and cedar-shake walls that made the room smell like sawdust. She looked around quickly and spotted a place at the bar where she then perched herself upon a padded stool, swiveling halfway toward the stage, which was across the room. From her seat she would have an unobstructed view of the band when they began their first set.

"What'll it be?" the bartender asked.

"Perrier with a twist of lime," she said automatically, but before he could move down the bar, she added, "and a Johnnie Walker on the rocks."

"You want to wait on one of those? For your friend?"

"No friend," she said. "They're both for me."

The bartender nodded slowly. "Black or Red on the Walker?"

"Red."

He placed two emerald green cocktail napkins in front of her, putting a short wide glass of Johnnie Walker on one and the tall, bubbling Perrier on the other. Francine passed him a ten, told him to keep the change. He was puzzled at first, even hesitant, then he took the bill, rang up the drinks, and put the five in the tip tray next to the register.

"You want a tab?"

Francine took the lime from the Perrier and gave it another twist before taking it out of the glass. "No. No tab. This will be it."

"I'm Chalie," he told her, pronouncing his name without the *r*.

Francine smiled. "And I don't need to talk to anyone."

Chalie rolled his eyes. "Hey, no problem, miss. I'm only here to serve."

To her immediate right were two people fidgeting on their stools, drumming their fingers on the bar. "Then serve them, Chalie. They look mean."

He shrugged and moved down the bar. "What'll it be?" she heard him ask.

Francine returned to her drinks with renewed interest. She drank half the Perrier, then she lifted the squat whiskey glass to her lips and held it there, letting the aroma of the golden liquid waft into her nostrils. She'd not held alcohol this close since 1965 and, until tonight, she'd not entertained the thought of ever holding it this close again. She knew the powers of the liquid well: that burning feeling on the first gulp, the warmth that would squeeze the pain out of her heart on the swallow, how her mind could transform anything bad that happened to her once she downed two or three glasses. She rolled the glass between her palms, listening through the din of voices and piped-in music to the rattle of ice in the glass. Looking down into it as if it were a crystal ball, she saw not the future but the past. She could remember with amazing clarity all of the nights after Tom left her, how she would lie to Emily and tell her she was going to play bridge. She would dress in something fussy and garish and stay out all night, leaving a sixteen-year-old Emily all alone in that large empty house. Often, she would stumble in around five or six and find Emily asleep on the couch, sometimes even on the living room floor where she must have been keeping vigil.

She would stoop down over Emily's curled-up body and shake her awake with every intention of apologizing for being out so long, but when Emily's eyes opened, when she sat up and stared with the eyes of judgment and contempt, Francine would start yelling. "Don't look at me like that, would you? I'm an adult. I don't have a curfew, young lady." By then Emily would begin gathering up her books and notepads (she was always reading or writing something), wordless, and the more quiet she was, the louder Francine yelled, until, exhausted, she would collapse on the sofa. It was then that Emily would come to her, sighing but dutiful nonetheless. She would slip her thin arms around Francine's waist. "You need a shower and a bed. You smell bad, Mom. Come on, I'll take care of you." And she could remember the last night she'd taken a drink: Emily, sixteen, was burning up with fever, her sweaty head bent over the toilet bowl. "Mom!" she had managed through the heaves. But she was too drunk to come to Emily's side, just a fraction away from loss of consciousness, unable to help her daughter, but worse, not even wanting to.

Francine was still holding the glass threateningly close to her lips. "What are you doing?" she said out loud.

"What? You want me to freshen that?" Chalie asked.

Francine put the glass down and pushed it away from her. "I don't want it. I don't want that," she said, her voice rising, pointing to the glass.

Chalie spoke to her hoarsely through clenched teeth. "Fine, lady. You don't have to have it, but keep it down, will you? You're gonna make people think I'm hitting on you or something."

She grabbed her Perrier glass, quickly drinking what little remained. "I have to go now," she told him as she picked up her purse. She wasn't even going to wait to hear the band; she wanted to set some things straight with Eva.

Francine pounded on Eva's door for several minutes before she heard the lock click and Eva turning the knob. It was clear to her that she'd woken Eva from a sound sleep. Eva was still wearing her jeans and shirt, but her short curly hair was mussed; along her cheek were the embarrassing red grooves one always got from sleeping in an odd position. It seemed Eva had fallen asleep with her face pressed against her watch.

"What time is it?" Eva asked, yawning, rubbing her face with both hands.

"Ten. It's early."

Eva yawned again. "Early for you maybe. What's wrong?"

"What's wrong? Let me in and I'll tell you."

Eva glanced backward into the softly lit room as if she were hiding someone in there she might not want Francine to meet, then she stepped back, giving Francine room to move inside. As soon as she was in the cabin, Francine closed the door and pressed her back up against it. "I believe I'm going to be tense," she said, to which Eva merely looked puzzled. "Is there anything to drink? I'm terribly thirsty."

Eva pointed to the top of the dresser. "Coke."

The bottle was warm, but Francine took it and a glass with her to the bed. She opened the bottle, poured some of the warm Coke into the glass, and drank it quickly. "You want some?" she asked Eva, who was now sitting next to her. Eva shook her head no.

"Did something bad happen?" Eva asked.

Francine was holding both the glass and the bottle so tightly she thought she might break them; she put both down on the floor by her feet. "I almost took a drink tonight. I mean, I *ordered* a drink. I held it in my hands even, and, Eva, that is not a good thing, not at all. No sir."

"I'm sorry. Maybe if I'd been with you . . ."

But Francine waved her hand. "No alcoholic ever stopped drinking because she had a watchdog with her." She took a deep breath. "I've disappointed you, haven't I?"

Eva was looking down on her own hands, stroking the tops of them as if she were trying to smooth out the wrinkles. "I just don't understand, that's all. After all you've told me. What I mean is, you've already lost one daughter, why risk losing another? Especially one who needs you right now?"

Francine turned, placing her arms in front of her for support, and leaned in close to Eva. "Do you know that in the nineteen years since Tom left I never once, not once, looked for him? What do you think of that, hmm?"

Eva made no reply and with that Francine stood up, one hand on her hip, the other beating at her chest while she spoke. "I thought he was going to come back. Can you imagine? I drank every day until Em'ly was sixteen, until she and my own mother had to put me away to dry out, because when I was drunk I could make myself believe anything."

"But that doesn't have anything to do with now."

"Yes, yes it does. A daughter's face is a mirror, Eva. She shows you every ugly thing you've been. She carries that, you know? I can't stand to look at Em'ly right now because when I do, she just reminds me that it was my fault her father left. I want to give back what I took away."

"Maybe you can't. Maybe you shouldn't. Maybe you should just be with her. It might be all she really wants."

Eva's words startled Francine enough so that she stood perfectly still in the room and dropped her hands by her sides. "I have to try."

Eva pressed her hands in on her thighs; she dropped her head, then looked up quickly. "How many more clubs on the list?"

"Four."

"All right. If anyone tried to stop me, I'd probably tell him that I know my Tony better than anyone, that I know what I'm doing. You want to go tomorrow night?"

Francine smiled. "Eight o'clock then?"

"Yes, yes. Eight o'clock. It's been boring faking an allergy anyway."

July ended in a fine, steady drizzle that turned the mountain air cool and the sky white-gray. At night the hard rocks glistened along the roadside, fog curled up around the lodge, settled in the valley. On the last night of their stay, Eva and Francine were going to tackle the final club on the list: The Starlight Room at the Starlight Pocono Hotel.

"And what's our next move if we don't find him there either?" Eva asked while Francine busily applied a dusky shade of eyeshadow—Midnight Muse—to Eva's eyelids.

"Please don't blink, Eva, you're wrinkling your lids."

"My lids are that way, Fran. I'm old."

Francine held Eva's right eyelid down with the fleshy part of her thumb. "I'll not hear the word *old*. We are beautifully mature."

"You still didn't answer my question."

"Well . . . " she said, "other lid, please." And Eva closed her left eye. "Well, I have a feeling about tonight."

"What if your feeling is wrong?"

Francine stepped back, still holding the miniature shadow brush between her fingers as if it were a conductor's baton. "I haven't thought past the initial feeling, but I won't give up. All right, now give me your lips."

Eva tilted her chin upward.

The Starlight Pocono Hotel had once been a Holiday Inn, and the owners, either out of sentimentality or lack of originality, had left the Holiday Inn green-and-blue decor intact. From what Francine could see the only changes made under the new management were in the ceilings, where billions of tiny stars had been painted on in gold and silver latex. The stars were distinctly out of place shining down on the hard-edged fifties-style couches and chairs, the large pots of fake blue dogwood trees and rubber plants. The Starlight Room itself was an improvement. The room was sparsely lit and the astral bodies in the high dome ceiling seemed, at least, to make more sense in the cocktail lounge.

At the table, Francine ordered her Perrier; Eva had switched to Scotch on the rocks. Both women were on their second round of drinks when the band members started making their way to the stage. They were wearing maroon three-piece suits and Francine frowned.

"What's the matter?"

"I don't think Tom would ever wear a suit like that."

"It's been a long time, Fran."

Francine turned her attention back to the stage where one of the men was lifting his clarinet from the stand. His back was still to the audience, and as he straightened up, Francine could see that he was tall, although she couldn't make out his age. In the split second between the time his back was to them and the time he turned around, Francine had already envisioned their reunion. But the man who turned around, bringing the clarinet to his lips, turned out to be a very light-skinned black man.

"Oh, my," Francine said, looking away. "Well, we can see it isn't him, can't we?"

They sat through one set, and when the band stopped for a break Francine got up. "I'll be right back, Eva."

She pushed her way through the crowd to the stage; when she returned Eva asked what she'd said to him.

"I said if I closed my eyes I would think it was Benny G. playing."

"Did you mean it?"

Francine gave Eva a long thoughtful look. "No. It was the only thing I could think of doing to save the evening."

They had one more round of drinks before paying the bill and heading out of the lounge. There was still some last-minute packing to be done, and Eva wanted to get up early the next morning, make the drive back to Roxborough before the traffic got too heavy on the turnpike.

"We'll go back to the cabin, maybe have some coffee," Francine was saying, but she found herself talking to no one because Eva had stopped by the door of the lounge. When Francine turned to see what had happened to her, she saw Eva pointing to a poster that wasn't there earlier when they'd gone in. It was set up easel-style to the left of the lounge doorway.

"Look, Fran."

In bold letters against a red background Francine read: APPEARING IN TWO WEEKS—THE BENNY T. GOODMAN BAND. THE NEWEST SWING BAND WITH THE OLDEST AND BEST SOUND.

Francine stood before the sign, looking first at it, then at Eva.

"Benny *T?* Do you think Tom would do that? Take on a name like that, a joke like that?"

Eva shrugged. "I guess it's possible, isn't it?"

Francine's eyes were shining. "That's the kind of talk I like to hear. Come on. Let's go."

"Where now?"

"To the front desk. I'm going to make a reservation. I'm going to come back two weeks from now."

At the desk while they waited for the clerk, Eva said, "What about work? Won't they need you there?"

She had devoted over ten years to SPSC, helping other people find ways to get their lives in order, ignoring the loose ends of her own.

"I'll take care of it, Eva. It'll be fine."

But Francine hadn't caught the look of worry in her new friend's eyes. In fact, she'd seen nothing but the fake stars in the ceiling upon which no one could make a wish or ever expect it to come true.

PART THREE

EIGHT

Holiday Night was Ocean Gate's biggest summer celebration. An invention of the Chamber of Commerce, the evening was designed to attract residents and visitors from other shore towns and, they hoped, attract some commerce too. In a town that still held fast to its blue laws, it had evolved into an evening of approved alcohol consumption, and those residents who owned both boats and houses on Ocean Gate's luxurious bay hosted the most lavish parties. Vanessa Thornton's had always been, through the years, the party to watch; because her husband had played tennis with Peter occasionally, Emily and Peter had always been invited. And they'd always gone.

People gathered along the banks of the bay to watch the long, slow parade of boats and cabin cruisers decorated with lights. As the boats passed by, guests spread out on the lawns, listening to music, dining on summer buffets of shish kebabs, seafood, and champagne, dancing on rented wooden dance floors under yellow and white canopies while their children ran about. The high point of the evening was the crowning of the Holiday Night Queen, a local high school senior, honored for her summer beauty and community activism. She would appear on the last boat in the parade, surrounded by her court, blossoming in the approval of the crowd.

On any Holiday Night afternoon a certain tension (otherwise

unfelt in Ocean Gate) grew as the traffic coming into town became unpassable and the traffic going out to neighboring towns, where people went to stock up on liquor for the parties, clogged street after wide asphalt street. But this year Emily had forgotten all about it until Gene reminded her.

He was standing out on the front porch when she and Lizzie returned from the beach.

"Quit working early today?" she'd asked him as she opened the gate. Although he never spoke of his play, Emily had learned to discern the sounds of his workday: his hour of early morning pacing, the voice of Billie Holiday from his record player followed by typing that was either intermittent or steady for several hours.

"You had a visitor," he said when she reached the porch steps. "I was going to come meet you two on the beach when this lady dropped by—a Vanessa Thornton."

"Oh."

Gene smiled, shoved his hands into his shorts pockets. He was standing just on the very edge of the top porch step, rocking on his sneakers. "Very southern belle."

"Yes, I know. I've been avoiding her all summer. Her little boy goes to camp with Lizzie. What did she want?"

"She wants you and Lizzie—and me," he said, "to come to her Holiday Night party. She said you always come and she wouldn't take no for an answer."

Lizzie tugged at Emily's hand. "Let's go, Mom. I can play with Jimmy."

Emily looked down on her. "You don't like Jimmy. You told me he's a crybaby."

"But I want to see the boats. We always go," she said, her voice turning to a whine on the word *go*.

"Yeah, Mom," Gene said, imitating her, "let's go. I missed it last time I was here."

Emily looked up at Gene and back at Lizzie; they were both waiting for her response. "You're a big help," she said to Gene. "I wasn't feeling up to seeing all of those people this year."

Gene looked thoughtful for a minute. He ran his hand through his thick hair, pushing it back off his forehead. "Well, you want me to take Lizard?"

Lizzie ran up the steps to where he stood. She grabbed his hand in hers and then stretched forward, reaching for Emily's. "No. I want you *and* Mom to go. Please?"

Emily looked at both of them, knowing that, if she went at all, she'd rather have Gene with them, but she wondered what everyone might think.

"Well . . . all right, *if* you both promise we'll go when I say. I mean, you'll go, Lizzie, when I say it's time to leave."

"I promise," Lizzie said.

"Me too," Gene said.

Emily laughed. "You can stay as long as you like. Who knows? You might meet some fascinating single lady."

Emily had noticed him girl-watching on the beach and thought him a rather smooth and surreptitious watcher at that, staring just long enough not to get caught. Once or twice she'd even noticed a woman turning back to look at him, but by then he'd always turned his attention elsewhere. What surprised her now was his unenthusiastic response to the possibility of meeting someone.

"You're right," he said, finally. "You never know who you might meet."

Emily said she was going to put the surf chairs around back, and she told Lizzie to come with her so they could wash off in the outside shower stall.

"By the way," Gene said, "she told me her theme is black and white. Does that mean I dress in both or either?"

Emily tossed her hand up in the air. "Whatever you like. Wait till you see the food—it'll be black and white too."

"You're kidding!"

Emily was right about the food: Russian black bread sandwiches with whitefish filling, white and dark chocolate mousse, white flounder served on shiny black plates. This year Vanessa had gone all out, hiring waiters and waitresses to serve the trays of finger food. And there were floral arrangements on the tables: big, clear bowls filled with black marbles, a single gardenia floating in the center. By nine thirty the party was in high gear, and each guest was given a sparkler that shot off snapping rays of white light. Emily was outside near the dock and she held her sparkler as close to her face as she dared. Well, Peter, she thought, you really missed one this year. When her sparkler burned out she turned to look at all the guests, at least seventy-five people, moving about on the back lawn and on the dance floor under the canopy. Vanessa had taken possession of Gene only minutes after they arrived, and she'd hung at his elbow most of the evening while he talked animatedly with these people he didn't know. Vanessa had introduced him as a "celebrity," and watching him handle the evening with such poise and grace, Emily could see how comfortable he was in the role Vanessa had assigned him. Around the house he seemed militantly unpretentious, determined to be a regular Joe rather than the successful playwright he was, but there, dressed in his white shorts and polo, very tan, tall and liquidly lean, Emily suspected it was *this* kind of attention that he thrived on, the kind of attention that pushed spouses and children far into the background.

When the music changed to the slow tunes, Gene put his wineglass down and danced with Vanessa. They were talking and laughing. Emily moved closer to the dance floor, out of the shadows, and watched, at first like a curious but uninvolved observer until, while watching them, she felt something unnameable shimmy through her. Whatever the sensation was, it made her turn away again, because accompanying it had been the desire to separate Gene and Vanessa. She threw back her shoulders, hoping to shake off the feeling, and walked back down the sloping lawn toward the dock.

Only minutes later, while she was staring out at the water, Gene came up behind her, cupping her bare shoulders in his hands. He pressed his face close to her hair and whispered, "Now that I've been nice to everyone here and danced with the hostess, am I allowed to dance with my friend?"

108 /

Without turning around Emily reached up and moved his hands off of her.

"I don't feel much like dancing," she said. "You go on though. You seem to be having a wonderful time."

Gene walked around her so he could face her. "And you're *not* having a wonderful time, is that it?"

He took his pack of cigarettes from his shirt pocket, tapping it against his forefinger. He pulled one from the pack and lit up, inhaling hard.

"I didn't say that. I said I didn't feel like dancing, that's all." Emily shooed him with her hands. "Go. Go dance, will you? Sometimes you just hang around acting like an older brother or a . . . guardian, as if I can't take care of myself."

In the moonlight the gray in his hair shone like threads of mercury. His eyes flashed and his jaw tightened. He tossed his barely smoked cigarette to the ground. "Sometimes you act that way," he said.

"I don't mean to," she snapped. "I've been taking care of myself since I was a kid."

He was nodding his head. "Okay, fine," he said as he started to walk off. "Let me know when you're ready to leave."

By the time he was halfway up the incline of the lawn, Emily was sorry for being so harsh. And she realized, her eyes following him to a small gathering of people, that she had wanted to dance, that she'd wanted to dance with him specifically; the realization made her feel raw and guilty. Watching Gene and Vanessa, she'd forgotten about Peter.

They stayed for another half hour, until Lizzie came to Emily and flopped into her lap.

"I can't keep my eyes open, Mom," she complained, rubbing them with her fists. "Can we go?"

Emily held Lizzie, rested her chin on top of Lizzie's head. "All played out, are you?"

Lizzie yawned and nodded. "Okay, kiddo, get up. Let's find Vanessa and thank her for having us."

Emily had to linger by the sliding glass doors of the family room until Vanessa could break away to say good-bye. In her inimitable style, second only to Francine, Emily thought, Vanessa rushed to them, a little breathless and smiling.

"Oh, I'm so glad you took yourselves out of the house tonight. Do you think everyone is having a good time, Emily?"

"It's your best party. The most original and beautiful."

"You think so?"

"I think so," Emily said.

"Good."

"We're going to be leaving now, though, and I just wanted to thank you for having us."

"Well," Vanessa said, leaning close, "I want to thank you for bringing along that wonderful man. He is, as we say down home, the kind to get your nose open," and she shook one hand rapidly.

Emily could see Gene out of the corner of her eye talking with Vanessa's husband, Mark.

"Emily?"

Emily turned her attention completely on Vanessa. "What?"

"Now I don't mean any disrespect. I know how close you and Peter were and all, but I'm telling you, if you had any sense you'd grab that one."

"Gene?"

"Don't be stupid. Don't you pay attention to anything? I watched him. Honey, when he looks at you there's such affection in his eyes. I may have captured him for the evening, dearie, but I was definitely not the object of his attention."

"Vanessa," Emily said evenly, "he's my tenant."

Vanessa laughed. "Yeah, well, you just keep on telling yourself that lie and you'll be kicking yourself come September."

One of the caterers called out to Vanessa from the kitchen window. "I have to run," she said. "And you'd better wake up and see how things are."

★　　★　　★

It was because she'd lain awake half the night thinking about what Vanessa had said that she felt so logy sitting in her surf chair on the beach now. The beach was dense with vacationing families burdened with towels and blankets, surf chairs, magazines, books, food, coolers, umbrellas, ointments, portable cribs, rafts and buckets, shovels and kites, Frisbees and horseshoes. The shoobies, day and weekend shore trippers, descended upon Ocean Gate ready to do battle with the elements. Only the residents arrived on the beach with a single surf chair, one towel, and a book, while the visitors arranged and rearranged their paraphernalia like interior decorators, paying no mind to the changing tides, until their campsite was wiped out in the far-reaching swipe of a wave. Emily had gotten Lizzie situated with her buckets and shovels just a little ways down the beach near the damp sand. There was a letter from Barbara in the mail that morning; she'd already read it once at breakfast, but she brought it to the beach with her anyway.

"Why don't you and Lizzie think about coming to Maine for a visit?" Barbara had written.

> I'm not sure I like the sound of the forced cheerfulness in your last letter. Don't send the tennis racket—bring it here yourself. Anyway, I am a stranger in a strange land and could use a good friend's company.

Emily reread the closing paragraph several times. She'd even brought a pad and paper with her thinking that she'd answer the letter immediately, but suddenly she could think of nothing to write and the idea of traveling to Maine to visit Barbara left her feeling cold. She dropped the pad and paper into her carryall, perplexed by her own reaction. Why not go? She was lonely; Barbara and Fred had been her and Peter's dearest friends for nearly thirteen years. How could it be that she didn't want to see the one person with whom she'd been so close—as close, in fact, as a sister? She pushed the thought away. In her mind the faces of Barbara and Fred were like thick, weighty pieces of Victorian furniture that she had to move across an unthinkably large room so she could make way for something white, shiny, light as doll furniture. She decided to read instead and burrowed in with her book, *Death: The Final Stage of Growth*.

Gene, on the other hand, had brought nothing with him to read, no pad or paper on which to write, and although her head was bent over the pages of Dr. Elisabeth Kübler-Ross, she could feel him thinking beside her. He hadn't even reached for his cigarettes, which she was holding for him in her beach bag.

Just as she completed reading the chapter that detailed the myriad ways in which the loss of a loved one brought spiritual strength and renewal to the living, Gene sighed—loudly.

"Why don't you go in the water?" she suggested.

He leaned sideways toward her then and peered over her left shoulder. "Why are you torturing yourself with that junk?"

"This woman," Emily said, tapping the center of the page, "is an authority on death."

He moved his head up and down in that measured, sagelike manner that was a bit pedantic, a bit paternal. "I see. Death is not the issue, Emily. It's life you need to deal with. Yes?"

Emily closed the book. "No. It's death that changed everything. I can only 'deal with,' as you put it, one major issue of humanity at a time. Right now, if you'd let me finish reading, the issue is death."

He was rubbing his chin, still moving his head up and down. "Suit yourself."

"That's big of you."

"Thanks."

As she reopened the book she heard him sigh again. "What is it now, Gene?"

But he didn't say anything. Instead he pointed down the beach, several yards from their chairs to Lizzie, who was working on an elaborate sand castle with two recently made friends for a day. "There is your reason for closing that book," he said.

She realized with embarrassment that it was the first time that day she'd really looked at Lizzie. She was gorgeous in hot pink and what surprised Emily was how alone Lizzie looked, playing with but set apart from the others. Seeing her daughter this way, Emily experienced a glimpse into Lizzie's future and decided that Lizzie would either become a diplomat or the victim of a horrible crime. A person like Lizzie—naturally gregarious, trusting, insightful—was either in control or controlled—there was no in-between—and the knowledge was sobering.

"You see," Gene said, "you cannot make a career of this sorrow."

"Put that in a Hallmark card," Emily told him, "or in a letter to your wife and son. You haven't seen *him* all summer."

"Jesus Christ, Emily."

She dropped the book in her lap, pushed her sunglasses down to the tip of her nose. "I didn't mean it."

"Sure you did," he said. She knew he was too angry to look at her. "You want to sit here," he continued, gesturing to her chair, "for the rest of your damn life remembering what you were and how it used to be with Peter and what the two of you planned together and blame everybody—including me—because it ain't gonna happen. Just like last night. You could have had a nice time. You chose not to, but you sure as hell were ticked off that I did. I write to Chris; I talk to him every night on the phone. We decided it would be better for him to be with Lottie right now. The point is" —and he shook his head, exasperated— "never mind. I meant what I said. You cannot make a career of this sorrow. Cannot," he repeated.

Unprepared for so much anger, Emily stood up and tossed her book on the chair. "I can be this miserable back at the house."

"Fix your suit," he muttered, "it's riding up in the back."

Despite the growing friendship between them, she felt he had no right to notice such things on her person and even less of a right to mention them. "You have—"

But he waved her on reflexively. "Save it, Emily. The most wonderful thing about you is your indignation, but I'm not in the mood today. Really." He looked at his gold watch and put up one finger. "You're about a second off. Aren't you going to walk away?"

She quietly resumed her place in her chair, amazed again that he seemed to know what she was going to do or say before she did or said it. Vanessa may have been right after all about her being the object of his attention, but Emily still wasn't sure why.

"You want a character?" she asked. "Invent one. You want a story? Write it. You cannot make a career of *my* sorrow. Put that down."

Staring straight out to sea, he said softly, "I have memorized every syllable."

It was almost six when they left the beach. The three of them walked home in silence, Gene and Lizzie just a few steps behind Emily, listening to the sounds of their flip-flops slapping the sidewalk. Emily was the first to reach the gate, and as she opened it she looked up at the house, seeing it in much the same way she'd seen Lizzie earlier—with a sobering recognition. As a child this same house had seemed twice as large and infinitely safer. Now the unrelenting sunny days had bleached the pale yellow paint to off-white and the red trim had become a muted shade of itself, shy and unremarkable. Even the glass tower seemed weary under the weight of so much heat. Although every evening she and Gene had tended to the lawn, keeping it mowed and trimmed, watering it, the grass remained a murky brownish green. She walked through the open gate longing to feel the same wonder and excitement that had overpowered her at ages four, five, six, seven on the first day of the summer season.

She couldn't have been inside more than a few minutes when she heard Lizzie call out from the kitchen, "It's Gene. He's back."

When Emily entered the kitchen, Lizzie was pulling him inside within the parameters of ceilings and walls, where suddenly there didn't seem to be enough space to contain him. His very presence swallowed the room and Emily felt herself take a sharp breath.

"You've got my keys, and my cigarettes," he said, pointing to her beach bag.

As she fumbled through the bag and then handed him his things, Emily wondered if the reason he and his wife had separated was just so she could breathe more easily. Whether he was on the beach with them or up in his apartment, out of her sight, still he had become as ubiquitous as cloud cover.

He was almost out the door when he asked if Emily was free that night. Still stinging from his angry speech earlier, she said, "No. I've got to put in an appearance at the White House."

He frowned but let the remark pass.

"Then meet me on the front porch at seven," he said. "The three of us can go up on the boards. There's something I want to show you."

Lizzie squealed because Emily had been remiss in taking her on the boards at night.

"Can we go on the rides?" Lizzie asked.

"Any ride you want, Lizard."

"All right," Emily said, "but I can't imagine what you have to show me that I haven't seen. I've been in this town for ages."

His smile was wry, smug. "That's why you've never seen this."

"We're passing the rides," Lizzie told him as he hurried them along toward Fourteenth Street. "You said any ride I wanted."

She was walking between them, each one of her hands secured in one of theirs.

"And I meant it, but first things first."

They walked against the flow of boardwalk traffic, seaside rather than arcade- and shopside, which made their mission that much more difficult. Gene steered them through throngs of sunburned tourists, babies in strollers, and elderly people walking three abreast, arms linked. He talked about his work for the Institute of Marine Biology in Mexico. "This was a year or two before Alaska," he said, giving Emily a time period for yet another of his careers, which were always borne out of his necessity to make ends meet while writing. She had learned throughout the summer that he'd been a cab driver in Las Vegas, that he'd engaged in some socially redeeming work with Indians in Santa Fe, that he'd been a magician's assistant for a week and a short order cook at a quintessential greasy spoon in the Midwest. Emily had mentally added a darker, subterranean theme to Gene's past, and in her mind saw him capable of extortion, bank robbery, pimping, and desecrating a church. These fantasies had led her to inquire, "Were you ever arrested?"

"Only for writing plays," came his answer.

Tonight, however, he was explaining the migration of the female sea turtle to land, where, under the most terrible conditions, the turtles laid their eggs and, after waiting for them to hatch, raced back to the sea. As was usually the case whenever he told one of these stories, the birth of the turtles was merely incidental to the story about ghost crabs—tiny crabs, he explained, that hid beneath the sand.

"They were vicious," he said.

"Like the huskies?" Lizzie wanted to know.

"No, Lizzie, different from the huskies. The ghost crabs are only doing their jobs. It's the only way they can survive," he went on, looking at Emily. "They pop out of the sand, just pop right up as the baby sea turtles are running back to the water. Then they capture the turtles, pull them into the sand, and eat them up."

Lizzie stopped walking.

"What's the matter, Liz?" Emily asked.

"Are they out there now?"

"See?" Emily said. "Can't you ever tell a tame story?"

"Nature," he said, "is not tame. And, no, Lizzie, there aren't any ghost crabs here. Come here," he said, pulling her over to the railing. Gene picked her up so she could stand on one of the rungs and he pointed out to the ocean. "Everything out there, even when you can't see it, moves in a rhythm. Every part of nature does its job. The mama turtles can't stay behind to protect the babies, and the babies need to learn how to take care of themselves even though getting back to the water means they may be captured by ghost crabs. Half of them won't make it," he said. "But the other half will. Like everything else. Like people," he said finally.

Lizzie was looking out toward the ocean, but Emily could see her absorbing every word, mulling it over.

"Are you sure they're not out there?"

"Yes." He lifted her off the railing and insisted that they press on. "Only two more blocks."

They stopped finally at a small tobacco shop, so narrow and long it looked like an alley. "This has been here forever," Emily said.

But Gene was already wending his way through the aisle to the cluttered counter in back. Lizzie and Emily made their way up the aisle where Emily could see Gene talking with the proprietor, an old man who looked as if he'd washed up on the shore several decades ago.

"I want to show them the dog," Gene said.

"Sure, but what're you buying?"

Gene glanced over the array of trinkets and snacks on the countertop and in the glass case. "These," he said, pointing to three packages of gum. After Gene paid him, the old man nodded toward the worn drape hanging in the doorway. "In the back there, but only for a minute, okay?"

Gene turned to Emily and Lizzie. "Come on."

The back room was crowded with furniture: small velvet settees, a scratched sideboard, a television set. Everything was imbued with the musky scent of the shore. Chained to the foot of an old armchair was the dog, a golden retriever, one eye raised to see who had entered. "Hello, boy," Gene said softly as he extended his hand for the dog to sniff. "I've brought my friends to see you."

The dog opened his other eye, licked Gene's hand, and seemed genuinely happy to see him. If she didn't know better, Emily would have sworn the dog smiled. "Say hello to Emily and Lizzie," Gene said, pointing to them. Lizzie let go of Emily's hand; she knelt down beside Gene and patted the dog.

"Good boy," Gene said. "Now stand up and show Emily what you're made of."

The dog wrestled himself to a standing position, and Emily saw that he had only three legs, two front and one hind leg.

"The dog's name is Oliver."

Emily shrugged. "So? So his name is Oliver and he has three legs. So what?"

"Barney Flood, the old man out front, told me that the dog's been with him over fifteen years. He used to take him fishing with him before the leg was amputated. The dog can't keep up anymore. The dog can't be anything but a dog, Emily."

Emily put her hands up, pushed outward as if Gene were close enough to touch. "Can we go now?"

"Oh, Mom," Lizzie said, "he likes me. Look." The dog was nuzzling her neck, licking her face.

Gene stood up and tapped the top of Lizzie's head. "Come on, Lizard. I think I've irritated your mother enough for one day."

Lizzie laughed, but Emily was not amused. "Come on, both of you. It's hot in here—and it stinks."

Outside again, walking back to the amusement pier, Emily said, "So far you've compared me to a baby turtle and a crippled dog. Have you got any more cute metaphors this evening, or will I get the rest of the lecture tomorrow?"

Gene caught her at the elbow, pulling her halfway around. "Hey," he said, "come here a second. Listen to me—"

"Lizzie," she started to say, pointing to her.

"Lizard's fine," he said, turning Emily so she could see Lizzie watching the other children on the bumper cars. "It's you I'm worried about."

He let go of her then and put his hands in his pockets. "I wasn't trying to be cute or glib or pedantic. I wasn't trying to be any of those things. Peter's dead, Emily, you're not."

"You don't know enough about my life to talk to me like this," she said.

He pressed his lips together, shook his head. "Maybe not, but I do know that not working, not letting yourself enjoy anything can't be good for anybody."

He walked away from her then and called to Lizzie, who accompanied him to the ticket booth. The two of them returned to Emily. Gene waved a long string of tickets in front of her nose. "You going to ride or mope?"

The pier stretched out over the water, and the strong wind from the sea lifted his hair off his forehead and blew a strand of hers across his lips. She took the string of tickets from him. "I'll ride," she said.

"Okay," he said, clapping his hands, "what's first?"

Lizzie liked the wild rides, the wilder the better, so Emily wasn't surprised that she chose the roller coaster first. They walked up the ramp, choosing a car near the front, then slunk down into it, Lizzie between them. As the car jerked forward, making its slow, suspenseful ascent up the tall latticework of hills and valleys, Gene put his arm around them, pulling them close. On the first steep downhill swoop, Emily let out a scream, but by the time they'd hit the third dip her screams had turned to laughter. The roller coaster hurtled them through the night, above the sea, clinging to each other, flying.

It was her mother who had introduced Emily to Chagall, but her father who'd taken him to heart. His favorite paintings were *The Birthday* and *Lovers Above the Flowers,* the paintings in which the man and woman transcended the physical world. "Aren't they happy?" he'd ask Emily, pointing to the picture. "Don't you wish you could do that with someone?"

After Maria died he looked at those pictures more and more, as if just by looking he could melt into them. Once when Francine was rattling around in the kitchen, clanging pots and pans for no good reason, Emily went into his study to get his signature on a permission slip for a school ski trip. They had all agreed that she shouldn't sit around mourning; she was young, they reasoned, and young girls should have fun. He'd already been in the study for hours, poring over legal briefs and talking to himself the way he always did when preparing for a big day in court. He must not have heard Emily's knock because when she walked in he looked up, at first startled then relieved that it was her and not her mother, who would have interrupted him carrying a spatula in one hand and a pot in the other, demanding to know where there was more whiskey. Emily noticed right away that the book of Chagall prints was open over his other papers. He took off his glasses, which he only wore when he was working, and rubbed his eyes.

"What's she doing out there, Emily?"

"You know."

He covered his face with his hands, a defeated act of decorum, thinking, Emily supposed, that if he covered his mouth and eyes she wouldn't see the frustration. In a dull voice he said, "I've told her a hundred times if I've told her once: you can't wake the dead with lids and pots." He pulled his hands away and slumped in his leather chair. "Is she drunk?"

"You know that too."

He shook his head from side to side.

"Listen, Dad, could you sign this? I didn't want to ask her." Emily slid the paper across the dry desk blotter, stopping short of his fingertips.

He lifted the thin paper. "A ski trip?"

"Just for a day. They say we'll be back by twelve."

He picked up the fountain pen and signed his name quickly. "Be careful," he said, handing the slip back to her. "If you hurt yourself I'll lose my skating partner, won't I?"

Then he eased both of his hands up on the desk, pushed himself up in the chair, which made the swivel mechanism squeak. "You're going to love it, you know. It will feel like flying." And he smoothed his open hand over the picture in the book. Then briskly he waved her on, asking her to leave him to his work so he could get some clarinet practice in before bed. As she was leaving the room, she turned back. His head was already bent over the book again; the desk lamp cast a white light over his hands.

"Will you and Mom be okay?"

Without looking at her he said, "In a while, I think."

As if he realized that she needed the reassurance of his eyes, he lifted his head and smiled.

NINE

Emily's mother couldn't have been home more than twenty-four hours before she summoned Emily, via the phone, for an audience.

"I'm back," she crooned through the wires. "Come to Philadelphia."

Not so much as a "Hello, Emily" had passed her lips.

"I've slit my wrists and broken both legs. I have a brain tumor, Mother, so you'd better plan on seeing me here."

"Em'ly, it's about to be ninety degrees, humid, and it'll be unlivable very shortly."

"That's exactly why people come to the beach. Come to the beach."

"This is no way to talk to your mother, who's been gone for two months."

"Oh, it most certainly is. You haven't even asked how we are."

"Hold on," she said. She clicked the hold button from her office, and Emily was treated to several minutes of a Mantovani rendition of "Bewitched, Bothered, and Bewildered" before her mother returned to the line.

"I'm your mother. I've known you all of your life. I would venture to say you've been doing absolutely nothing with your time. So, get in the car with my granddaughter and come up here. I'll buy lunch."

"We're not supposed to have lunch until Christmas."

"Well, then, let's be reckless."

An hour and fifteen minutes later, Emily and Lizzie stood in the front foyer of what used to be Nana Irene's home. Emily's recollections of the house were few. She used to come to Nana's for the holidays when she was small, but those visits decreased and then vanished altogether once Maria was born. Then, after Maria died and her father left, Emily rarely had reason to come to Philadelphia to visit her grandmother; Nana always came to see them in New Jersey. The only regular visits she'd made to her grandmother's occurred during the time Francine was in the sanatorium. By then Emily was in college, so she came, with Peter, to check on Nana, who was slowly fading from old age and illness. Not long after Francine was released from the sanatorium, Nana Irene passed away, leaving the house, as she had the summer house, to Francine. Francine lived in the upper two floors of Nana's elegant brownstone while the first floor, with its marble entrance, living room, and sitting rooms, had been converted into the offices of SPSC. Emily avoided the house whenever possible. In fact, she was considering turning around and walking out, making up some excuse for Jane, the secretary, when a door opened off of a tunnellike hall and her mother, accompanied by a couple in their mid-thirties, walked toward her. The woman who appeared with her mother held wadded-up tissues in one hand and with the other clung to her husband as if she literally could not walk without him. The man was sweating despite the air-conditioning. They both turned to thank Francine, and she shook their hands with Emily's favorite kind of handshake: taking both of their hands into both of hers. Emily heard her mother promise them that she'd be in touch soon and then add, "Whatever you decide, you must do it guiltlessly. Understood?" They whispered an almost reverential yes; Emily marveled that her mother could be as reassuring with them as she was intractable with her. She also marveled at how her mother looked. First of all, her suit was lilac, a color whose very name could make her mother's skin crawl. "It reminds me of Easter," she used to say, "and Easter reminds me of lilies and they—I don't like lilac. Period." And yet there she was in lilac neck to knee. Emily wondered if her mother was going color-blind.

As the couple headed for the door, her mother's eyes fell on her and Lizzie.

"Elizabeth! Come let me hold you." She half stooped and held her arms out to Lizzie, who walked to her grandmother slowly, cautiously. Her mother held Lizzie for a moment. "Well, you're very tan, Elizabeth."

Lizzie wriggled out of her arms. "I always look like this in the summer," she said.

As Francine straightened up, she ran her hand over Lizzie's bare shoulder. "Of course you do when you live at the beach," she said, but her eyes were on Emily.

Now it was Emily's turn. She and her mother moved toward each other at the same time, giving each other one of those barely there kisses.

"Your eyes are dark right here," Francine said, dabbing her finger under Emily's eye. "You're not sick?"

"No."

Then she took Emily's wrist and felt along the inside of it. Her mother thought that with her fingers pressed against Emily's skin she could read illness or a fib. A rapid pulse was an indication of a quick lie. Emily had never thought to use the technique on her. Up close, Emily could see that the high color in her mother's cheeks, which she'd first attributed to new blusher, was really her own natural glow. Her avid gray eyes seemed lit from within. Something— or someone—had excited her. She looked like a woman in love.

"What's this about?" Emily asked, fingering the collar of her mother's suit.

"Who said that 'a rose is a rose' nonsense? Gertrude Stein? A color is a color."

"What's going on with you, Mother?"

Francine pulled Lizzie next to her and put an arm around Emily's waist. "Let's just go to lunch. Are you hungry, Elizabeth?"

Lizzie nodded, then addressed Francine rather formally. "Grand-mother?"

"What is it, Elizabeth?"

"I'd like it if you called me Lizzie or Liz or Lizard."

"Lizard?"

"That's what Gene calls me."

"Gene?" She turned to Emily.

"The boarder, Mother."

"Oh, well, I will try to remember Liz or Lizzie. I'm not fond of lizards though."

When she walked back to the office to get her purse Lizzie asked what *fond* meant.

"When you're fond of someone it means you like them more than a little but not quite love."

"She doesn't like lizards."

"No."

"Does she like me?"

Emily pulled her into the folds of her skirt. "She more than likes you."

Francine had made reservations at The Garden, an expensive restaurant with a menu far beyond Lizzie's unsophisticated tastes. All Lizzie wanted was a Happy Meal from McDonald's. Emily pacified her with a Shirley Temple and told her if she ate the broiled potatoes from her plate she'd buy her a Happy Meal for dinner.

"I suppose I didn't plan very well," Francine said.

"You're out of practice, that's all." Emily didn't mean to offend her, but she saw her mother's eyes cloud over immediately. "I'm sorry."

She shrugged. "Apology accepted."

After their food was served, Francine asked how the new book was coming.

"Mommy's not writing a book," Lizzie offered.

"Well then what *is* she doing?"

/125

Lizzie looked at Emily. "She's getting tan too."

"That's it?" Francine asked.

Emily concentrated on cutting her veal. "What can I say? Writers are very boring people. Boring when they are writing because they're self-absorbed and boring when they're not because, if you're not doing your work, what else is there to do? My house is clean though. My lawn looks good. Peter would be very proud."

Emily heard the disapproving click of her mother's tongue. "Then I have the perfect solution for your boredom."

Emily looked up from her plate.

"I have to go away again—just for a little while, understand, and Jane can handle my end of the organization, probably blindfolded. I just don't want to leave her completely at sea until the end of the summer, and I was thinking . . . I was thinking you could come by the office—just two or three days a week. Maybe seeing these people will help you."

Emily swallowed and put her fork down. "I grew up with those people. Honestly, Mother, what I need is—" Just then she caught sight of Lizzie's concerned stare and she lowered her voice. "What I need is—"

But Francine cut her off before she could say, "What I need is you." "What you need is to begin."

"Begin what?"

Francine sat back and took a long sip from her water glass. "To grieve."

"I thought that's what I've been doing for seven months."

Francine gestured to the air. "Look at you, all lovely and tanned, saying Peter would be proud as if he's going to show up tomorrow and pat you on the back."

"Isn't that what you did?"

"Elizabeth, I mean Lizzie, aren't those potatoes wonderful?" Francine asked.

"Mother."

Francine kept her head down and pushed her string beans around on the plate. "Don't repeat my mistakes, Em'ly."

"Then stop making them."

Francine's eyes cut to Emily; Emily shook her head, wondering why it always ended up this way between them, no matter how hard they tried to be civil.

"Why do you have to leave again?" Emily asked, breaking the silence.

"I'm thinking of starting new branches of SPSC in the mountains."

"You don't have to go there to do that. Ever heard of the telephone? Well, no, of course not. I mean, you never pick one up to call us or anything, do you?"

Emily expected a sarcastic reply, but apparently none was forthcoming. Her mother suddenly seemed weary of their bickering and said, "I have to see the real estate I'm buying, don't I?"

"I guess so."

"Em'ly, will you help me out then? Could you manage it?"

On principle alone, Emily wanted to say no. She wanted to say, "Why should I help you again? I helped you get a bath, I helped you wake up in the morning when you were too hung over to move, I helped you stay *alive,* for crying out loud." But she felt her resolve weakening seeing her mother in lilac, one arm draped along the arm of her chair, and thought perhaps the way to get closer to her was to step into her shoes for a while.

"I'll see if I can work something out, Mother."

"Good," was all she said.

Emily and Lizzie stayed on in the city after Francine returned to work. They took the tours in Independence Hall and the Betsy Ross House, rode in a horse-drawn carriage through the historic district of town, and later found a McDonald's where Lizzie could have, at last, her Happy Meal. Emily didn't feel quite ready to return to the shore, so she asked if Lizzie wanted to see a movie. They'd not been to the movies since Peter died, and when Lizzie said yes, Emily found an *Inquirer* and scanned the listings for a suitable show. After dinner they walked up Nineteenth Street and slipped into the cool theater armed with Junior Mints and popcorn.

/127

The sun was setting behind the tall brick buildings when they came out of the theater; the streets and sidewalks were nearly empty. Unlike New York, which was always pulsing with activity, in Philadelphia there was, especially in the summers, a quiet time between the flurry of daylight and the onslaught of the night people. Lizzie had lost her former perkiness, her hair falling in wisps around her face.

"What do you say we head for home, kiddo?"

"Carry me to the car."

They were almost out of the city, stopped at the last red light before the approach to the bridge, when Lizzie shouted, "There's Daddy." She tapped her fingers on the window. "There he is."

To their right was a man in a beige suit crossing the street. In the dusky lavender light he *did* look like Peter. The stoplight changed to green and the driver behind Emily blew his horn.

"Get him," Lizzie said.

The man stepped inside an office building just as Emily pulled out of the intersection.

"It's the wrong way," Lizzie said when she saw that Emily was not turning the corner.

"It's not Daddy, Liz. Daddy is dead."

Lizzie curled her legs up under her, then rested her head against the inside of the door. She pulled her bottom lip out, poking at the slick red insides.

"Don't do that. Your mouth will freeze that way."

She let her lip snap back into place like a rubber band. "That's not true."

"I'm sorry, Liz. The man looked like Daddy."

"You didn't look so you don't know."

"Lizzie."

She closed her eyes, lifted her chin in rebuke. "It was him."

By this time they had crossed the bridge and stopped at the tollbooth. Emily had driven into an exact change lane without the exact change; she had to fumble through her purse for the money. Cars honked behind her while Lizzie, who could have helped, watched her scramble for the money. As soon as the toll bell rang, Emily snapped at her. "You could have done something, you know. You heard those people honking."

"I'm not fond of you now," she said.

"Guess what, kid?"

There was no answer from her.

"I'm not fond of you either."

In the heat of that exchange Emily was reminded of herself, much older than Lizzie but equally stubborn, arguing with her mother. The day after her father had left them, she'd asked Francine when they were going out to look for him. They were sitting at the kitchen table and Francine was drinking whiskey from a chipped "Flintstones" juice glass.

"And how do you propose we do that? He took the goddamn car. There's seventeen feet of snow out there. Look!" she yelled, reaching behind her, roughly pulling aside the curtain.

"We'll walk."

"We're not going anywhere. I told you, Em'ly, a man does not leave for good without his bathrobe."

Emily began to cry. Francine dropped her head onto her folded arms and mumbled, "He'll be back. Say a prayer to St. Jude."

"What good will praying do?"

Francine pulled herself up straight; there were circles under her eyes from not sleeping, from crying. "He's the patron saint of hopeless cases, of the impossible, of those who are in despair. Are you in despair?"

Emily nodded yes.

"Then say this." She pulled a small, green plastic booklet from her bathrobe pocket. It was the size of a matchbook. Inside was the prayer in the minutest print and a silver template of St. Jude's face.

"While I pray, what are you going to do?"

"Drink."

Emily had pushed the miniature booklet across the table then and left it there.

★   ★   ★

Lizzie slept in the car, but had she stayed awake, Emily would have told her that she understood. She would have told her how she used to think she saw her own father crossing a street or behind the wheel of a passing car all the time. How she had waited outside a movie theater through a double feature in the cold because she had spotted someone with his lazy walk and irregular features buying a ticket at the booth. She would have told her about the time when she, a grown woman with her own family, had frantically chased a man through four subway cars in New York.

She had just come from a meeting with her editor, Jill, and the illustrator of the next Flora book. It was rush hour. In the subway station the press of bodies, the smell of wet wool, smoke, and stale urine made her feel as if she were a part of an aching yet vibrant world. She let herself be pushed into a waiting car, grappled for a hand strap since there were no seats. She was crushed in against the other passengers when she noticed the man at the front of the car. His back was to her, his coat collar turned up toward his ears so that strands of gray and brown hair curled over it. He turned to the side, just for a second, but Emily was certain that his nose could belong to no one other than her father. She pulled her handbag closer to her and looked back up just as he was passing into the next car. "Please," she said, "please excuse me." She stepped and pushed over and between people, trying to reach that door at the end of the rocking car. People grumbled and reprimanded her, but she kept pressing onward, sweating with the exertion of moving through the crowd. When she opened the door at the end of the car, the forceful blast of air knocked her off balance. She hit her shoulder against the metal doorframe, and in the second of recovering her balance lost sight of the man. She had not found him by the time she exited at Penn Station. The train screeched into the black tunnel and only after it disappeared did she see her shoulder bag, gaping open like a wound. Her wallet had been stolen.

TEN

Someone was sitting on the porch steps. As Emily pulled into the driveway the headlights illuminated a woman, sitting with her knees drawn up, her arms clasped around her shins, chin resting on her knees. The picture of the diminished college girl who'd been stood up by her date, her forlorn, solitary posture might have triggered Emily's deepest sympathies until she realized that the woman was Margot Compton. Emily knew her instantly, not by her face, which she had turned toward Emily as she got out of the car, but by the angular hand that fluttered across her forehead to wave away a fly or a moth.

How long had she been sitting there? Emily wondered. Had she been waiting at all, or having come by the house, seeing it dark, had she simply wanted to sit on Peter's steps thinking she wouldn't get caught? Emily was astounded by the woman's gall; sleeping with Peter had been a minor infraction compared to this. Emily poked her head back in the car to check on Lizzie. She was still asleep.

"Hello, Emily," Margot said as Emily walked across the lawn. She rose slowly, almost theatrically, letting the ankle-length skirt float about her. She seemed ready to deliver a soliloquy.

"I don't think you should be here. Do you?"

"There's something I want to ask," she said, her voice quivering on the last word. Emily's mind ran immediately to clothes, Peter's clothes. She believed Margot wanted a shirt or a pair of socks, a relic to cling to.

"I don't think there's anything you could ask for that I would agree to, Margot."

She shifted her weight, back and forth, left to right, and back again. Her arms were folded across her stomach; she made a sound, a small sound like a whimper. She looked badly in need of comfort—Emily was not far gone enough in her own pain not to recognize it in the eyes of someone else—but she had come to the wrong place for commiseration.

"Whatever you have to say, please say it and then leave."

She took a deep breath. "I would like to put flowers on Peter's grave."

With that said she let her head roll forward, as if the words had sucked the air out of her.

"There are flowers on his grave." In fact, there weren't. Emily had not been able to bring herself to the cemetery since the day the headstone was implanted.

Margot brought her head back up, haughtily this time. "No there aren't. I've gone. It's empty."

"Come down from there. Come off of our steps." Margot stepped down onto the walk. "No, you may not put flowers on his grave, although God knows I'd have to stand guard there night and day to keep you out. Why are you doing this?"

"I loved him."

"He never spoke of you," Emily said. "It was over."

Margot smiled then, nothing so bold as a grin, but there was no denying the supercilious nature of the smile. Had she been a famous actress she would have been the sort to write one of those inflammatory autobiographies, claiming affairs with dead actors who could not refute her stories.

"I want you to get out of here, and I don't want you to come back or ride past the house."

She walked past Emily, stopping just long enough to say, "Only his death ended what we had," before she hurried off down the walk and out the gate, letting it slam behind her. Emily watched until Margot turned the corner, then she carried Lizzie from the car to her room where she undressed her quickly, letting her sleep in only her flowered panties.

Her head was swimming by the time she went into the yard to smoke. She turned and faced the house, believing that Margot's having been there, on its steps, had defiled it in some way. She couldn't have been more of a trespasser had Emily found her in her bed. Margot had succeeded in planting the worst doubt in Emily's mind: that the affair had not ended at all, had merely gone underground, become more discreet, and that she was not only a widow, but a cuckolded widow as well. She exhausted herself with thoughts that led to no conclusion until finally all she wanted was sleep. She went inside to take up her usual place on the sofa, determined to dream of Peter, to conjure a visitation from him that would reassure her.

She dreamed of a New York City where everything looked as it did in reality except for the streets, which were wide waterways. It was night, pitch and starless, uncommonly still. Suddenly from the center of the waterway she emerged naked, arms upraised and radiant. On a street corner, the one nearest to her, was a man, and when his face came into focus it was Gene, dressed in navy blue and smiling like a saint. He reached down, cupping some water in his hand, and sprinkled her with it. She repeated the gesture, sprinkling water at him. As she moved toward the sidewalk, he was holding a towel, dark and velvety, big as a blanket, which he wrapped around her. "How fast can you run?" he said.

What woke her was not the strangeness of the dream but the music. The song, something smoky and old, the recording of a woman singer she was not familiar with, drifted through the vents. It was the music she'd grown up listening to at home. It never mattered what the lyrics actually said; the sentiment was always the same: Do you love me, did you love me, will you ever love me again, Big Boy/Mama or whoever?

If Gene was a fakir, she was the snake charmed by the music. Before she could think about what she was doing, she traveled up the back staircase. She tapped a couple of times before Gene, wearing only gray sweatpants cut off at the knees, opened the door. A cloud of smoke hung around him; his silvery hair was slick.

"The music woke me," she started to say, but he somehow knew she had not come there to tell him to turn it down.

"Come on in." He took her hand.

"Ah, no." Emily looked past him, could see the table by the window cluttered with papers. Cigarette smoke streamed up from an ashtray, a small vapor trail. "I don't want to disturb you. You're working."

"Then what do you want?" he asked, not unkindly.

"I'm not really sure."

"Emily, I'll take a break. I'll even give you a cigarette."

"I don't smoke."

He put his hands on his hips then, looked around him on the floor as if the words he was searching for were scattered about like so many dropped clothes. "I've watched you smoke your cigarette every night. For two months. Do you know Chekhov's 'Lady with the Dog'?"

She could recall most of the story readily, about a womanizer who falls in love with a married woman who is vacationing alone except for her dog, which she takes everywhere, even to their trysts. His question implied some kind of test. "I vaguely remember it."

"Well, you're the lady with the cigarette." He reached for her fingers again. "Come in, Emily."

"I should have figured you for a voyeur," she told him. They had smoked so many cigarettes between them that the ashtray overflowed.

"It's not as if I needed binoculars. If you didn't want me to see you, you wouldn't have chosen the front yard."

Emily rolled the tip of her cigarette back and forth over the ashes. "Sounds like something my friend Barbara would say. She's a psychologist. She used to live right down the block there," Emily said, pointing out the window. "They moved in June. Great timing, huh? She has this theory about the public nature of nervous breakdowns. Jimmy Piersall, for instance."

"The baseball player."

"You got it."

"I remember the movie. *Fear Strikes Out,* with Karl Malden and Anthony Perkins."

"Very good. Well, anyway, she cites Jimmy Piersall as a popular example of the public breakdown, you see, because he climbed that fence like a caged animal in the middle of a game. She believes people fall apart in situations where they can be helped, or at least witnessed, by a cast of thousands."

"What do you think?"

"I think a lot of times they do it alone, actually."

Gene smiled. "I detest psychology."

"Ah, you know, don't you, what the good doctor would say to that, yes?"

"That I detest it because I fear its validity. Yes, yes, I know."

Emily stubbed out her cigarette, folded her hands, and leaned in against the table. "What else have you seen from your little window there?"

Without blanching or blushing he said, "I saw you talking to that woman tonight."

This shocked her and she told him so; his light had not been on when she pulled into the driveway.

"I was working," he said.

"In the dark?"

"Hey, I do my best work in the dark." If not for the dryness of the delivery she might have thought the remark a seduction. He was, after all, half dressed, it was after one, and she had come to him. Then there was the music. He replaced each album with another, and it was all plaintive and steamy as only the blues could be. He explained that the singer was Helen Humes, extremely talented and underrated, that he'd come across her by accident. "When I heard this on the radio," he said, and he moved the turntable arm to the cut "Every Now and Then." "I think you'll like this."

He stood hovering over the turntable as if he could see the music rising up from it. After the first chorus, he turned from the stereo and held his arms out. "Dance?"

He didn't hold her close, but they moved around the floor a great deal. Gene knew the patterns of a real slow dance and Emily had to pay attention to her feet and his, which were moving her now to the right, now back, now to the left and up. She and Peter had danced in that clinging random shuffle of the sixties when couples wrapped both arms around each other and ground their hips together hard, and all the mystery of slowly discovering the warmth, the texture of another strange body was dissolved in the first touch. Her and Peter's style of slow dancing left nothing to the imagination. What she was doing with Gene left as many options as one could imagine or invent.

She disengaged herself from him as soon as the song ended. He pretended not to notice her discomfort by rushing back to the stereo, lifting the arm, and scratching the record as he did. "We don't need the music if you don't want it."

"I do though. Put another on."

He did but he turned the volume down. "You're a wonderful dancer," he said.

"It comes from years of ice skating with my father."

"He was a figure skater?"

Emily laughed and sat down at the table. "No, he was a lawyer, but he loved to skate and he loved to play the clarinet."

"Has he been dead long?" Gene asked. He sat down on the other side of the table.

"I don't know. He, uh, he left us when I was fourteen. We've never heard from him since. Christ, it's always so embarrassing for me to say that to someone for the first time. It's hard—being left that way, you know—because, because you never know if it was your fault."

"Yes, I know."

"Not your father too?"

"Na. Lottie. Only in that case it *was* my fault." He lowered his head, began picking at his cuticles. He rarely ever spoke about himself or Carlotta; the act of disclosure made him seem vulnerable. "You both work very hard for a goal, in our case it was my success, then it happens and you look around and . . . well, you've heard and seen it before—you got where you wanted to go, lost each other along the way. A very old story."

"You two looked very happy when you stayed here last."

Gene nodded. "That summer was the beginning of the end, I think."

"Maybe there's still a chance. You have Chris."

"I'm almost fifty," he said. "That's twenty years too old to believe in enormous changes." Then a pause that couldn't have been more palpable had he written it into a play elapsed, and he said, "I'll get you something to drink."

He brought back to the table with him two glasses of wine and a white paper bag filled with nuts. They picked out the cashews and the macadamias. "Here, take the Brazils," he said. "I don't like the Brazils." He pushed a handful of them in Emily's direction.

"You shouldn't buy mixed nuts if you don't like all the nuts, Gene. I don't like them either." But she shoved them around on the worn Formica tabletop. She'd read once that certain African tribes used beans and nuts as game pieces, so she kept arranging and rearranging them in rows and shapes as if she knew what she was doing.

"So what did she want?" Gene asked, cracking a cashew between his teeth. "Wasn't that the woman who drove past the house?"

"I need another cigarette."

Gene lit it for her and she inhaled deeply, taking a moment to feel the heat in her throat. "Yes. It was her. Apparently you're not such a good sleuth because she'd been waiting on the goddamn porch half the evening it seemed. She looked a little wilted. I'm such an ass I even felt a little sorry for her. Anyway, what she wanted—you're going to love this—was to ask my permission to put flowers on Peter's grave."

Gene refilled Emily's wineglass while she was talking, and as soon as he drew the bottle back from the lip of the glass, she sipped most of it and asked him to top it off again. "I've had the worst day. First my mother, a story herself. Then on the way home Lizzie tells me she's not fond of me because I won't go racing through the streets of Philadelphia in pursuit of a beige-suited man she thinks is Peter. And what do I come home to? A dead man's mistress who asks if she can put flowers on his grave. She reminded me of a Girl Scout. Would you like to buy a box of Samoas, and can I go with you to the cemetery someday? She could have just put them there. Do secret admirers ask permission to be intrusive? But it wasn't about the flowers."

"No. It wasn't."

Emily slammed the glass down and wine spilled over the top. "What do you mean, 'No, it wasn't'? You sound like a therapist."

"I'm agreeing with you, for Christ's sake. You're right. There was nothing polite about it. After all, she didn't ask you if she could fuck him, did she?"

"You don't have to be crude about it."

"No, I don't, but you do. Toughen up, lady."

Emily narrowed her eyes at him. " 'Toughen up, lady'? This woman succeeds in planting the worst suspicions in my mind, suspicions I can create all by myself, thank you, and I'm supposed to toughen up? Very athletic advice."

Gene was laughing as she'd not seen him laugh all summer, baring all of his perfect white teeth.

"It's not funny."

"I'm sorry," he said, catching his breath, "but you're great when you're angry like this."

"Oh, thanks."

138 /

He cleared his throat, composed himself. "Listen, she's the one who isn't sure if he ever really cared."

"And how do you know that?"

"By her walk. I'm very good at walks. Your depressed walk, for instance, is very different from your angry walk, which is very different from your purposeful walk."

"Be serious."

"I'm being serious. She walked away like a woman who'd not gotten her way. Her shoulders were thrown back too much—a definite sign of masked defeat."

"You're crazy. Why should I believe you? A spy."

"Because it's my job to know the difference between a stomp and shuffle, between walking lightly and walking determinedly across the stage. Yes? I'm a between-the-lines man, Emily." Then he slid his arm across the table and touched one of her fingers with his. "Besides—and I'm guessing now, an educated playwright's guess—that Peter's affair happened about four years after Lizard was born, just around the same time you hit the big time with your blue bird books—"

"She was four and a half."

"And you were busy writing and answering mail and giving little talks at conferences, reviewing books—"

"No conferences, but you've got the rest," she said.

"And he was just chugging along, doing his job, feeling left out. And there she was, and he thought you wouldn't even notice, when in fact, he *wanted* you to notice. And you did. Finally."

He tapped her fingernail.

"Leave it to a man to take the man's side."

"Hey, Emily, don't you know by now I'm on your side?"

The music stopped and this time Gene didn't move to replace the record. Now the only other sound besides her own voice was the ocean in the distance, a sound like static. She had completely lost track of time while confiding in him the things that only Peter and Barbara had known. Without knowing how, she was telling him about her earliest memories at the house, how she and her

/139

mother would come off the beach around dinnertime, shower in the outside stall, then hurry, wrapped in thick towels, to the house. "She would slather this white cream on both of us, then dust me in powder. 'We are sea nymphs, Em'ly. We are mermaids,' she used to say, and it would give me the chills. There was something sly working in her voice." She told him about the excitement of Friday evenings. "That's when my dad would come down here. I just lived for the moment his car pulled into the drive. He would be rumpled, a little sweaty from the long drive, but it never mattered." And after that she logically and unself-consciously progressed to Maria.

"She died in 1963. It was devastating because she'd only been in the instituition for about three months and . . . well, my parents felt responsible. She died in November. We buried her four days before they buried Kennedy. The day of his funeral I watched the television. I went up to my mother's room asking if she wanted to watch with me.

"She was lying on the bed, fully dressed right down to her pumps. She was even wearing her good pearl earrings and the matching bracelet. She would do that, get dressed every day with the best intentions, then sit or lie down for hours. When I asked her to come downstairs with me, she lifted herself up and threw a pillow at me. 'I've had enough mourning for one week, Em'ly. What you can do is get me another drink.' I threw the pillow right back at her and walked out. Oh, I sat in front of the television listening to the commentators talk about the grief of a nation, the grief of the world. I was crying with them, but not for him. I've always felt a little guilty that I couldn't have more sympathy for the president."

Gene was fiddling with an empty matchbook, curling it into a tight tube. "Why didn't you ever write about it?"

"Just because it happened is no reason to write about it."

"True, but if Flora's flown the coop, why not try something different?"

"I'm under contract. In fact, just the other day I got an impatient phone call from my editor. Flora's been very good to us. There's been talk of a stuffed Flora toy to package with the books. CareBears, Paddington Bears, and Floras. I'm an industry. I can't just stop."

They'd eaten all the nuts except for the Brazils, and Emily was beginning to feel queasy. "I've been asked to work at something that has nothing to do with writing." And then she told him about SPSC.

"You going to do it?"

"I told her I'd try to work it out, but how? What would I do with Lizzie? With Barbara gone I'd have to leave her with a stranger and after today I'm not sure that would be so good for her."

Without hesitation he said, "I'll take care of Lizard. I would like to."

"You've got the play to worry about. I'd be entrusting my child to you."

He reached for the empty pack of cigarettes, crushing it emphatically in his hand. "Oh," he said, "I'd keep the rough stuff to a minimum."

"I'm sorry. I don't know what I was thinking. You're a daddy yourself."

In her dream he had harbored her from the cold with a towel. In real life he was beginning to bring evenness to her days and now her nights.

"I would like for you to take care of her."

"Good," he said.

This pact would change them, and she felt no desire to be anywhere else but at this house. She would write to Barbara, stall the visit; there was nothing for her in Maine that she couldn't get here. That night they became a family—not happy, not unhappy—but in a category that Tolstoy may have considered and judiciously decided to forego. They became a nothing-else-for-us-to-be family. The worst kind.

ICE, 1963

"She blames me, you know."

Emily and her father were walking the beach bundled in extra scarves and thick woolen hats. They had come to the shore to check on the house, to make certain it hadn't been vandalized, to be sure the pipes had not frozen from disuse, and to estimate the repairs come spring. Always when they had finished their inspection they would walk down to the beach and out on the narrow slick jetty. Sometimes they brought an aluminum thermos along and drank hot chocolate. They would sit on the very edge of the jetty, passing the cup between them, the steam licking their cold noses while the ocean spray settled around them.

Today, however, they'd brought no thermos with them and had come to the beach only because Emily wanted to. Her father did not have his arm slung around her shoulder as usual, his excuse being that his new parka, down filled and made of nylon, was awkward and slippery against hers. "I was the one who insisted on the institution. I want you to know that, Emily. It was my idea in the first place."

Emily tried to walk faster so he would be out of breath and unable to say anything as they trudged toward their jetty. She wondered how long they would do this, both he and her mother, taking her aside to slander themselves now that Maria was dead.

"There's our spot, Dad," she said, pointing ahead to their jetty. "Why don't we race?"

She started to jog ahead of him, but when she didn't feel him gaining on her the way she'd expected, she turned around. He was on the sand, on his knees, pressing his gloved hands against his thighs. His dark skin was ruddy from the wind; he was breathing hard and, she thought at first, coughing. Rolling violently to his right was the ocean, and behind him the December sky was a brutal gray. He was sitting on his heels like a man who'd never seen this place before, who wasn't sure how to walk the terrain.

When she called, "Dad," insistently, he never lifted his head, so she ran back, stood before him, her knees level with his eyes.

"Dad, please get up," she said, "the sand is cold. Your pants will get wet." Still he didn't look up, so she knelt down too. She had never seen a man cry before; she dared not touch him until he wiped the tears from his face. She grabbed the thick elbows of his coat sleeves, and with all the effort a fourteen-year-old could muster she pulled him up, the way she'd tugged her mother out of bed that same morning. Both times she'd felt as if she were pulling suicides from the ledge of a building.

"Come on, Dad. Let's go home."

ELEVEN

Connie and Martin Dill looked at Emily imploringly from their side of her oak desk at SPSC. She'd been working for her mother for over a week, and she had decided that she did not have a natural disposition for this kind of work, which required her to hear from couples things that she believed were most private, sacred even. She felt the limits of her empathy being stretched tight, like skin over a drum, and longed for a sudden but not permanent shock of deafness to overcome her. Since her mother had left no notes as to how she should carry on, she waded through the days like someone entering a murky pond unsure of the shift in depth beneath her. She'd written lists of things to say to these couples, tag phrases such as, "You have a special child with special needs." She found, however, that when it came time to utter these lines the power of the words flagged. Wasn't every child, disabled or otherwise, special? And so most of the time she said very little and gave in to compassionate nodding, a noncommittal "I see" or a lame "I understand."

From the moment they'd entered her office, Emily knew that the Dills were not going to let her off so easily. Although they looked completely unmatched as a couple—she, composed, tall, fashionably dressed, and he, heavyset, short, with large uneven features and an outlandish multicolored tie—the Dills had, either through years

144 /

of living together or out of some deeper, more mysterious means that linked husbands and wives, affected the same unrelenting gaze in their brown eyes. We have come to bare our souls, the look said, and Emily wished for the anonymity of a priest in the confessional, shielded in the dark by that perforated screen that kept the sinner separated from the arbiter of absolution.

She reached to her left for a pencil and held it at each end as if this miniature barrier might ward off the sting of anything they had to say. To her surprise it was Connie Dill who spoke first, in a voice suitable for a public speaker or a stage actress. She explained that her seventeen-year-old son was partially handicapped, profoundly retarded, and given to spontaneous, unpredictable outbursts of violence that on one occasion had left her with a broken arm, on another two broken fingers, and on yet another a hairline fracture in her left foot. The whole time she was speaking, Martin Dill tapped his foot regularly against the carpet, the muted thump punctuating his wife's sentences. "We need help," she said frankly, and Martin Dill made a noise that was part sigh, part grunt. Emily looked at him and then away. Before she had time to prepare herself for him, he was out of his chair, leaning on her desk, his heavy face close to hers. He smelled of English Leather.

"She won't let us put him away, Mrs. Hansen. We have two other children. I'm forty-six years old. My blood pressure is one forty over a hundred. I'm going to die of a stroke. Talk sense to her."

Exhausted, he sank back into his chair, resumed tapping his foot, and stared forcefully at Emily.

Emily felt her stomach roll over, felt the hairs at the back of her neck stand up. It was not part of her job to convince either partner to keep a child or send a child away; the only thing she knew how to do with any success was to tell stories, to reach people—children— through metaphor. Neither allegory nor a bedtime story was going to soothe the Dills. Unlike the other couples she'd been seeing who'd already come to a meeting of the minds, the Dills wanted an assessment and a decision from her, placing her in the role of

/145

prosecutor and judge, Solomon and Pontius Pilate, all rolled into one. She cleared her throat and delivered the speech about the purposes of the organization, how it was a source of counseling and a hot line for programs of support. "We can't decide anything here today in this office. You'll have to make an appointment with one of our counselors, a professional, an expert who will listen, who can guide you properly."

"See," Connie Dill said to no one in particular. Her comment sparked a furious response in Martin Dill, who stood up once again, this time his face blustering.

"Do you want to know what he does, Mrs. Hansen? He goes to the toilet," Dill shouted, "and he puts his face in it. He doesn't care if somebody left piss unflushed—he dips his face in it. Like this."

With that said, Martin Dill turned his back to Emily and, using the arms of the chair for support, dipped his face onto the seat and yanked it up again, shaking his head so dramatically, Emily thought she could see the beads of toilet water.

"Disgusting," he said, shaking his head. "We've given him seventeen years of our lives. I'm forty-six. I have high blood pressure," he repeated, his voice winding down, his hands slipping into his pockets. "I could die of a stroke," he said, chanting the words.

Connie Dill reached for his hand and guided him back to his chair. The shock of his open display had left him looking utterly helpless and bewildered. "I'm not a cruel man."

Emily saw the tears welling up in his eyes. She and Connie Dill both reached for a tissue at the same time.

"Take this, Marty," his wife said.

He took the pink tissue, blew his nose.

"You're a wonderful man, Marty," his wife told him.

Watching them, Emily was filled with the desire to lay her head on the desk, to pound it lightly against the green blotter.

When the Dills seemed to have gathered their composure, Emily gave them the name of the counselor most suitable for them, led them to the reception area, and then made a return appointment with them. Then, in the way she'd seen her mother do it, she

146 /

turned to Martin Dill first and took both of his hands in hers. She did the same with Connie Dill, adding that SPSC would help them, that perhaps they might need extra day-care help with their son and not need to institutionalize him at all. They smiled, weak smiles, thanked her, and walked away, leaving her with the image of their penetrating eyes still etched in her mind.

"Where, oh where, is dear little Mary? Where, oh where, is dear little Mary? Where, oh where, is dear little Mary? Way down yonder in a pawpaw patch." The voices were coming from Emily's kitchen. One was Lizzie's, a shaky soprano, and the other was Gene's, gravelly from dedicated smoking.

"Take it," Emily heard Gene say, and Lizzie sang out, an octave higher. "Come on, boys, let's go find her. Come on, boys, let's go find her. Come on, boys, let's go find her, picking pawpaws in a pawpaw patch." Lizzie then told Gene to take it and he sang the last chorus, a repeat of the first with a variation of Mary putting her pawpaws in a pawpaw basket. On the sound of a lid dropping, Emily entered the kitchen through the side door.

"What's a pawpaw?"

Lizzie sailed across the room to hug her. "Hi, Mom. Did ya hear?"

"I heard. What's a pawpaw?" Emily looked around her usually tidy kitchen. There were pots and lids, bottles and jars everywhere; something was cooking in the large stainless steel pot on the stove, and Gene was standing by the sink twirling lettuce in the plastic spinner, flicking drops of water on himself and the countertop. It was clear that Lizzie had set the table: the napkins were on the right, one place setting was missing a spoon, and she'd given the three of them salad forks—the size she used—for the main course.

"It's an apple," Gene said. "At least that's what I was told when I learned the song. You look beat, Emily."

"One very distraught couple today," she said, the image of the Dills still fresh in her mind. "They cried. It took me back, I'll tell you."

"Want to talk?"

But Emily indicated Lizzie with a slight nod of her head and mouthed, "Maybe later."

"No crying here, Mom."

Emily brushed Lizzie's hair from her eyes. "Yes, I can see that. What on earth are you making?" she asked Gene.

But Gene didn't answer. He cocked his head toward Lizzie, barely smiled, and yet Emily knew that he was leaving the story of dinner for her to tell.

Lizzie took Emily's hand and guided her to a kitchen chair, climbed onto her lap. "Weeell," she began, "we went to the bay for crabs and we picked them—"

"No, we crabbed for them," Gene said, correcting her gently. He was now slicing tomatoes with a vengeance.

"And we crabbed for them," she said. "Then we boiled them to death."

She rubbed her small hands together.

Gene had abandoned the tomatoes and was attacking an onion, wiping at his eyes with the back of his hand while he chopped, leading her. "But we didn't catch any—"

"Girls!" Lizzie shouted. Then she pulled herself up so her lips were nearly touching Emily's and whispered, "You don't kill the girls, Mom."

"Lucky for us, huh?"

"And what did the man who rents the boats tell you, Lizard? Tell Mommy."

She pulled back very proudly and said, "That I caught—I mean, crabbed . . . ?"

"Caught," Gene said.

"That I *caught* more crabs than any other kid."

"Wonderful. That's wonderful."

"Goddamn onions," Gene muttered.

"Watch your language, please," Emily said.

"Sorry. I meant darned onions," Gene said. "Enough." He pushed the cutting board away from him, whipped a paper towel off the rack to wipe his eyes.

"So we're having crabs for dinner?"

"Good, Mom."

Gene sat down, sniffling, still wiping his eyes. "Crabs and spaghetti, salad, watermelon for dessert, and an insouciant Hawaiian Punch with the meal," he said, kissing the tips of his fingers. "We'll be ready to eat in five minutes."

"I'll go wash my hands," Lizzie said.

"Well, dear, would you like your pipe and slippers now or after dinner?" Gene kidded.

Actually she was enjoying this domestic reversal, but she said, "You didn't have to go to so much trouble, you know. Hot dogs would have been fine too."

He was using a dish towel for an apron, had it stuffed in the waistband of his track shorts. He pulled it off and waved it at her. "Don't be ungrateful," he said, snapping the towel in the air. "And don't be too grateful either—you've got cleanup duty."

When it was time for cleanup, however, he didn't leave it just for her. While she loaded the dishwasher and scoured the pots, he took care of the crab shell disposal, dumping them in plastic bags first, then in brown paper bags, before taking them out to the trash. "I don't know how you two would survive without me," he said before he bounded out the side door with the bags in hand.

It was that comment, spoken offhandedly, that made Emily wonder how they *would* survive without him—their boarder, teller of gruesome tales, landscaper, cook, baby-sitter, confidant. She wondered if it were possible that he needed them as much as she and Lizzie seemed to need him. She looked out to the back section of the yard where Lizzie was trying to climb one of the two sturdy maples near the garage. Gene must have seen her footing slip at the same time Emily did, but his reflex to warn her was quicker, oddly, than Emily's.

"Lizzie!" he bellowed. "Get out of that tree before you break a leg." Then he came into view under the window, waving at her. "Come on. Right now."

She shimmied down the trunk, obeying him without question, just as she would have had it been Peter and not Gene. She ran to him, giggling, and crashed into him, burying her head against his stomach, stretching her small arms around his waist. He stooped over, wrapping his arms around her shoulders, bringing his chin to rest on her head, then he reached down, patting her lightly at the top of her behind. "We can't have you falling out of a tree and getting hurt. You climb when you've got someone close to catch you, you understand?" Because her face was still pressed against him, her yes was muffled, but when she pulled away from him, she said, "Then come close," taking his hand and leading him back to the tree.

Lizzie had inherited her father's athletic grace; she had no trouble getting up the thick trunk, scaling it with her sneakered feet and small fingers like a cat. Gene stood close by, shadowing the trunk, his head thrown back, his arms flung open wide, her safety net. The water was still running into the sink, but Emily was motionless, holding a lid and scouring pad under the stream of water, watching them. On the descent, Gene talked Lizzie down, telling her where to place her feet, when to hug a branch tight and when to let go. At that moment Emily felt as if she could float out of her own body, transport herself from this warm summer evening to the cool caverns of an ice rink. She was little again, as small as Lizzie, her fingers tingling with the cold, her father's voice guiding her through a jump; how effortless it seemed to fling herself into the air, knowing he was there to catch her.

Lizzie was down now. "Nice job, Lizard," Gene told her, ruffling her hair. The longing Emily felt just then frightened her; it was so ripe with contradictions. She longed for Peter to be in that yard with Lizzie, yet at the same time she was filled with affection for Gene. But there was another, trickier desire at work in her, dark and disturbing, the desire to be in Lizzie's place, to *be* her, with all three of them—her father, Peter, and Gene—waiting, with outstretched arms, for her to fall.

Even several hours later, Emily could not forget this image of the falling child. It burned in her mind with the power of a high fever, and before she knew it she found herself sitting at her desk in front of the typewriter she had not touched in months. Lizzie was asleep, and because he'd spent the day taking care of her, Gene was upstairs working, playing his Helen Humes music, her voice delivering a perfectly gorgeous rendition of "Stardust" so affecting it seemed tailor-made for the evening. It had been humid most of the day, but the moisture had blown off and the balmy breeze that replaced it rustled the wind chimes that hung off the back deck next door. With the sax hauntingly underscoring her typing, Emily began a story.

Four Reasons Why I Never Went to Bangor, Maine
by Emily Hansen

1. I have a recurring dream—many people do—but my dream only visits me when the conditions are right. If I go to bed early and fall asleep beside my husband, I don't have the dream. It's the other nights, after I've read, replaced the buttons on a shirt, washed the stray mugs and spoons in the sink, and finally settled down on the couch, that I find myself nodding off, basked in the blue haze from the television screen. I snuggle up with the eiderdown quilt and fall asleep there; the dream drops in uninvited and plays itself out like a record.

I am in a car, in a Volvo or a Mercedes. I'm in a car unlike the one I own, which is a '67 Chevy, rusted out in the body, cancer on the black vinyl roof, in need of brake fluid after a long drive. Sometimes I must manually pull the choke to get it started. It refuses to die and I should probably be grateful since I can't afford to replace it. Anyway, in the dream Volvo I feel safe. I have not one but two spare tires in my trunk. My tank is filled, and I have money in my pocket and in my purse.

Other drivers seem respectful of me on the highway. They smile at me as we wait in line at the tollbooth. I appear to be a well-cared-for woman behind the tinted windows. The Volvo and I are on the way to Bangor, Maine, because that is where my husband purchased the summer cottage, located on a beach with enormous black jetties and multicolored rocks stretching out for miles. It's late August and the flies are a nuisance, but anything is bearable in Bangor, Maine. When I arrive at the cottage, my husband greets me with a wet kiss and eases his hands up under my blouse to cup my breasts. "I really missed you," he whispers. The dream ends here.

I awake with lines on my face from the rumpled quilt, with the television fuzzy and an ache in my stomach. We have no cottage there or anywhere.

2. When I was twelve Janet Penny was my best friend (best friends seemed yearly then and twelve was the year for Janet). Her parents owned a trailer in Bangor, Maine, and her father also owned the largest dry cleaners in Stratford, New Jersey. Every August he closed up shop to take the family to the trailer.

All that summer we hung out in the dry cleaners and Mr. Penny let us work the revolving rack that held the freshly pressed clothes. The clothes whizzed past us; the odor of cleaning fluid and plastic lingered everywhere. Mabel Barley, a stout black woman with a face like Aunt Jemima, stood at the steam pressers, her thick strong arms lifting the press and slamming it down again in a graceful, methodical motion. Sweat rolled off her cheeks, but she never complained about the heat. She just kept pressing and hummed to the tunes on the small transistor radio she kept on a table near her.

"Don't you girls have nothing better to do than spin that rack?"

she'd ask. The truth was that after the first week of freedom from school, summer was already boring.

"Look outside!" she'd holler over the hiss of the steam presser. "It's a day for young girls to be splashin' in the sun."

"I'm learning the trade," Janet would tell her.

Mabel would always let out a hoot. "No offense to your daddy, but I sure hope life does you better than a career in the trade. Find yourself a prince, Lady Jane, and let him do the sweating."

"You have a prince, Mabel?" I asked.

"Do I look like a woman's got a man spinning cartwheels over her? Now do I, Lisa?"

"Well, why don't you?" Janet asked.

"Cause I got fat, mean, and ugly, I s'pose."

We believed in princes then. We didn't want to get fat, ugly, or mean, and when we weren't in the dry cleaners we sat in the Pennys' kitchen at the table, flipping through *Teen* magazine, waiting for breasts to sprout on our chests, waiting for my first period to arrive. Janet had got her period in the spring; she was a woman as far as I was concerned.

Often we also spent hours trying on clothes in her room, which was at the top of the Victorian frame house. The attic had been converted into a room just for her, though at the time we couldn't have understood the true meaning of a room of one's own. We tried out new makeup techniques with her mother's old and cracked compacts. Sometimes we dialed Janet's number on the phone and hung up quickly so it would ring, and we'd each practice talking to the boyfriends we'd imagined had called us. When we grew tired of these games, we sat outside in the grass under the weeping willow tree in her yard making promises we could never keep: that neither one of us would have a boyfriend unless both of us did; that we would have a double wedding and a double honeymoon and double pregnancies and live next door to each other

until we became double widows or double grandmothers, which-
ever came first.

July was nearly over when Janet asked me if I'd come to Maine
with her in August.

"What's it like there? What do you do?"

She shrugged. "Same as here—only it's better. We can swim."

"We swim here."

She smiled at me. "But my cousin Chuckie and his best friend
Ted are coming, and I think Chuckie likes you."

I had only met Chuckie once before, at Janet's birthday party in
June. She had had a barbecue birthday party at night with Chinese
lanterns strung in a large square around the patio. Chuckie was tall
and blond and tough looking. He danced with me twice and threw
pebbles from the driveway at me the rest of the evening, laughing
the whole time.

"Well?" Janet asked me. I knew she was thinking that we'd have
double boyfriends in Maine. I said yes.

Bad luck or real life stepped in and Ted came down with a case of
the mumps, so in the backseat of the Pennys' station wagon,
Chuckie sat between Janet and me. The car rocked over the bumpy
roads and whipped along the smoother highways, and through all
of it Chuckie balanced a Monopoly board on his lap. Janet grew
sulky when I bought Park Place and won the game.

"I don't want to play anymore," she said darkly, and she turned
her face to the window.

While she sat staring out at the smokestacks and refineries of
north Jersey, Chuckie leaned against me and swiftly kissed me on
the cheek. He smelled of the red licorice he'd been chewing throughout the Monopoly game; the kisses I've enjoyed most since then
always remind me of licorice.

We seemed to pass through New York State before we even
knew we were in it, and in New Haven, Connecticut, we stopped

at Mr. Penny's brother's house. The brother was a slight, red-faced man who wore his cotton shirt sloppily—shirttails hanging out, buttons missing. He was nothing like Mr. Penny, who was also slight but was neat and clean. He insisted that I call him Uncle Jim, but I didn't. I just started talking to him if I had something to say, and the most I had to say was, "Please pass the mashed potatoes," at dinner.

Uncle Jim begged us to stay the night instead of driving on in the dark. Janet and I asked if we could use our sleeping bags and camp in the yard. Chuckie smiled and thought he might like to camp out with us, but Mr. Penny reminded him that girls our age giggled all night about nothing.

Chuckie sneaked me another smile, and later, when Janet carried the extra blankets out to the sleeping bags, he tugged my arm while we were standing near the screen door. He kissed me again, this time trying for my lips but catching me on the chin, then he hurried off and disappeared into the den.

Sometime in the middle of the night I had to use the bathroom. I didn't want to go into the house alone so I shook Janet, who was snoring loudly beside me. I couldn't rouse her. I shook her several more times but only managed to stop her snoring. She rolled onto her stomach and burrowed deeper into the bag like a turtle retreating into its shell. I nudged her one last time. She only groaned and curled up some more, her rear end sticking up toward the sky.

Inside I didn't even bother to turn on lights; instead I felt my way to the second floor and used the bathroom quickly, hoping I hadn't disturbed anyone. As I was washing my hands, though, I heard footsteps in the hall. I thought immediately of Chuckie and his last kiss. There was a tap on the door.

"You okay in there? It's Uncle Jim. That you, Janet?"

"No. It's Lisa," I called out hoarsely.

"You okay?" he asked again.

"Sure."

He said nothing else. I heard his footsteps again and then I left the bathroom. I was still at the top of the stairs when I heard my name.

"Lisa. Lisa," Uncle Jim whispered.

When I turned to the voice he was standing at the end of the hall, his pajama bottoms down around his knees. It was too dark to actually see the private parts he was exposing, but I imagined them, thick and hairy. What I could see were his eyes shining, and I could make out his crooked white teeth, neon teeth, through his grin. "Lisa, sweetie," he said.

For what seemed like more than the several seconds it probably was, I stared at Uncle Jim, then fled down the stairs. I let the screen door slam behind me as I raced into the yard. When I reached my sleeping bag I climbed in and bit the downy inside to muffle my crying. I cried until I fell asleep.

In the morning Mr. Jim Penny made himself scarce, claiming an important appointment in town. I begged Janet's parents to let me go home. I was homesick, I lied, and I just couldn't imagine staying in Bangor. Mrs. Penny took me in her arms and smoothed back my hair, telling me in her soft voice what fun we would all have. "And Janet will be so lonely without you," she said.

"I want to go home. I'm sorry, but I want to go."

Mr. Penny phoned my parents and everyone finally agreed that I could manage the Trailways ride home alone. On the bus I filled the empty seat next to me with my belongings. Before the bus pulled out of the depot, I saw Chuckie standing below, waving me off. Suddenly he brought his hand to his mouth, then blew me a kiss. I wasn't interested. One day licorice-smelling Chuckie would be a man. I closed my eyes, partly because I was tired and partly because I thought I might cry again. I pretended to sleep the entire ride back to New Jersey.

Janet called me when they returned from Bangor, but I could

never bring myself to tell her about Uncle Jim. I never told anyone. I never saw Janet again either. In the fall we started high school at different schools, and whenever she called I made an excuse not to talk to her. For a year after that, I dreamed of that hallway in New England. Slight, sloppy men still unnerve me.

3. I'd been married a year when my parents announced that they would vacation in Bangor. They hadn't been on a real vacation in years. They were day-trippers, taking time off for a quick trip to the shore or to places like Longwood Gardens or Washington, D.C. They'd gone to Washington to see the monument eleven times.

And Lincoln. For some reason my father was hooked on the Lincoln Memorial. My father had fancied himself congressional material; he'd been involved in small-town politics for years, but he would never go further.

"This year we're going north," he told my husband and me, "to Bangor. Yankee country. Lisa almost made it to Bangor once, didn't you, Lisa?"

I cleared away the remains of the chicken paprika and collected the dirty plates.

"Yep. Almost made it to Bangor."

"But she got homesick," my mother added for my husband's benefit. She could never resist the chance to tell a story about me. "She had to come home on the bus alone. She moped for the rest of that summer too. And you never did see that Penny girl again, did you? Why didn't you?"

I looked at the three of them sitting around the dining room table, the expectant silence growing larger. "Her uncle was a flasher."

My husband choked on his wine.

"A flasher? You mean he showed you—*himself?*" my mother asked.

"Yes, himself, Mother. When I went inside to use the bathroom he hid in a corner with his pants down. I couldn't stay. Who knew what lunacy I would have been up against in Maine."

"Jesus," my husband said. "Jesus Christ."

"It was far from a religious experience."

My mother tapped her fingers on the table. "Religious. Do you hear her being glib, Arthur?" she asked my father.

But my father sat rigidly in his chair, acknowledging no one. His face was pale. "The bastard," he whispered furiously after a while.

"Daddy, it was a long time ago," I said coolly, although I was secretly bursting with love for him at that moment for absolving me of the doubt that I had done something to make Uncle Jim act that way. "Do you want more wine?"

My parents couldn't have been in Bangor more than two days when the phone call came. I was sitting on the couch struggling with a needlepoint. It was a tedious and not very enjoyable pastime, but my husband worked long hours. I missed a stitch and jabbed myself with the needle before I managed to pick up the phone.

"He was on the jetty when it happened," my mother said, her voice chillingly even and toneless. "I was snapping a picture of him," she added, as if this had somehow caused the stroke. As he stood out on the jetty, he had shouted to my mother that it was more beautiful than the Lincoln Memorial.

I've always wanted to stand in the spot he last stood in. The exact spot. Every year after his death I would begin talking about Maine. I would begin telling my husband in March that's where I wanted to go for summer vacation. He would placate me for months, promise me one of those promises that are lies, that this would be the year. Seven years later I still hadn't been to Maine and I didn't love him anymore either.

4. My husband is still here in the house with me and our daughter. More and more now I sleep in the living room, dreaming, dreaming. Tomorrow, I tell myself, tomorrow I will say that I'm

leaving. My Chevy won't take me far; neither will my purse. But I feel it, feel the decision moving into place like a rook on a chessboard. It will not be an easy game. And so at night, after my dream, I go into the kitchen and watch another life. I watch my neighbor's house from my kitchen window. It's August again and it's vacation time for many; it's vacation time for them. And guess where they're going with the camper and their child? Just guess.

At 6:30 A.M. the grass is dew speckled. The new-day noises are muffled and distant: the guttural rush of a car engine, the rhythmic click of John Barker's black leather shoes on the sidewalk, the slam of another neighbor's front door, the Wilsons' retriever yapping. I stand at my window and look out on my neighbor's driveway. Bill is outside checking the tires, testing the lights on the camper. He looks up to his kitchen window and his wife, Lynn, appears. She holds up a lime green thermos and waves it. "I'm ready when you are," he shouts to her. Then he checks the outside faucet and the coiled green garden hose, jiggles the handle on the garage door, piles the redwood benches on top of the table, pulls his daughter's tricycle close to the side of the house. With his hands on his hips he surveys his yard once more and, finding everything in order, he walks to the car and gets in. Lynn and little Shelley come running out of the house. Shelley's arms are loaded with dolls for the long ride.

As the car and camper back out of the driveway, I wish them the times of their lives, though they can't hear me. I push back my hair, finish my last gulp of coffee. I imagine them on the black highway, singing, stopping at the Howard Johnson's for lunch, pulling off to the side of the road to rest or stretch. Bill looks up and sees me watching. He honks his horn and smiles. I wave and mouth the words: "Have fun. Have fun in Bangor, Maine."

Emily woke to the feel of hot sun, what she thought was hot sun, on her shoulder. She had fallen asleep at her desk somewhere around four in the morning, her head wedged in the crevice of her folded arm, but as her eyes fluttered open she felt the sun moving, felt pressure inside the warmth and, still half asleep, murmured, "Peter."

"It's only me, Gene," he said, pressing her shoulder more firmly, shaking her. "It's nine thirty, Emily."

His hand, heavy on her skin, shook her once softly. She sat up, blinked herself awake. "Oh my God, where's Lizzie?"

He squatted down close to her chair; his smell, fresh from a shower but tinged with the scent of two or three hard-smoked cigarettes, was intoxicating, like the fruit-wood smell of those potpourris she cooked on the stove at Christmas.

"She found you sleeping here this morning. She came upstairs, knocked on the door, and, I swear to God, like a sixteen-year-old she asked me if we could let you sleep and surprise you with breakfast. The kid knocks me out sometimes," he said, laughing.

"Yes, sir," Emily said, "that's my baby."

Outside the window, the locusts were rattling off their morning signal of another humid day. Emily arched her back in a stretch, smoothed her hair with her hands. At one point the night before, her and Gene's typing were in syncopation, so loud and even they had obliterated the other night sounds: the wind chimes, the raspy breeze, even Helen Humes.

"I wrote a story," she said, her voice tentative, rising on the word *story*.

Gene glanced past her to the papers on her desk. "Yes, you certainly did."

When she tilted her head, raised her eyebrows expectantly, he merely shrugged. "Well, if you're waiting for applause you ain't gonna get it from me, darlin'. Go take a shower. Lizard and I will be waiting for you upstairs," he said, backing out of the office.

Emily stood up, one hand on her hip. She flicked the edge of the papers with her fingernail. "Nothing like a word of encouragement to start the day."

He turned on that comment, strolling down the hall, and called back to her, "I don't congratulate professionals for practicing their profession."

He was halfway down the hall. She picked up a small, slim notepad and rushed to the doorway, then she threw it at him, aiming for his calf. The notepad missed, but Gene turned around.

"It's not a children's story," she said, "and—and it's good."

He waved his hand at her. "We'll see."

"You're infuriating," she said.

"Go take your shower. Come on, breakfast awaits."

TWELVE

" 'His hair was already beginning to turn gray,' " Gene read. " 'It struck him as strange that he should have aged so much in the last few years. The shoulders on which his hands lay were warm and quivering. He felt pity for this life, still so warm and exquisite, but probably soon to fade and droop like his own. Why did she love him so? Women had always believed him different from what he really was, had loved in him not himself but the man their imaginations pictured him, a man they sought for eagerly all their lives. And afterward, when they discovered their mistake, they went on loving him just the same. And not one of them had ever been happy with him. Time had passed, he had met one woman after another, become intimate with each, parted with each, but had never loved. There had been all sorts of things between them, but never love.

" 'And only now, when he was gray-haired, had he fallen in love properly, thoroughly, for the first time in his life.' The end," Gene said, snapping the book shut.

Emily was being lulled by his soothing voice; all of his years of writing for actors and listening to actors speak his words had left him with the ability to read the contents of a cereal box, as well as this Chekhov story, with a curious mixture of passion and control.

When he closed the book her eyes opened. She'd been reclining in her surf chair and now sat up. "That isn't the end of the story."

Gene put the book down in the sand beside his chair. "Sure it is."

He was putting his sunglasses on, and as he did, she took hers off, nudging his shoulder with them. "That isn't the end. Why'd you stop there?"

Over the summer his thick hair had grown so long it now fell from a center part into waves along his temples; he continually pushed it back from his forehead, raking his fingers through it, a gesture that made him seem exasperated. "And why isn't it the ending?"

"Because he's in love. He's got to decide to do something. I know they decide something at the end."

He moved his head in her direction; even behind his sunglasses she knew his eyes were fixed hard on her. "You're dissatisfied with the ending?"

"Yes, because—" Then she noticed just a hint of smile beginning at the corners of his mouth. She had rewritten her own story twice in a week and had given it to him. "This is a sneaky way of telling me you don't like the ending of my story, Gene."

He was still staring at her, now turned halfway in his chair so his shoulders and chest blocked her sun. "The ending is fine," he said, "it's very moving, but I think its center is missing. I want to know more."

"About her marriage?"

He shook his head. "No. About why she can't go stand on that jetty where her father last stood unless someone takes her there? Why isn't it an easy decision, if, as she says, she doesn't love her husband anymore?"

His question was the same one that tripped her up after each revision. "Because she's . . . afraid."

"Of what?"

Emily looked down into her lap, studying her fingers as they folded the stems of her glasses in. "I don't know."

"Well, when you do know, you'll have your story—or a book. That way you structured it, like miniature chapters, it might be a book."

"Or a play? Like acts of a play?" she kidded.

"Leave the plays to me," he said, just an edge of the competitor in his voice, "and you write the books." He flung himself up from the chair then, adjusted the waistband of his trunks, pulling them up over a slice of untanned skin, and extended his hand to her. "Come on, let's go in the water with Lizard."

"You go. I'm going to read the real ending to Chekhov while you're swimming."

"Read it after I leave."

"Leave?"

"Two days, Emily. I leave in two days. You'll have plenty of time to catch up on your reading then."

Her watch was strapped to the handle of her straw carryall and she peeked at it, as if it were a calendar that would tell her he'd gotten his dates mixed up. "Next week," she said.

But Gene shook his head. "August twenty-sixth. I've got a production meeting in New York on the twenty-seventh and Chris comes home on the twenty-ninth. The end," he said.

"Go in the water. I'll be down in a second."

He tossed his sunglasses onto the seat of his chair and walked to the water, kicking up sand in his wake, shouting to Lizzie for her to take his hand. Emily sat there, a little dazed, wondering how she'd let herself be so unprepared for his leaving, how she could have blotted out the date like that.

She reached across his chair, lifting the book out of the sand where he'd planted it. The book was old and dog-eared, an anthology of Chekhov's stories and plays. As she flipped through the pages, she noticed Gene's underlinings and margin notations; like a Braille reader, she let her fingers roam over his penned-in words, interested only in the touch of her skin against the ink he'd put there. Then she flipped through the tissuey pages to the last page of "The Lady with the Dog" and found what Gene had edited out: "And it seemed to them that they were within an inch of arriving at a decision, and that a new, beautiful life would begin. And they both realized that the end was still far, far away, and that the hardest, the most complicated part was just beginning."

Late that evening Emily took the back outside stairs to Gene's apartment, but his place was dark, the door was locked. She returned to the front porch, where she smoked six or seven cigarettes in a row, drawing on them more violently than usual so that she was queasy, dizzy by the time she saw him approaching the front gate. It was after one.

"What are you doing out here so late?"

The wait, coupled with the chain-smoking, had left her feeling frayed and inarticulate. All evening she'd mentally prepared a very long-winded good-bye speech, but now that the time had come to deliver it, she realized that saying good-bye was the last thing she wanted. "Just thinking it's a shame you couldn't stay on. The shore's more beautiful in September. I'll be done with SPSC, thank God. I could write; you could write. Lizzie'll start school in a week. We'd have someone to throw the crab shells away." Inside a tinny voice was saying, "I'm going to miss you terribly."

He had sauntered up the front walk but stopped short of the porch steps. His hands were in his pockets and he shrugged, jutting his arms out to the side like handles. "The crabs will be out of season soon anyway, and, well, there's Chris. He's got school. And Lottie, she—we have things to straighten out before the divorce. I've already taken more than I should have."

"Taken? I don't understand."

Now he seemed to be the one having trouble with words. "Let's just say that I thought a lot about your sadness when I was working on the play."

"We use what we can."

"Yeah," Gene said, "something like that."

Almost imperceptibly, his physical presence seemed altered, a subtle change, like the shift in light in a room at dusk; already he was becoming memory.

/165

"Well, your staying on was just a thought. Lizzie will miss you."

"We'll stay in touch," he said, moving off of the walk sideways, almost a dance step, onto the lawn. "Don't worry."

And so two days later, with as little fuss as possible, Gene left them. At midmorning it was raining, the hard gusty rain they had longed for all summer. Emily held the umbrella over his head as he loaded his belongings into the car, while Lizzie, reluctant to say good-bye, stayed on the porch watching pensively. The rain was splattering his hands as he shut the trunk. "Wait a second," he said to Emily, and the next thing she knew he was dashing up the front walk. He grabbed Lizzie quickly, giving her three kisses—one on her forehead and one for each cheek. "Be good, Lizard," he said before he ran back to the car. He was soaked by the time he dipped his head under the umbrella. "You take care," he said. Swiftly, Gene kissed Emily's cheek, then got into the car. She stood at the front gate, waving at the tailpipes as he made a left and sped off toward Ninth Street.

Several days later her mother sent word that Emily should carry on with her duties at SPSC in her prolonged but unavoidable absence. A note, of course, only slightly less cryptic than her father's had been. "I will be back, but not yet. I'm going a little westward and will call." Emily stared at the words, wondering if her mother meant to write wayward instead of westward or if westward was just her code for AWOL, wacko, off the wagon. And how, now that Gene was gone, was she supposed to carry on with her duties, which weren't truly her duties at all? Whenever she flicked on the television at night she half expected to hear a report mentioning her mother with film to follow. It would be a grisly scene, with her mother, dressed to the hilt in something beautiful, being dragged from the scummy depths of a river somewhere west. Over the rainbow. East of the sun, west of the moon, like a character in an Irish folktale. It was frightening, the knowledge that she'd been orphaned too, and it occurred to her that if she needed a blood transfusion all of the compatible donors had left for parts unknown, unless they could draw blood from Lizzie—her type— but could they siphon enough from a six-year-old to save her?

PART FOUR

THIRTEEN

Francine was asleep in the bus when it hit the pothole, slid into a skid, and crashed into the metal railing on the shoulder of the road. She had been dreaming of an event that had never taken place in her real life, but had appeared so often in a dream that she had assimilated it into her past. This vision had come to her most regularly during the year and a half she spent at Green Hills sanatorium where, battling the d.t.'s and acute depression, she waited like an old woman in a home for Emily's weekend visits. During the first months of her drying out she talked about the dream freely, as if it were a plan that could come to fruition. Once when Emily visited her, Francine said, "Em'ly, I hope you're practicing for the show. You wouldn't want to disappoint your father or Maria."

"There is no show, Mother," Emily had told her, "and no father and no Maria."

"That's what these doctors keep saying to me."

"They're telling you the truth."

"I don't like it. Not at all."

"You don't have to like it, Mother, you just have to accept it."

The dream went like this: Emily, Francine, and Maria (a different Maria, a child with normal limbs, no palsy, and no seizures) were in the back of a motor home while up front Tom held the wheel steadily. They were on their way to Hollywood to perform at the

Hollywood Bowl for a sell-out crowd. What made them special was the fact that both Emily and Maria were musical prodigies and Francine herself was known as one of the best singers of her day. Tom, of course, was the leader of their group and played his clarinet. The dream always ended at the part when the stage began to rotate and they were washed in blue-gold light as the cameras flashed and the audience roared its appreciation. When Benny T. Goodman's traveling bus began its skid, it coincided with the rotating stage in Francine's dream so that, at the point of impact with the guardrail, Francine's head thumped against the metal rim of the seat and she called out, "We've made it!"

Magic Eddie, the keyboard player, had been lounging in his seat, his back to the aisle, so he toppled to the floor like a sack of groceries. He looked up at Francine, his wide eyes rolling in his head, and said, "We ain't made nothing, Ms. Perone. We had ourselves an accident."

The bus, a reconditioned yellow school bus that had been painted black and redesigned with bunks for the band members, a kitchenette, and broom-closet-size bathroom, tipped to the right. Porky "Stix" Billings appeared from the bathroom demanding to know what had happened. Ray, the bass player, was still sound asleep despite the uproar and would probably stay sound asleep until someone slapped his face with cold wet hands to rouse him. Benny T., who had been driving the bus, rapped against Francine's window, calling out, "Everybody all right in there?" While Eva, who had been riding up front with him, kept asking if the bus was going to explode.

Now that Francine could plainly see that she was not in the motor home with Tom and her children, she reached up, jiggling the latches, and pulled the window down. She knelt on the seat and stuck her head outside. "Where are we?"

Benny T. scratched the top of his head, looking from the front of the bus back up at Francine. "You okay, Fran?"

"I think so," she said, rubbing the back of her head. "Where are we, Benny?"

Benny glanced around him, up at the sky, out toward the highway, and around the back of the bus, then he smiled. "Wake up and smell the coffee, Fran. We're in Kansas."

"I had a feeling we were going to meet with disaster. I was thinking it last night, even though I didn't say anything to you. I was thinking, whenever two grown women our age take off like a couple of delinquents—and that's what we're doing, Francine, being delinquent—well, that's the first sign that disaster is about to strike. I know when I know."

Eva was pulling clothes from her suitcase like rabbits from a magician's hat.

"What kind of phrase is that—'You know when you know'? You know *what?*"

"What you feel, Fran. What you know without being told."

Eva had already emptied the contents of one suitcase and was working on her smaller overnight bag. Francine slumped on the bed and watched.

"I'm too tired to follow this line of thinking. And, my head hurts. Do you have aspirin?"

"Do I have aspirin? she wants to know," she said to the room, throwing her hands up. "Yes, I have aspirin, and I used to have good sense and a brain before I took up with you."

Francine let her head flop forward, pinched the bridge of her nose with her thumb and forefinger. The ache that had started at the nape of her neck had worked its way to the front of her face. "For God's sake, Eva, we have not had a disaster. The bus hit a pothole and lost a wheel. You make it sound as if we're fugitives from the law, running around the country with gangsters."

Eva was holding a cardigan sweater in her hands and stretched it out tight; Francine could hear the fabric snap. "Gangsters, musicians—same thing."

"Oh, fine. Just point me to the aspirin, if you please. I'll consume the entire bottle, and then you'll be done with me and you can get on the next plane out of here and go back to Roxborough."

/171

Eva tossed the aspirin bottle at Francine. "With the luck we've been having, you won't die. You'll just go into a coma for the next twenty years, and your poor daughter and I will have to go to the hospital every day to see you withering away."

Francine's fingers fell away from her nose. She was sitting close enough to Eva's suitcase to reach for Eva's wrist as her hand dipped inside to pull out more clothes. "You would come visit me every day for twenty years?"

Eva thumped her hands against her thighs, dropping the nightgown she was holding back into the suitcase. She started to laugh, which also made Francine laugh.

"Well, you wouldn't deserve to have visitors," she said. She sat down on the bed too, the suitcase between them. "But I would come, I guess. I came here, didn't I?" she asked, gesturing to the Holiday Inn room.

It had been the fortuitous attraction of Benny T. Goodman to Eva at the Starlight Room in the Poconos two weeks earlier that had started Francine thinking. What better way to find Tom Perone, if, as she suspected, he had left her for a life on the road, than to travel with a real band? Who would know better the night spots they were likely to find him in? Who would know music agents, inside information about the nightclub circuit groups better than someone like Benny T., who had traveled throughout the country time and time again? Although she'd been disappointed to discover that Benny T. was not her Tom using an alias, she couldn't have been more pleased when, during the band's break, he zeroed in on her and Eva's table, introducing himself to Eva with a shy gentlemanliness that was in such contrast to his rambunctious onstage personality. He thought Eva was a woman he knew, someone from his very distant past. The fact that she wasn't, however, didn't seem to bother him in the least from what Francine could see. He bought her a drink, asked how long she'd be staying in the Poconos, asked her if she'd like to meet him for dinner the following night before the show. At first Eva was visibly flustered. Francine watched her twisting the thick gold wedding band she was still wearing a year after Anthony's death, slipping it up and down her finger, but never over the knuckle, never completely off and on.

He excused himself when it was time to start the second set and asked her to really consider his request for a date. As he walked across the dance floor back to the stage, Eva turned to Francine.

"I can't go on a date," Eva said. "I've been married since I was twenty years old."

"Eva, you're a free woman now."

"But, Fran, it's only been a year. And anyway, what's the sense? He'll be gone after they finish the week out here, and . . . and we'll go home, back to our lives. It's silly. I don't think it's for me."

Francine's eyes were on the band members. "Maybe we won't go home," she'd said. "Maybe we did find the man we've been looking for."

And that was all it took. Eva did have her date with Benny T. and discovered that the initial stood for Tartaglione, his real last name. She also learned that he was sixty-two years old, originally from Philadelphia, that he had known Anthony's partner's brother Phil, and that he had gone to high school with Phil's second cousin, Mike DeBusco, who, it turned out, had played trumpet in Benny's first band, the Tremelos, when they were all in their early twenties. Naturally, Eva remembered the Tremelos well—she and Anthony had heard them once at a wedding—and so, within the time it took to order a steak, eat it, and drink several cups of coffee with their pie à la mode, she and Benny felt like family to each other. Of course, Francine's last name was her calling card. Italian is Italian is Italian. When she explained to Benny why she and Eva had come to the mountains in the first place, he was sympathetic; when she asked if she and Eva could travel with the band, he thought they were joking; when she said how much it would mean to her daughter, Emily, if she could find Tom Perone, he said, All right, sure, sure, you can come. Francine hadn't even minded that he couldn't take his eyes off of Eva when he'd said it.

And so the unlikely ensemble had finally arrived here in Wichita,

/173

Kansas, after a detour through Philadelphia, where Francine, informing no one, not even Emily, that she'd returned (for fear that she'd change her mind), parked her car and stole away on a bus with Benny, Eva, and Benny's reluctant, disgruntled band. Their final destination was Las Vegas, where, if it didn't happen before then, Francine was sure she'd find Tom.

Unlike the fantasies of life on the road she'd indulged in as a young woman, Francine would have been the first to admit that the cozy, smoke-filled lounges and elegantly appointed supper clubs with dim lamps in the center of the tables were of an era past; that musicians were no more lyrical or mysterious than anyone else—in fact, they were less so; and that life lived out of a suitcase was limiting. She was a woman who liked furniture, the scent of her own linens, and having such things along was impossible when traveling across the country with four men in a black school bus. And even though they'd only been in Wichita for a few hours, she wasn't wild about the city either. To her Wichita seemed like the end of the earth, desolate, even though the city was by no means small. Anywhere west of Pennsylvania, however, and Francine conjured images of wheatfields, flat, motionless plains in patchwork designs for mile upon endless mile. She couldn't get the song "Wichita Lineman" out of her head even though she'd never liked it. She'd always thought Glen Campbell's voice was just short of apathetic.

She dared not mention any of this to Eva, who had finally emptied the contents of her suitcases into the dresser drawers; she felt obliged to sustain the illusion of their big adventure in order to prevent Eva from lapsing into a funk.

Francine shook three aspirin into her palm and was on her way to the bathroom for a glass of water when Benny called through their door.

"I'll get it," Eva said. Francine couldn't help but notice how Eva's mood improved at the sound of Benny's muffled voice through the door.

"Where's Fran?" Francine heard him ask once he was in the room.

"Taking pills. She has a headache. What are you all worked up about?"

"Who's worked up?" Francine said, standing in the bathroom doorway, still holding the half-filled glass of water.

"I've got news, Fran," he said.

"About the bus?" Eva asked.

Benny touched Eva's shoulder lightly. "The bus is fine. Mechanic says he'll have it fixed by the time we're ready to head out. It's other news," he said, turning to look at Francine.

"Don't say a word yet," Francine said. She disappeared into the bathroom and splashed some cool water on her face, but it didn't help her composure the way she thought it might. When she came back into the room she asked him to sit down, so he sat on the edge of the bed and she sat right next to him. She held her head high and stared straight across the room, her gaze lighting on a mundane piece of contemporary art that was hanging on the wall. "All right. What's the news?"

She could feel him reaching for something in his pocket, heard the rustle of paper being unfolded, and then Benny's sigh, his preamble to formal speech.

"I've been checking around with some agents," he said, "and I found this." He tried to push the paper into Francine's hands, but her hands were folded tightly in her lap. She didn't budge.

"Just tell me."

"There's a guy named Tom Riley, plays clarinet, has a band called the Jazz Lights. They were here in Wichita about a week ago. They're headed for Vegas, Fran. They'll be playing there just about the time we roll into town."

For a moment the only sound she could concentrate on was the clinking of dishes being piled onto the lunch cart outside in the hall. The angular lines of the painting she'd been staring at blurred suddenly. Without moving her head she opened her hand and waited for Benny to slip the piece of paper into it. When she felt it against her palm, she looked at the words: *Tom Riley, Jazz Lights, Vegas.*

"Riley is my maiden name."

"Yep," Benny said in a whisper.

"This could be him," Francine said, turning to look at Benny. Eva was standing just behind him, her hand on his shoulder.

"Yes, yes it could," Eva said.

There was no accounting for the panic she suddenly felt except to say that, after all this maddening pursuit, her race headlong into the past would be complete; she would be faced with the task of reconstructing her life at the late age of sixty. It occurred to her that she had never considered the possibility that he might not want to come back, not even for Emily. Well, I can't think about that now, she thought. And the choked feeling in her throat was gone, passed away like a menopausal hot flash. She threw her shoulders back and smiled bravely for Benny and Eva.

'What do you think of the name Jazz Lights?" she asked Benny.

Benny looked from Francine to Eva, as if he were waiting for Eva to cue him, send him a silent, sharp message with her hazel eyes as to how he should interpret what Francine knew must have sounded like an ordinary and detached question. Then Eva's eyes caught hers and she smiled, Eva smiled, Benny shrugged and waved his hands. "Hell, I think it's a damn nice name, Fran. Damn nice," he said.

"I'm willing to forgive you," Francine mumbled.

Emily bent her head toward her mother's chest to hear the words. They seemed to be coming from deep down in her rib cage rather than from her lips.

"What did you say?"

"I'm willing to forgive you," Francine repeated.

Emily sat by the hospital bed wearing her navy blue peacoat and beret, one hand gloved, the other bare and clutching the bed rail. "Forgive me for what?"

She expected her mother might say, "For putting me here, that's what."

Francine rolled her head back, her unmade-up face floating up from the pillow, as fragile and opaque as papier-mâché. "For dying," she said.

"I'm here, Mother. I didn't die."

"Maria," Francine whispered before she closed her eyes.

FOURTEEN

Emily stands by her car along the side of the highway. The sky is as dark and threatening as the sky in The Wizard of Oz *just before Dorothy is knocked unconscious. It's windy and it's raining and she has no coat, no umbrella. She stands shivering, hugging herself, her blouse so soaked through that the outline of her bra shows; her nipples show through the wet bra. Since there is nothing to do with the broken-down car on a deserted highway, she begins to walk, one thumb stuck out like a hitchhiker, the other arm folded across her stomach, flimsy protection against the wind and hard rain. The man passing by in the car, the one who likes women's breasts more than their legs or faces, might pick her up just so he can stare at her nipples as she sits passively in the passenger seat beside him. At a stoplight he will reach across the leather seat and cup her breast in his hand. His breath close to her neck will be warm and slightly stale with the scent of that morning's coffee, but she won't mind. In fact, she will arch herself up to greet his touch. "What do you want?" he'll ask. "To be eaten alive," she'll tell him.*

The fantasy was outrageous, but it was not the first she'd entertained since Gene returned to New York. It was, however, closer to reality than any of her other fantasies because she *was* stranded, in her Toyota, in the rain, on Ocean Drive instead of a deserted highway, and try as she might to restart the car, all she got when she turned the key was a click. She tried again, remembering words like *alternator* and *solenoid*. If one was dead there would be a click but if the other was dead there'd be nothing, not a sound, and only Peter had known the difference. Of course, had she paid any attention to what he was saying when it had happened in the past, she would know what to do now, but she hadn't. There'd been no reason.

This was the third incident in three weeks in which she'd sat or stood helplessly, remembering words that were of no use to her. When the hot-water heater broke, shedding gallons of water on the utility room floor, she threw towels down thinking *valve* but not knowing which one to turn. And then only a week later, while she was washing dishes, the pipe under the sink broke apart like a hand grenade, spewing garbage remains and more water on the floor. "Trap," she'd yelled at the plumber over the phone, "the trap broke."

And now here she was at midmorning on the twentieth straight day of unrelenting rain in a useless car. Her first thought was to get out and abandon it, just leave it there and walk two miles to Lindsy's showroom and pick out another Toyota. "Trade in?" the salesman would probably ask, and she would shake her head no. "I just left it where it died," she'd tell him. After all, how bad could abandoning a car be? Certainly not criminal, certainly not as inhumane as leaving a wife and kid. Sitting there, her breath fogging up the windows so that the world outside was just a hazy blur, she thought she understood why her mother ever began to drink in the first place: it was because she knew too many words for which she had no use, the biggies like *death* and *desertion*.

Emily reached forward and rubbed the inside of the window with the back of her hand. There was a phone booth on the corner of the next block, and she knew that three blocks beyond the booth was the Diambrosio brothers' gas station. She pulled her keys out of the ignition, pushed open the door and her umbrella, and walked in the cool rain to the booth. It was no surprise to her that the phone was out of order. Often after the tourists fled Ocean Gate the residents would find phone cords snipped in the phone booths, lawn furniture missing from rental properties, screen doors confiscated, walls with holes in them. She cursed under her breath and continued to walk to the Diambrosios'. There she explained that her car had died and she needed a tow.

The mechanic interrogated her while his head was bent over the guts of another car inside the station. "Did you gun the engine?"

"No."

"Any sound at all?"

"A click."

"Is the battery charging?"

She hadn't noticed. She had forgotten to look at the red indicator.

"I don't think it's the battery," she said.

The mechanic looked up, wiped his hands on a rag that was poking out of his back pocket. "You don't."

"No, I don't."

"Okeydokey," he said, "we'll get you towed and check it out." He waved the rag in the direction of a beat-up chair against the wall. "Have a seat."

She dropped the keys into his greasy palm. "I think it might be the alternator," she said suddenly, trying to impress him with her command of auto lingo, "or the solenoid." He smiled politely, then dismissed her, shouting across the garage to a Sammy to get the tow truck.

Two hours later Emily drove to the Foodtown, a newly installed battery charging the Toyota's engine. The mechanic had cast her a look of barely restrained superiority when he announced that it was neither the alternator nor the solenoid. Emily consoled herself with the thought that maybe this was *all* he knew in the world as she scribbled out a check for eighty dollars. That amount when added to the $275 for the new hot-water heater and the $150 for the new trap meant she had spent an extra $505 in three weeks' time. For once Emily was actually relieved that her mother seemed to have fallen off the face of the earth; as long as she stayed away, Emily could keep her part-time job at SPSC, a big help with these surprise expenditures.

She had planned to do a major food run, but it was already close to one, half the day shot in the cold, dirty Diambrosio garage, and she had to be back by three to meet Lizzie's school bus. Inside the supermarket she stalked the aisles, list in hand, picking only the absolute necessities from the shelves. She made a left off of the cereal aisle, almost toppling an end display of Cheerios, when her cart clipped the edge of a box. Her hand shot out to steady the display, and when she looked up, she was looking straight into Margot Compton's eyes. Their carts were facing each other, inches apart, like bumper cars on the boardwalk, Emily thought, waiting for the electrical jolt to set them in motion.

Margot's cart was empty, Emily noticed, yet she gave the impression that she'd been in the store for hours, simply wandering. Everything about her had changed. She was pale; she wore no makeup, which left the traces of dark circles under her eyes there for anyone to see. Her hair had been clipped shorter, to chin length, but it was not clean. It lay flat against her head. Her trench coat flapped open and Emily could see that she was wearing a navy blue sweatshirt and sweatpants, but they were certainly not the chic matched sets most of the ladies in town wore food shopping. They, too, were unclean, rumpled, in fact, as if she'd been sleeping in them for days.

"Excuse me," Emily said, angling her cart around Margot's, but Margot made no attempt to get out of the way. Emily sighed. As much as she disliked the woman, she wasn't in the mood for a scene, nor did she want to know why Margot was here instead of at school, looking like one of those street women Emily saw more and more of whenever she went into the city to work. She wondered, too, what Peter would think if he could see her now.

"Margot, please excuse me," Emily said.

Margot's eyes burned on her as if she could see right through Emily, as if she could see in Emily something Emily had failed to

/181

recognize in herself. Margot opened her mouth to say something, but no words came out, just a sound, a soft *ahh*—like the sound Maria used to make when she needed something; it triggered a paroxysm of compassion in Emily so strong that she reached over and touched Margot's wrist, asking, "Are you ill?"

Margot snatched her wrist free and in a voice of unexpected control, she said, "We're blocking the aisle and you're wasting my time." She took two steps backward, pulling her cart with her, clearing the way for Emily. As Emily rolled her cart past Margot, Margot said, "I go to the cemetery twice a week." And Emily recognized the look in Margot's eyes; it was the same look of superiority the mechanic had given her earlier. She realized too that Margot was proud of her deteriorating looks; she was stricken and she meant to prove it with a vengeance, to wear her bleeding heart like a badge so anyone could see the mistress grieved for him more than the wife. Emily felt herself breaking out in a cold sweat. She pushed on, wanting to be far away from Margot, turning into the next aisle quickly.

Outside it had stopped raining. Emily loaded the groceries into the trunk. She looked north of her to where cars were speeding quickly around the circle; less than half a mile away was the cemetery. The thought of that icy cold day in January made her legs tremble. Everywhere, even outside with a stiff breeze blowing, the air had smelled just like the funeral home—medicinal and cloying—and standing by the casket listening to Father Catalano's final prayers, she had suddenly grabbed her mother's arm, digging her fingernails into her coat. "That smell, Mother. I can't stand the smell," she'd hissed. Francine did not hold her; she just patted the hand that was clutching her for dear life and said, "It's almost over, my baby." But even back at the house, while she tried to hold herself together for those who had come to pay their respects, she'd felt the odor clinging to her, as if it were oozing from her own pores. At one moment she even slipped into the bathroom, un-zipped the dress, pulling it down to her waist, and before the bathroom mirror, she sniffed under her armpits to be certain that the smell was not emanating from her. Francine was on the other side of the bathroom door when Emily came out; the narrow hallway sealing off the bedrooms from the house proper was lit dimly by two Colonial wall sconces, and as the winds outside howled, one candle flickered.

Her mother's face was in shadow. "You were in there a long time, Em'ly."

Secure in the strained light, Emily said, "It should have been Daddy we buried today, not Peter."

Francine reached up to touch the scarf at her throat. Emily saw a glint of gold on her mother's hand; she still wore her wedding band. Emily had buried her own with Peter, but she felt no less married to him for the gesture.

"You want your father dead?" Francine's voice was conspicuously soft, almost tender.

Emily shook her head, feeling ashamed of what she had said. "I just want things in a natural order. If I had to bury my husband, then I want my father here. I want . . . one of them, Mother."

Francine took hold of Emily's elbow. "There's no such thing as a natural order. I thought you knew that by now. Come," she said, prodding her, "you have guests."

Late that night, before she changed into the bathrobe and went outside to smoke for the first time, she had washed the dress, ruined it, in fact, because it was wool and should only have been dry cleaned. She'd held it, wet, pressed to her face, but the odor was not gone.

She looked once more in the direction of the cemetery. "I can't go there," she said to herself. She unlocked her door and slid into the car. The smell of Peter alive was smoke.

She drove slowly because she was still feeling unsteady after the encounter with Margot; she didn't trust herself not to ram the back of someone's Mercedes if she applied more than adequate pressure to the accelerator. It was the supreme irony, she thought, that Peter, who'd brought Margot into their lives in the first place, was free, his soul at rest, while she was left to face his mistake and its repercussions over and over.

He was a good man who had made one error, one that had almost cost them their marriage, and sometimes Emily wished that Peter's reason for the affair had been the result of the kind of passion heroes are made of instead of the contemporary disease of restlessness. The night he confessed she already knew what it was he intended to tell her, but hearing it, having a shape and a sound to what she'd begun to suspect, made the affair seem tantamount to first-degree murder in her mind. She'd wept, stormily at first, before lapsing into the prolonged painful sobs that made her throat sore. "Is her house clean?" she'd asked him, finally, because during his confession he'd complained that she was too fastidious, too perfect. This from the man who organized his gardening tools, compartmentalized his drawers, arranged his clothes in a hierarchy of design and color.

He blinked, then cast a look around their living room, which glistened and smelled of lemon oil.

"Not as clean as this."

And with that she had determined his punishment. For two months she didn't clean. The bathtub grew a flaky white ring, the dishes piled high, caked with egg yolks, rotting bits of vegetables. She threatened to walk out if he dared to tidy up a single thing. He was forced to wear the same socks several days in a row until one night, as she was placing more dishes on the drainboard, he said, "Emily, you've got to stop this."

"I'm just giving you what you want."

He was sitting at the kitchen table and he flew out of his chair, turned the faucet on full blast so it splattered on the dishes and on them. "For fucking Christ's sake, what I want is for you to forgive me!"

His face was raw with anger. She reached across him and turned the faucet off. "You'll have to wait."

And wait through it was what they did, until all the dishes in the house had been used, until she had to dip into the good silverware for a fork or a spoon, until she could derive no more satisfaction from watching him leave the house in the morning in a plaid work

184 /

shirt and a pair of jeans, carrying a briefcase. They'd run out of soap and shampoos, laundry detergent and Brillo pads. Only Lizzie was kept neat and clean while they tripped on the toys Emily had stopped insisting she pick up.

All through that autumn Peter raked the leaves in the yard, working with the sullen resignation of a prisoner on a chain gang. In the late afternoons he pushed the leaves into piles for Lizzie to romp in, and after she spilled them all over the yard, he raked them into heaps again. One evening after supper, wearing the faded suede jacket he reserved for cool-weather yard work, he went out, filled the metal trash can with the leaves. He struck a match and leaned on the rake, watching as the leaves took to the flame. Black smoke swirled in the wind, mixing with the briny smell of the sea, while Emily watched from the kitchen window, her hands plunged deep into the sudsy water of the sink.

Peter didn't come in that night until after Lizzie was asleep. Emily was picking clean laundry from a big wicker basket, folding Lizzie's small socks and undershirts. He came to her boldly, rubbed the back of his hand against her neck, and she shivered.

"The yard looks nice," she said.

He peeled off his jacket. There was no light in the small laundry room save for the thin fluorescent over the utility sinks.

"Start the new book yet?" he asked.

Shorthand. The steno of a long marriage. Slowly they had begun to trust the language of penance and forgiveness. Later they had taken large mugs of steaming coffee, a flashlight, and the first draft of the new book up to the tower, where, before settling in on the damp floorboards, they had looked out its long windows, watching the twinkling lights on the bridge of the causeway that led into Ocean Gate. From the tower they had a panoramic view. To the left they could see the white tips of the waves rolling inland and beyond that the terra-cotta rooftop of the Music Pier, where the summer concerts were held. They could make out the flapping American flag at the high school and the old-fashioned striped awnings of Sloan's, the oldest guesthouse in the town.

After a while, Peter sat down, his legs spread out wide on the pine floor, and she sat between them, her back resting against his chest, the top of her head fitted against his neck. She shined the flashlight over the manuscript.

"Flora's betrayed by her best friend in this one," she said.

"Just read," he said, clamping his arms high around her, just under her breasts.

If a house could have sighed, Emily believed theirs had that night; if it could have spoken to them, it would have been one word: *sustain.*

What could Margot Compton know of this? Emily was thinking. She made a right onto Fourth Street and took the turn into the driveway wide, had to cut the wheel sharply to avoid crashing into the lilac bush. Emily sat in the car for several minutes, gazing up at the tower and its rain-speckled windows. She gripped the steering wheel until her knuckles blanched and then she saw him, the same man who picked her up on the highway that morning . . . *Now he is dressed in white painter's pants and a cap. He climbs a steel ladder and paints the house from the top of the tower, working down. His bucket is large, huge even, and she wonders how he holds it so casually. The paint is white and he covers everything with it—the lawn, the marigolds and shrubs, the windowpanes—erasing her past with his brush. He comes toward the car, tipping his cap up, but he is no one she knows—just the faceless man who disappears just when she is about to touch him.*

FIFTEEN

King's Row Publications
22 Park Ave.
New York, NY
September 21, 1982

Dear Emily,

Why is it that a relatively successful author does not own an answering machine? Is there some kind of law forbidding such necessary equipment in Ocean Gate-by-the-Sea? You know I hate to write letters—you know I hate to write, period—which is why I'm an editor and you are a writer. You have forced me to type this. What's going on? Why are you not home diligently creating another wonderful story about your incomparable, dauntless blue bird, huh?

I know I should mind my manners and ask how you are feeling, but you have never responded well to sympathetic questions—at least not from me. If there's some terrible problem, please be in touch soon. If there's no terrible problem, please be in touch soon. I need to talk books, particularly book contracts.

Yours in constant need of good fiction,
Jill

Dear Jill,

I don't have an answering machine because whenever we have indulged in phone conversations in the past, you yell. No one wants to come home to someone yelling on a machine. And how would you know whether or not I respond to sympathetic questions since in the eleven years we have been associated I don't think I can recall your ever having asked one? But this is beside the point.

Just so you can rest easy, I have been writing since August. I know I am late. I know you can sue me. I know these things, but I cannot push books out. Also my time has been short-circuited by the fact that I've had to tend to my mother's organization since her unexplained and bizarre disappearance earlier this summer. I now have one dead sister, one dead husband, one missing father, and a missing mother whose only clue to her whereabouts puts her, as she says, "somewhere west." Also we had Gene Lisicky, the playwright, here this summer as our boarder and he and Lizzie became very attached. So add to my list of missing and dead persons one very sad little girl who is counting on me, her only surviving and sane relative, to give her attention. She has begun first grade, and we all remember how traumatic that can be.

I probably won't be calling; I know I'm not going to buy an answering machine, so throw caution to the wind and call, or we can continue to write letters. I am bereft, Jill, a word that sounds so elegant gliding off the tongue I hate to part with it as a state of being. If I were to apply for a job now and the application asked, What is your present status?

I would have to write *bereft*, boldly, darkly, and in a sneer if there were a way to write a sneer. I'm sorry I couldn't respond more cheerfully, but circumstances haven't been what they used to be.

Love,
Emily

2032 Coors Drive
Bangor, Maine
September 23, 1982

Em,

I can't believe I haven't heard a word from you in over a month. Are you all right? I would have called but the ceiling in our bedroom collapsed—we were not in bed at the time—and the damages are running us into unexpected thousands. Postage stamps we can afford.

I had so many things I wanted to ask you, but now I can't think of one that matters except: Is it getting any easier? Fred and I were disappointed that you weren't able to get away with Lizzie before school started to spend some time with us. I feel terrible that it's worked out this way; I never expected to be so far from you at a time like this. We want to keep that invitation open-ended. We want you to feel free to hop in the car or get on a plane whenever you decide you can.

I was sitting here alone in the living room the other night remembering the time you and Peter got dressed in your pajamas. What was it, November? And you two came down to our house at ten P.M., holding your pillows, wearing slippers, just to keep Fred company because he had the flu. God, those were great times. None of the kids were

/189

born yet, and we were still young enough to be ridiculous. Well, I miss you—we miss you—and it was sad to realize that you wouldn't be showing up at the door dressed for sleep anytime soon.

Little Fred and John started school, and so far, so good, but they're still asking when we're moving back home. Maine will take a little getting used to. How's Lizzie doing? And your mother, what about her? She hasn't started drinking again, has she? Listen, please be in touch soon, okay? You didn't tell me much about the summer in your last letter.

Much love always,
Barbara

September 25, midnight

Dear Barbara,

Sorry to hear about your ceiling. I'm having similar problems here, only they all seem to be fixed on water. The trap broke, the hot-water heater broke, and just a couple of days ago the car battery died, but I was in the rain when it happened, so I count that among the water-associated disasters.

I can't believe you remembered the pajama gag. About a week ago Lizzie was trying to do her homework, and I was sitting with her (strictly for moral support; she really hates it when I try to help) and for some reason I asked her if I'd ever told her the story of the pajamas visit. Well, her pencil broke and she got very huffy, blaming me for distracting her. "I can't concentrate when you talk to me," she said. How's that for a wiseass kid? Of course, had it been Gene, she would have been all ears and smiles, hanging on his every word. All summer he told little stories, allegories about everything. It was quite nice. Anyway, I was thinking about the pajamas because looking at Lizzie, her head bent over the composition book, I remembered that this was the night she was conceived. I never told you that, did I? That after we drank all that wine, after you and Fred went off to your bedroom to sleep, Peter and I sneaked out of the guest room. It seemed more delicious to us at the time to camp out on your living room floor. I don't know, but the mixture of the wine and the initial silliness of the evening, the furtiveness of being in someone else's house— well, we made love in your living room. What began as a prank ended up giving us our most profound joy. When I told Lizzie the story, I left out the part about her conception, but she loved the story even without it. Then she went back to alphabetizing her words. A few seconds passed and she said in a low voice, her eyes never veering from the work in front of her, "I love Daddy."

Which leads me to your question about whether or not life is getting any easier. You know what it's like here by the end of September. There's just a little over a handful of summer people who come in on the weekends, trying to stretch out the season, but everything's closed up and what else is there to see in this town other than the boardwalk and the ocean? It's colder than it should be at this time of the year; I think we're headed for an early winter. When I used to come here as a kid to check the house with my father in the winters I used to feel privileged, as if we were on some special secret mission and the town as well as the house belonged to us. With you and Fred here and Peter alive, who paid any attention to the desolation of a shore town out of season? I hate to admit it, but I think the only things holding me together right now are SPSC and Lizzie. I go into Philly three days a week, shorter days now that Lizzie is in school, and on the other two I try to write and I answer letters. Jill is about to have my head. I wrote a story with Bangor, Maine, in it and have written a new one called "Real Love." How's that for an original title? They're not children's stories, but I haven't told Jill. Actually, I started writing again when Gene was here. "You cannot make a career of this sorrow," he told me, which seemed to get through to me more than all of Dr. Kübler-Ross. He had this way of getting through to me. I can't explain it.

Oh, I almost forgot—it was so unnerving I must have blocked it out—but I literally almost ran into Margot at the Foodtown. She looked awful and she was her usual arrogant self, sure to inform me that she visits Peter's grave twice a week. I still haven't been, and now that I am nearing the one-year anniversary of his death, I'm even less inclined to go. No, it's not easier. It isn't. Everything I remember seems so fragmented, almost unreal.

I can't come to see you yet either, but thanks for the open-ended invitation. Work keeps me here. I have no idea whether or not my mother has started drinking again. I've heard nothing from her since the end of August. But this is not unusual, right? When have I ever been able to count on her for anything? Sometimes I think I gave birth to a daughter as a test of my mettle as a mother. Imagine God as the Supreme Psychiatrist, asking will she or won't she repeat her mother's behavior. Ah, well.

Don't call—save your money for renovation. My love to all of you.

Emily

Dear Emily,

I am not in Nova Scotia, even though the picture on the postcard is a picture of Nova Scotia. In about a week, a Mr. and Mrs. Clemente will come to the office; she'll talk about her card reader, Madame Rosa. Humor them. They come every October. Tell Jane not to take more than twenty new cases. Keep up the good work.

Love,
Mother

Memo to SPSC Staff

In a brief message from Nova Scotia, my mother, your leader, extends her congratulations to all of you for carrying on in her absence. She also extends her deepest gratitude for your patience and your consummate professionalism in accepting me as your interim supervisor.

We have been asked not to accept more than twenty new cases until her return (still undefined), and when the Clemente couple arrives next week, we have been asked to be gracious and cordial.

If any of you have any problems that need immediate attention, please feel free to air your suggestions and complaints with me. Keep up the good work.

Emily Perone Hansen
Supervisor

263 E. 69th St.
New York, NY
27 September 1982

Dear Emily,

I know I said we'd stay in touch and I know you well enough to realize that you probably think I've forgotten all about you and the Lizard. I have not. I've spent most of the month getting to know Chris all over again. He's grown about two and a half inches, but at least he's with me now where I can watch him growing—or try to. Several possibilities for producers on the new play fell through earlier this month, but after a lot of begging, pleading, and lying, I think we've got our men. It's going to be a busy fall.

Lottie has been having some problems; I feel I must be supportive right now despite everything, despite the fact that we're supposed to be finalizing joint property, custody, visitation rights—all the rules and regulations of ending a marriage, which there seem to be more of than for beginning one. She noticed these white spots on the inside of her wrist around midsummer. They are the size of a dime but the derm men, those wonders of medical knowledge (if it's dry, wet it; if it's wet, dry it), do not know what's causing them. She will try more derm men, although I've already told her that she might as well see a chiropractor for all she's going to find out.

I assume you're hard at work, writing away, now that you don't have to go to the city. Also, I know I could have picked up the phone and said all of this, but it seemed more appropriate somehow, for us, that I write you. Drop me a line and let me know how you are, and Lizard too. Didn't she start first grade?

Fondly,
Gene

September 30, 1982

Dear Gene,

I'm still at SPSC. My mother sends postcards from places where she isn't. I suppose she fears I'll track her down. Lizzie misses you, she misses Peter, and she hasn't had enough of a normal life so far to miss that.

I'm so glad you wrote. Yes, I did think you'd forgotten all about us. "We'll stay in touch" is up there with those other great lies like "The check is in the mail," "My dog ate my essay," and "I never received a bill for those purchases." Also you are well aware by now of my startling track record of being remembered. Oooh, that sounds awful. Pretend I didn't say that.

We are keeping busy. I have enclosed a new story. Feel no obligation to read it. So far, I've managed to stall Jill about the new Flora books, which I haven't even thought about, but I'm going to be in big trouble soon, I think.

Sorry to hear about Lottie; glad to hear about Chris. I spent so much time this summer talking and you spent so much time listening, I realize there's so much about you I don't even know. We will be eternally grateful to you, however, for making this past summer a sane one.

Best to you always,
Emily

3 October 1982

Dear Emily,

"Real Love" is wonderful. I think it's time for you to make a decision. Yes? I have the feeling you're finished for good with Flora Flamingo.

/195

By the way, in case no one has told you recently, you too are wonderful. I know you don't think so, but I believe your mother's being away has probably been good for you. You are a very strong lady, lady. What else could possibly knock you down?

Give Lizard a kiss.

Love,
Gene

October 5, 1982

Dear Gene,

What, no complaints about the ending of the story? No mandatory comparisons to a master? I'm shocked—and thrilled. Thank you, thank you.

Lizzie sends a kiss back and wanted to know when you were returning. I felt I should be honest and told her maybe never. This concept is not one that sits well with her, as you can imagine.

It is very cold here already, very much the weather of last year, which makes me think about those last months with Peter. When he still had enough strength, we would sometimes walk the beach in the early morning. He wore two jackets and two hats, which made his face look so small. He never wore gloves. He'd rather let his fingers turn raw than not be able to feel the heat of his cigarette in his hand. I had to keep one arm around him, to support him, when we walked. You know, we never said much of anything on those walks and I keep asking myself why. Did we think we were somehow going to trick fate? Were we thinking that if we didn't speak of an end, there simply wouldn't be one?

I would like to write about this, this grief. I think perhaps it is as passionate a state as any, and yet it seems so interior, so static, so . . . private. Any ideas?

Love,
Emily

10 October 1982

Dear Emily,

I have thought long and hard about your question, especially in light of the news that Lottie will see an oncologist next. How frightening that word must have been for you. There are new spots, now on her neck, the size of quarters. The other day Chris asked, in the inimitable style of all children, "Is Mom fading, Dad?" For once, I had no tale to tell to allay his fears. I was struck dumb and could do nothing but hold him. What must the image in his head be? I thought. The parent fading into a ghost?

And so my answer is that this grief is not as interior as you think, Emily. It has many faces, many gestures. Retreat is only one. I did not have a story for him, but I have one for you. Bear with me; it is old and I can't remember where I heard it.

There was a boardinghouse, and in it there lived three women. One had lost her husband, one had lost her mother, and the other, her child. The owner of the boardinghouse wanted to measure their pain, so he called in the resident wise man (there are always resident wise men in these stories), and he asked him if he would look in on each of these women. He had seen them himself already; he knew what answer he was looking for.

The wise man took the key and climbed the stairs. He opened the door to the first room, where the widow lived. She was sitting on the floor, tearing at her hair. She was pale and he could tell by the scratches on her face and the blood on her fingers that she had hurt herself. "Why do you brutalize yourself so?" he asked.

"I am crying my pain away," she said.

He went to the next room, a little ways down the hall. There he saw something quite different. The woman was beautiful and well groomed. She seemed to wear a transfixed smile all the time. She was sitting at a loom and the results of her weaving were all around her on the floor. She continued to smile when he looked in.

"Why do you weave so much?" he asked.

"I'm working my pain away," she said.

In the third room, the woman was not alone. She was with a man and both were naked in bed. She was astride him, moving over him ferociously.

"I'm sorry," the wise man said, "but isn't this the room of the woman who lost her child?"

Between breaths she cried out, "Yes, yes! I'm fucking my pain away."

He closed the door and returned downstairs.

"Well," the landlord said, "which one suffers more? Which loss has caused the greatest sadness?"

The wise man handed the landlord the key. "Their grief is equal," he said.

The landlord scoffed. "That's absurd. Only one is crying and the third acts like a whore!"

And the wise man said, "But all three are locked in their rooms."

I have no advice, Emily, except to say that everyone will know what you mean when you write what it is you have in mind. Think about it. More later.

My love,
Gene

"Do you want to stop somewhere for lunch, Mother?"

The question hung unanswered between them in the car for several seconds. Emily reached forward and turned up the volume on the radio. The Four Tops were singing "I Can't Help Myself."

"Mother? You want lunch?"

Francine had her chin poised in her hand, her elbow resting on the inside arm of the passenger door. "No. What is this music, Em'ly?"

"Motown."

"That's the name of the group, Motown?"

"No. The style of the music. The Motown sound. It comes out of Detroit. Didn't you listen to music in there?"

"There" was Green Hills. A year and a half had passed since Francine went into the sanatorium, but it might as well have been five. Her mother seemed completely disconnected to the world outside despite Emily's faithful weekend visits.

"We listened to the Beatles and Elvis Presley, Mozart, Barbra Streisand, Steve and Edie, Mel Torme, and the old stuff. How are the Beatles?" she asked, as if Emily were personally acquainted with them.

"They're fine."

Francine tapped her hand against her lap; Emily saw her foot tapping to the music too. "Well, I like this Motown sound," she said. "They're black, these boys?"

Emily smiled. "Yes. They're black singers, Mother."

"Best in the universe," Francine said.

An hour later, Emily pulled into the long driveway at home. She let the car idle for a minute while she kept a close eye on Francine. She had no idea how her mother would react to going back into the house. Earlier that morning Emily bought bunches of fresh flowers and put them in vases throughout the house, in every room, in fact, except the kitchen and Maria's old room. She'd had the drapes cleaned and the floors waxed and buffed the week before. She'd cleaned out the refrigerator and filled it with fresh fruit, cottage cheese, milk, butter, eggs, orange juice. She'd restocked the pantry with cereals and canned goods, and figured she'd let her mother decide what kinds of meats and vegetables she wanted. She'd hunted through every nook and cranny of the two-story Colonial house, making sure there were no little bottles of Johnnie Walker hidden away. She found one slipped down inside the tube of a fresh roll of toilet paper and she threw it away.

She packed her mother's drinking clothes—neon-colored miniskirts, boots, bell-bottom pantsuits—in a box and put them in the basement, so all that remained in her closet were her few good Chanel-inspired suits, her Jackie hats, her fur, several slim-heeled pumps, a pair of flats and her bedroom slippers, her best blouses, and her knee-length skirts. She was going to need to plump up her wardrobe considerably, but Emily thought that would be just one of the many things they could do together now that she was well, now that she was like the other mothers.

Her biggest problem regarding the interior of the house had been the living room couch. The upholstery was stained with blood and vomit, the putrid remnants of Francine's last drinking binge. Because she was embarrassed to have the upholsterer see it, Emily saved money from her part-time job at the university bookstore and borrowed money from Nana Irene to purchase a new couch. She found one almost like the old one in style, but in a shade of creamy eggshell instead of pale blue. She had consulted her mother's doctors about the photographs on the fireplace mantel.

"She had pictures of my father, and me and Maria," she told them.

Emily was worried that the slightest evocation of all that had gone on in the house would send her mother off the wagon again.

"Leave them there," the doctor told her. "She carries them in her memory anyway. They can't hurt her now."

Emily wished she could have been as sure of that. She didn't trust him completely, so she removed two pictures— the wedding picture and Maria's christening picture—and left the others standing.

Emily cut the engine. Francine was staring up at the house.

"Are you ready?" Emily asked.

"You've kept the place nice," Francine said, reaching for the door handle.

"Peter helped me on the weekends, usually after he drove me up to see you. He's good with lawns, don't you think?"

Francine nodded. "Better than your father was. Remember how there used to be those zigzag patterns left whenever he mowed—as if he couldn't keep track of what part of the lawn he cut?"

Emily honestly couldn't remember; she always thought of her father as an interior man, and he'd always hired landscapers, but she said yes anyway.

They both got out of the car at the same time. "That Peter seems like a nice fellow, Em'ly. Does he play an instrument?"

"I told you, Mother. He's tone-deaf."

"That's a good thing. Does he have a sport?" she asked as they walked to the door.

"Tennis," Emily told her.

"That's a good thing too."

Emily unlocked the door and pushed it open, then she stood back out of the way, so her mother would be the first to enter.

"Oh, I smell gardenias, Em'ly."

"I bought them this morning. They're all over the house. Go ahead inside. I'll get your stuff out of the car."

When she came back inside carrying two bags, Francine was nowhere in sight. "Mother?"

"In my room," Francine called.

Emily lugged the heavy bags, which were filled with clothes, magazines, and books, up the staircase. She found her mother standing before her bedroom closet, one hand on the glass knob.

Emily dropped the suitcases. "I cleaned out some things. I hope you don't mind."

Francine shook her head. "I was only interested in this," she said, pulling out the bathrobe by its hem. "I suppose your father's bought a new one by now."

"It's been four years, Mom. I think he probably has."

She let the robe drop from her fingers. It was late afternoon; the setting sun left just a faint orange glow over the white chenille bedspread and the dark mahogany furniture. Emily was holding her breath, waiting for some indication from her mother that she should come closer, that she should hug her—something, a flutter of an eyelash, a flick of the wrist or sigh, something that said to her, "After all that's happened, at least I have you." "I Can't Help Myself" rang in Emily's ears.

When Francine looked directly at her, finally, Emily thought that at last the moment had come.

"I want to sell the house, Em'ly," she said, "and everything in it. There's nothing for me here now."

Nothing for you here? What about the new couch, the gardenias, the cottage cheese, the landscaped lawn, a whole life? Emily swallowed the words, like swallowing rough stones, like swallowing fire. She hated her mother. She loved her. She knew they would never be close.

/203

SIXTEEN

Emily made the list on a yellow legal pad. It was short so long as she left out fantasy items such as flying a plane over the Pacific and spending a night in jail. She wouldn't feel her life was a failure if she never did either of those things. But there were others that seemed far more important, at least now; they seemed immensely important to her now.

Things I've Never Done in My Life
1) Made love to anyone except Peter
2) Gone to Europe
3) Checked into a hotel alone
4) Taken a train ride other than the metroliner to New York
5) Lived anywhere but New Jersey and Philadelphia
6) Written a novel
7) Stopped wishing that my father would show up on the doorstep; stopped wishing for a sister
8) Broken a contract

She stared at the last item and then she ripped a clean sheet of paper from the pad and started figuring. King's Row had given her $40,000 for the two-book Flora deal, half of which she'd already received and put into an account for Lizzie. She and Peter had decided that they could use the money to save for Lizzie's college education. Peter's medical plan had covered eighty percent of his medical expenses, but they came in over $150,000, which left her with $18,000 still owed to the doctors and hospital. There was no mortgage on the house, but if things continued to break apart as they had in September, she knew she would need some savings to cover those expenses. She and Peter had $2,000 in their own savings account, and his pension paid out forty-six percent of his salary, which gave her an income of roughly $16,000 a year before taxes. She would make about $10,000 if she worked part-time at SPSC for a whole year—before taxes. And she couldn't bank on selling short stories for a living. She figured some more, making column after column of numbers, trying to come up with enough money for four years at Harvard and a wedding reception at the Plaza Hotel, and anything else Lizzie might want in the next eleven or so years. She reasoned that since Lizzie had been deprived of a father at an early age, of cousins and aunts and uncles, she should at least be able to attend the college of her choice. After all, a mind was a terrible thing to waste.

After she added, subtracted, divided, and multiplied for nearly an hour, she tore the paper up, took it to the powder room, and flushed it down the toilet. She didn't want to be like those women in the boardinghouse, defined only by their losses. She returned to the kitchen and crossed Europe, a train ride, and the hotel off her list. She had survived so far without them, and would continue to survive. That would cut expenses considerably. Then she circled "Broken a contract." She studied the words for several minutes. If she had to, she would take any job, two, doing what she didn't know, but she would force herself. And she could always sell the house if Lizzie wanted to go to Harvard. In eleven years a property like hers, a block from the beach and historically certified, could even make her a millionaire. What she knew she could *not* do anymore was write children's books.

So it was no surprise to Emily when Jill phoned and said she'd like to get together for a "little lunch." It was her euphemism for a big talk. On the phone all Jill would admit to was that she'd found the stories Emily had sent her *interesting,* a word that when applied to blind dates and writing signaled a red alert.

"Can you get up around the end of the month? I can clear away the afternoon of the thirtieth."

"That's the day before Halloween."

"So?"

"It's my wedding anniversary."

"You were married on Mischief Night?"

"Yes. It seemed appropriate. A combination costume party and wedding with us dressed as the bride and groom."

"Jesus."

"I'm kidding. It was a small quiet ceremony with our very small families; Peter's parents and my mother were the guests. We went out to dinner afterward."

"Well, can you do it? Might be a good time for you to be out of the house anyway."

Emily was thinking the same thing. The year before she and Peter had finally defrosted the top of their wedding cake. For twelve years it sat in the back of the freezer, wrapped in layers of waxed paper and aluminum foil. She believed it was tampering with good fortune to open it and eat slices from it on their first anniversary even though the tradition was supposed to bring the couple luck. Then last year, months before he died, she decided it was tampering with good fortune not to, as if the cake could somehow invest him with good health. Of course, only in her damned Flora books could she assign magical powers to a cake. As it turned out the cake was inedible. The pearly white frosting had turned yellow, the shade of weak urine; it was hard as a brick. She had wept when she unwrapped it.

"I'll be there," she told Jill.

They met at a quiet Mexican restaurant on Thirty-fourth off of Park. Margaritas were the drink of the day, and Emily ordered hers frozen and salted and finished it before Jill had sipped a third of hers.

"How was the train ride?"

"Fast. I took the metroliner."

"Who's got Lizzie today?"

"She's staying at my mother's place in Philly. Jane, the secretary, was nice enough to volunteer to take care of her; that way I can pick her up on my way back to Jersey. I'm taking the four o'clock train back. You're not drinking."

Jill looked down at her margarita, but she gently moved the glass aside and folded her hands.

"You look like a school principal, Jill."

"I feel like one, let me tell you."

Emily had already made up her mind that, no matter how much Jill bullied her, yelled at her, or threatened her, she was going to return the $20,000 and say good-bye. The waiter, dressed smartly in a red bolero jacket and red tie, stopped to take their order.

"I'm not eating," Emily said, "but I'll have another margarita." Drinking in the afternoon was another item Emily had forgotten to add to her list.

Jill collected their leather-bound menus and handed them to him.

"I'll have the seafood frittata and the house salad."

Once the waiter was gone she laid her finely manicured hands out in front of her, took a deep breath. "All right. I was going to try to be delicate about this, Emily, but instead I'm going to be blunt. Where is the Flora Flamingo book for which you've been contracted—a contract, I might add, that you are now over a year late in honoring?" She reached down then and brought up a slim, expensive leather briefcase from which she took Emily's stories. "And what is it you want me to do with these?" she asked.

Emily felt the pulses behind her knees and in her neck thump. The waiter returned with her margarita, but suddenly she didn't want it. She licked the taste of salt from her lips.

"I wanted you to see what I've been doing."

"You're a children's writer. Why should I want to see these? I want the bird with the weird legs and an answer for everything."

Emily leaned forward; she struggled to keep her voice down. "I can't write about fucking Flora, Jill. I don't know how to think like that anymore. I can't remember what it was like to believe that way, all that sappy optimism in the face of disaster."

Jill's cheeks reddened. It surprised Emily. Jill was always so tough. She sat back and began to pick the polish on a perfectly good nail. "I can't do anything with these stories, Emily. And I'm not even sure you can. What are you going to do? Throw ten years' worth of work, successful, money-making work, down the god-damn toilet because you've somehow got it into your head that you should be Joan Didion instead of Maurice Sendak?"

"Plenty of writers do both."

"Then do both, for pity's sake. Write all the short stories and adult novels you want, but finish Flora. Do that too. One doesn't cancel out the other, Emily. You're a writer, no matter which way you want to cut it." She arched an eyebrow, chewed the inside of her cheek. "Anyway, are you really in a position to give back twenty grand?"

Emily felt her resolve dissipating and thought for a minute that she was being stupid about the whole thing, burning her bridges behind her at the worst possible time. She stared into Jill's eyes, wanting to say, "I'm fine now. It was just a passing loss of my senses, pay no attention, two new Floras you shall have." But the words wouldn't come. She had started writing Flora stories when she was seventeen; there were tons of manuscript pages no one had ever read and never would. That blue flamingo had been her friend, the sister who didn't fit in, and she had reincarnated her time after time for years.

"Flora's gone, Jill. I'm sorry."

After lunch, when Emily handed Jill the check, Jill held it out between them, giving Emily one more chance to change her mind, but when Emily shook her head, Jill folded it in half, slipped it into her purse. "I'm not going to make this official right away," Jill said. "Maybe you shouldn't have signed anything when your personal life was in so much upheaval. Maybe I should have seen that—"

"Jill—"

"No, I mean it. I thought if you just kept doing what you've always done it would have been the best thing for you."

Emily touched the sleeve of Jill's jacket. "It's no one's fault. I thought the same thing too."

"Well . . ."

"Yeah, well. I'm sorry."

Before Emily stepped into the waiting cab, Jill said, "Talk to someone, Emily."

Emily was sure Jill didn't mean that very second, and she was even more sure she meant a therapist. In the cab as she was being recklessly wheeled through the city, toward Bloomingdale's where she'd kill some time before meeting her train, Emily realized that the person she wanted to talk to most was only blocks away. "Let me out here," she told the cabbie, who deposited her somewhere in the East Fifties. She had to walk a block before she found a pay phone, and on the way she passed a woman in a pink tutu, a man carrying the head of a bear costume, and an ape carrying a briefcase. Nearly everyone she passed that afternoon was carrying a costume box or a part of a costume—devil horns, angel wings, animal masks—for their Halloween parties. The spirit of the afternoon was festive and menacing, and feeling it envelope her, too, she found the paper with Gene's address and telephone number on it and dialed.

"Jesus Christ, Jesus Christ." He kept saying it—it must have been at least four times—when he heard her voice. "Jesus! What a surprise you're in the city. Why didn't you let me know you were coming?"

"I tried to get you a few times, but there was no answer."

"Jesus Christ."

"Gene, I won't be able to see you at all if you keep me on the phone invoking the Son of God all day. I've got to make the four o'clock train."

"I'm moving."

"This minute?"

"I mean, I'm moving tomorrow. I'm packing now. There are boxes—do you mind boxes? Come for a visit."

"I don't mind boxes."

"You've got the address?"

"In my hand."

He then launched into what Emily thought was an unnecessary description of the building, which was a brownstone, the location of the doorbell, the size and shape of the carved lions at the base of the front steps, the color of the door.

"Two sixty-three East Sixty-ninth, right?"

"Between Lex and Third. There are lions—"

"—at the base of the steps," Emily said. "I'll see you soon."

She scanned the streets looking for an empty cab, but in the crunch of traffic she doubted any cabbie's ability to get her there faster than her own two feet. By the time she spotted the lions, serene and aloof at the foot of the steps, she had broken out in a light sweat. She took a deep breath, smoothed her windblown hair, and went up to the front door.

The interiors of the houses she had known had always been the province of women and Gene's apartment was no different. Things were missing from the high-ceilinged rooms. Two chairs, most likely black mahogany, must have stood on the other side of the oversize Oriental cocktail table where now there was only a couch, but the chairs had left their impression, like irregular footsteps in sand. Afterimages of a wife's presence hovered in the cool air, even though Gene had not kept the place up. Dust was everywhere, a thin veneer of it, fallout from a deceased marriage. Passing the open door to the bathroom, Emily saw towels hung haphazardly on the rack, but they were expensive, thirsty towels, the kind women craved in a shade of peach men simply called pink. The bathmat matched. They had to make their way around cardboard boxes whose lids were open revealing porcelain objects, books, pieces of teak and brass, records. One box overflowed with ivory moire: drapes that once covered the long windows where now the white metal rods hung in place like unsheathed bones. There were faded spots of wallpaper in the living room where pictures had been, but over the fireplace two Schiele prints were still in place. One was a drawing, a nude with a yellow towel, a scurrilous drawing of a splay-legged model, her pubic hair as dark and prominently sketched as her black stockings, which clung without the aid of garters to her legs. Her armpits were unshaved and the careless tilt of her head, her apathetic eyes, said simply, "Take what you want, use it, use me."

The other was a watercolor, the kaleidoscopic, circus colors—reds, bright yellows, and blues in stripes and checks—made an odd contrast to the subject matter, which was a girl, seemingly very young, prone, her skirt hiked up to her waist, her raw white ass, the pink swell of her vagina, her stark white legs presenting themselves, once again, for use. Her eyes were closed and it seemed that whatever was about to be done to her—fingering, sucking, licking, screwing—she intended to sleep through it, not so much as letting out a sigh of protest. Emily assumed that what was missing from the apartment belonged to Carlotta; these Schieles, then, belonged to the tender-hearted Gene.

"You don't like them," he said, coming up close behind her.

"The Viennese were nearly pornographic."

"There are enough art critics who would agree with you, Emily."

"I guess I expected to see Monet."

Emily turned away from the mantel then, saw Gene shrug his famous shrug. "I don't like things diffused for me."

He took her elbow then and moved her down the hall to a room drenched in sunlight from a lead glass window. "Look out here," he said, beckoning her with his finger. "It's a nice garden, isn't it?"

She looked down on the foliage, on the carefully designed and scrupulously kept flower beds. "So that's how you knew so much about the lawn and shrubs?"

/211

He rapped his knuckle against the window, looked at her, bewildered. "I told you about the garden."

"No."

"Well. I thought for sure I had. I won't have a garden at the new place."

"Oh. Then will Carlotta be living here?"

Gene guided her back toward the kitchen. "No one will be living here."

They were now standing in the kitchen; rather, Gene was, while Emily hung back by the doorframe. "Where will she go?"

"She's with friends right now. Chris is here with me and he'll come with me to the new place. We haven't settled much of anything really, with all these doctor's appointments and tests. They still haven't figured out what's causing the loss of pigment. Lottie's been very down."

He was busy uncorking a bottle of wine and it was then that Emily let her eyes stray from him to the kitchen cabinets. There were photographs stuck up on them—photographs of Lottie and Gene together, Lottie, Gene and Chris, and a few of other people she didn't know. When he noticed her looking he said, "I went a little bonkers when I came back here. It felt lonely so I tacked up pictures. Helped me remember that for a while I had an intact life."

It was so unlike him to show the least bit of self-pity and it took Emily aback. In the summer he'd seemed so sure that his marriage was beyond repair, that the decision to part had been mutual; this display of nostalgia confused her.

"Where will you go?"

He handed her the wineglass.

"I'm subletting from a friend. How is it?"

"Subletting or the wine? I'm afraid I'm not an expert on either."

Gene smiled. "At least you haven't lost your sense of humor," he said, clinking his glass against hers.

"No. Just an editor, not more than a half hour ago."

He put his arm around her shoulder. "Ah, this sounds portentous to me. Who dropped whom?"

212/

"I dropped her, or it. I'm not writing the Flora books."

He gave her shoulder a slight squeeze. "Come on, let's sit."

They sat together on the sofa, close to each other at one end, and Emily relayed the content of her lunch with Jill. "I spent a long time thinking about this, especially after you wrote that letter about the three women. I calculated income and every possible disaster that could hit me and Lizzie in the next twenty years, and finally, well, it just didn't seem worth it to keep plugging at something that was . . . that was finished a long time ago."

He rubbed his wineglass between his hands. "I hope your decision wasn't based solely on that letter, Emily."

"Uh, well, of course not, but, Gene, it did put some things in focus for me. There's nothing wrong with that, is there?"

He smiled again, but Emily sensed that it was forced. She'd made him uncomfortable, but she wasn't sure how or why.

"No, there's nothing wrong with it."

Her eyes traveled back up to the Schieles, to the question of use. She looked back at him.

He wanted to know all about Lizzie, what she was going to be for Halloween.

"Rainbow Brite," Emily told him, "and it was hell trying to come up with that costume."

And he wanted to know about work, her other work at SPSC. She told him about the Clementes. "They have a profoundly retarded daughter and six other children," she said. "Anyway, for the past five years or so, they've come to SPSC every October. One of the counselors says that they're like the patient with an obsessive concern, the kind that never really wants to solve the problem but doesn't want to stop therapy either. Well, Mrs. Clemente is a devotee of the tarot, and she's got it in her head that my mother should have hired her as a consultant. She claims that she can read the auras of special children and their parents, and that her card reader, Madame Rosa, could help the couples decide the best course of action for their kids and themselves."

"Are you serious?"

Emily gulped the rest of her wine and nodded. "Oh absolutely. She even gave me this," Emily said. She leaned over and took a Xeroxed sheet of paper from her purse. "Look," she said, handing it to Gene, "I've been carrying it around for a week."

Gene held the paper in his hands and Emily read over his shoulder:

Readings by Madame Rosa
SICK? BLUE? DISCONCERTED? If so, here is a message of hope! Do you wish to know: If your sweetheart is true? Who and when you will marry? How soon you will make a change? What you are best adapted for? If you can trust your friends? Why your love acts strange? If you are unlucky?
AVAILABLE FOR HOUSE CALLS OR PARTY GATHERINGS

"This is great stuff," Gene said, laughing. Emily took the paper from his hand.

"Yeah, I thought the same thing. Maybe I could—"

"Put it in a story," he said.

Emily nodded. She shoved the paper into her purse; he lit a cigarette and offered her one, but she declined.

"Emily?"

"What?"

"It's great to see you. I mean it. You look, well, you look terrific."

Emily felt a chill at the back of her neck. He looked terrific to her too, more handsome than she remembered, grayer, wiser around the eyes. She said thanks and then, "So, where's Chris?"

Gene checked his watch. "He's at school, then soccer practice this afternoon."

"Is he good? I mean, a good soccer player?"

"Team captain," Gene said, stubbing out his cigarette, turning slightly as he did it, as if he intended to move closer. She stood up, an abrupt and awkward leap from the sofa, and blurted out that it was her wedding anniversary.

She suddenly felt that she shouldn't have come, especially not today, and, at the same time, more than anything, she didn't want to be anywhere else. With him, she felt her grief shrink back, a curled fist.

"I should go," she said. "I have to catch the train and pick up Lizzie."

He held her with his eyes before he finally stood up. "Want more wine maybe? Coffee? I can make you coffee."

She shook her head. "No. I really have to go."

"If you had let me know ahead of time we could have planned . . . something, dinner maybe."

"I didn't even know I'd be calling until I did it."

"You may always call," he said, walking away toward the desk near the door at the end of the hall.

"Well, let me know when you're settled. We'll try again."

She was speaking to his broad back and could see that he was writing something. He turned around, handing her a small slip of paper. "Here's my new address. The phone's the same. Call me."

She took the paper from his hand, but she didn't know how his arms went around her, only that they did, tight around her waist, his palms dry and warm, pressing in on the small of her back. He kissed her, not insistently, on the mouth, just dryly enough for her to decide if she wanted more, how much more, and how long. His erection poked against her skirt, made her own groin ache to respond and frightened her at the same time. Her hands were flat against his shoulders, fluttering against him, beating him back, but not. He smelled of every good thing she could ever remember— ice, summer, her father's voice, Lizzie's skin after a bath, earth on Peter's hands. Before he tried to kiss her again, he looked at her as if she were something delicious, something he'd heard of but had never touched or held this close. She loved him and it was love, returned to her, that she saw in his eyes. If there was a moment to speak of it that should have been it, but they heard a key in the door, a slam, then "Dad!" from downstairs in the foyer. His arms fell away from her; the moment was gone.

The sight of Chris, so much like Gene, with Gene's dark hair, those same brown eyes, made her feel ashamed, as if Chris knew instantly what she and his daddy were planning to do. Chris exploded into the room, knapsack dancing off of one shoulder, shirttails out, and Gene recovered his wits quickly, Emily thought, a trick all parents, discovered by their children, had to learn as well as they'd had to learn to change a diaper.

"Hey, sport, this is Emily. Remember her from the beach?"

Chris was sizing her up, calculating the situation. "No," he said, not impolitely, but Emily could make no mistake about the lack of warmth.

Gene ruffled his hair. "Well, it was three years ago. What happened to soccer practice?"

"Called off." He threw his knapsack down on the seat of a nearby chair, staking his claim, protecting his father, and, though she wasn't there, Emily guessed, protecting his mother, from her, from this she-devil stranger in his house.

"Well, go get changed and then you can help me pack up the rest of this stuff."

Chris stood woodenly in the doorway.

"I'm going to see Emily out," Gene said, firmly.

"Nice to see you again, Chris," she said to him, but the child refused to smile. She turned to Gene. "Listen, I can see myself out. Thanks for the wine—and the talk."

"Emily—"

"I'll see you," she said.

She could feel him behind her on the stairs, but midway down he stopped following her. As she opened the first set of doors to the vestibule, she turned halfway, wanting to tell him, "Do it again, kiss me again and make the pain go away." But all she saw when she turned around were his feet, disappearing up the winding staircase.

★   ★   ★

216 /

"And, Mom, Jane even let me look through the Rolo—, the Rolodes?"

"Rolodex."

"She said I could look up the names when she called them out. I told her I knew alphabetical order."

"That's nice, Lizzie. Eat your steak. I cut it up in little pieces so it's easy to chew. Go ahead."

Emily pointed to Lizzie's plate where ten little wedges of steak lay untouched.

Lizzie frowned. "You burned it, Mom."

"It's charbroiled. I charbroiled it, not burned."

Lizzie poked at a piece. "Looks burned to me."

The steak was burned. And it was tough, and because she could think of nothing but Gene since she left New York City, she had made a mess of dinner and now her poor child would go hungry because it was clear to Emily that Lizzie was not going to sit at the table until nine o'clock to chew the meat, which was how long it would take a six-year-old with those small teeth to eat it.

"Would you like me to make you something else, Liz?"

"Yeah, fish sticks."

"Fish sticks?"

"Jane had them for lunch. She let me taste them. They're my new favorite food."

Emily sighed. "We don't have fish sticks. Second choice."

"Hot dogs?"

"How many?"

She held up two fingers.

"Can do," Emily said. "Broiled or boiled?"

"Any way you won't burn them."

"Smart aleck. You act as if I gave you burned food every night."

While Emily boiled two hot dogs, Lizzie went on and on about Jane and how she'd let her try the typewriter and the Xerox machine, how she let her sit in the swivel chair at her desk and spin, fast, three times. "It was like the time Daddy took me to his office."

"You were four years old. You remember that?"

"I remember everything about Daddy," she said, shoveling a forkful of corn into her mouth.

Emily turned back to the stove, poked the hot dogs in the pot with the sharp tip of a knife. One minute she was wishing for amnesia and in the next she was wishing for the phone to ring; it was as if her mind had only two switches: remember nothing and Gene. His name flashed in neon inside her forehead, alternating with Peter. The ache behind her eyes was so intense, she feared she might have a stroke right in front of Lizzie.

The hot dogs plumped up. Emily always had to overcook them just a bit so they would plump almost to bursting. Lizzie loved them fat. She turned down the burner under the pot and popped two hot dog rolls into the toaster oven for thirty seconds.

"Okay, Liz, here they are—two unburned hot dogs."

"Make the valley," Lizzie said.

Making the valley was something Peter had taught her. He would slice Lizzie's hot dog down the middle, making a deep ridge in the center, then he would fill it with a thin stream of mustard. Sometimes they'd pretend the mustard was volcanic ash, other times it was a river, and when they were low on mustard, it was just a brook. Emily used to get angry with him for teaching Lizzie to play with food, but he'd insisted it was educational. "Think of it as a geography lesson, Em."

Emily made the valley. "What do you want, Liz? Lava, rivers, or brooks?"

"Just put the mustard on," she said. "It doesn't matter."

Emily wanted to say, "You mean it doesn't matter now, because I'm doing it and not Daddy?" And she had to remind herself that, dead or alive, Lizzie was at that age when all girls were daddy's girls. And who better than she would know that your daddy didn't have to be there to make it so?

All Emily wanted to do was get through dinner, clean up, get Lizzie into bed, and then sit in the living room with her pack of cigarettes, where she would smoke and wait for this ridiculous morass of feeling to pass into something more familiar, something she knew how to live with, a certain dullness, a certain numbness that until that afternoon only Lizzie had been able to break through.

But the feeling did not pass. If she could have seen it, the feeling inside would have been white light, like the picture of the burning heart of Jesus on the holy cards they used to pass out in grade school. She had smoked most of her cigarettes. She turned on the television, switched channels rapidly, blips of pictures flashing on the screen. Then she turned back when she thought she spotted *Brigadoon*. It was *Brigadoon,* a movie that had inspired her faith in the fairy tale, that had inadvertently inspired her to write for children instead of cynical adults. She stood before the screen listening to Gene Kelly telling Cyd Charisse that he "canna leave her, canna leave this place." All he had to do was believe that the little Scottish town of Brigadoon, that woke up for one day every hundred years, really existed, and he could go back. He "would na have to leave her" ever again. They could dance those elaborate dances on the sharp rocks in their bare feet and never suffer a scratch.

When the phone rang, Emily turned off the television and walked slowly to the kitchen. On the third ring she picked up, it was Gene.

"I would have called you earlier," he said, "but I figured you had to get the Lizard in bed, and I had my hands full with Chris here."

"He's not upset, is he? He looked confused this afternoon and, well, a little miffed maybe?"

Gene cleared his throat. "He's having his problems with this separation. Seeing you here . . . look, you know how kids are."

"Yes. I know." "And how are you?" she wanted to ask. "How are you now?"

"What are you doing? Did I interrupt your work?"

She supposed the right answer would have been yes, but she said, "No, I was watching *Brigadoon*."

"I remember that one."

"It's still the same," she said. She had no idea what she meant by that, but it was the only thing she could think of at the moment.

"Emily, listen. Our lives are not what you might call, at the moment, playing out the best-case scenario. It's been a bad time here, and God knows you've had your share there—"

She didn't want him to explain, so she said, "Gene, it's all right. I mean, I wasn't expecting that you'd want to see me or anything. I know what this call is about."

"No you don't," he said.

"I don't?"

"No. What I'm trying to say to you is that I haven't stopped thinking about you since you left. Actually, I haven't stopped thinking about you since *I* left—there—this summer."

"Thank God you said that."

"Emily, I want you very, very much. I—"

"I want you too. I do." It was so easy to say, it amazed her.

There was a long pause. "Gene?"

"I'm here." He paused again; she could hear him lighting a cigarette, blowing out smoke. "I want to see you, and I've been sitting here half the night trying to figure out how. I can't leave the city because we're in the middle of casting, the move is tomorrow. You can't come here because of work. Then there are the kids."

"I'll come there," she said. "Next week Lizzie has a day off—teachers' convention. She loved being with Jane today because she let her type and use the Rolodex. She wouldn't mind going there again. I don't think she'd mind."

"What day?"

"Thursday. And I don't have to go to Philly that day either."

She heard the flipping of pages, an appointment book, no doubt, and the sound made her wince, just a little.

"All right. I can move things around. They can survive without me for one day. Actually," he said, laughing, "they hate having me around during casting. I never agree with the choices."

The next bit of logistics was more difficult. They had decided the when, but there was still the where. Gene was not comfortable with his place because of Chris, and she couldn't blame him.

"Do you know the Westbury? It's very nice. How about that?"

She was relieved that he didn't say the word *hotel,* and she knew the Westbury: expensive and charming, a doorman, sometimes a red carpet on the sidewalk, limos pulling up to the curb. She could see them heading out to Central Park in the late afternoon, she could see them drinking coffee at the tiny Left Bank café around the corner. And she could see that after this first time, maybe the second, they would find a way to close up this distance and travel.

"I know it. Sixty-ninth and Madison, right?"

"Yes."

She told him it was okay, it would be fine, that all she wanted was to be with him. and he apologized, several times, that it couldn't be at home, but she told him not to worry and she was glad knowing that, despite what she said, he would worry. Someone, this man who'd dropped unexpectedly into her life, would worry about her. They talked for nearly forty-five minutes. He confessed that he had wanted to kiss her on Holiday Night standing by the bay on Vanessa's lawn, and in the roller coaster when she finally laughed as they careened down the chute, and that night upstairs in his apartment when they danced. "You were so beautiful," he said. And then she was able to tell him how she watched him with Lizzie under the tree from the kitchen window, how she realized that night she didn't want him to go. And Chekhov, they talked about Chekhov and the morning he woke her in her office from her sound sleep. "Your hand felt like the sun," she said. They went on and on, regretting the moments they'd let slip by, planning new ones, and in this way, hearts to the line, they were becoming lovers.

/221

SEVENTEEN

He sent her a Helen Humes album, Federal Express; he sent a bouquet of baby's breath to Lizzie; he sent her a copy of his last play, *Thetis Island,* inscribed: *To Emily, with my affection, Love, Gene*—also Federal Express—all within a three-day period. And then, when there was only one more long day for her to wait through, one more night to toss on the couch, imagining how she would make love to him, what his skin would feel like under her tongue, how willing she would be to do anything with him, anything he wanted—he called.

She was so happy to hear his voice, she didn't detect the strained huskiness of it at first. Before he'd been able to say much of anything, she told him how good she thought the play was, how sure she was, without even knowing its title, that this new one would make him a household name. "They'll put you on the cover of *Time,*" she said.

"I don't think so," he said. There was no playfulness in the remark.

"You sound funny. Is something wrong?"

He hurriedly said, "Emily, I have a problem," and she suddenly knew that the problem was not a business meeting he couldn't get out of.

"What is it?"

She could feel her insides getting hard, preparing for a blow. This internal stiffening was something she'd learned to do at an early age, similar in its way to learning how to rub her stomach and pat her head at the same time. As long as she concentrated on one, she could blot out the other.

"It's about tomorrow. Jesus . . . Emily. I don't think that we should go ahead with this."

She was in the kitchen. The remains of breakfast were still there. An opened jar of grape jam, a half-eaten slice of cold toast, a spot of black coffee in the bottom of her mug. She made herself sit and started picking at the crust of the toast.

He began an explanation, a monologue really, about how people too often do things, hurt each other, by going ahead with plans that in their minds sound wonderful but in actuality are filled with "boomerang effects." He said that the more he thought about it, the more he realized that what they were about to do was not going to be entered into clearly. Their "four eyes weren't open." Their lives were too chaotic.

"You are making an ass of yourself," she said. "What is a boomerang effect?"

"It's—" He paused. "I don't know what the hell it is, all I know is that something about this doesn't feel right. Not now. Emily, don't you agree with me that something about this doesn't feel right?"

She paused, trying to gather words that made sense because none of this was making sense. "No. I don't agree with you."

"I don't want to take you to a hotel. We don't belong in a hotel. It makes it seem so casual. I can't be casual about this."

She felt the heat rising in her throat; her own breath smelled sour to her when she exhaled. "Do you think I'm being casual? We have kids, we're hundreds of miles apart from each other; of course, it's going to feel awkward." And then, against her better judgment, or maybe because she never thought she'd have the chance to say it, she blurted, "I'm not being casual. Don't you know I'm already in love with you?"

"Yes," he said. "I think a *part* of you is in love with me." And

/223

she was about to cut in, to shout, "How do you know, how dare you tell me what parts of me are in love?" when he said, "The same part of me that's in love with you, that's been in love with you from the first night I watched you from my window."

"Gene—"

"Let me finish, Emily. Let me say this or I might never say it, and I need to say it."

"Well, I don't need to hear it. Damn you, I don't need to hear this now. Just hang up, hang up and call back and start over."

"Emily!"

"Don't yell. Why are you yelling?"

"I'm sorry. Listen to me, please?"

She bit down on her lip; it started to bleed and she wiped her mouth with the back of her hand. "All right."

"I think," he said, sighing, "there's another part of me that still loves Lottie. And I know there's a part of you that is still very much in love with Peter. If it were a ways down the line, if we could be sure we were really free of those feelings, then tomorrow would be right. In fact, it wouldn't be tomorrow, it would have been last week, the day after you left. I wouldn't have let you leave at all probably. Maybe I would have dumped Chris in the car, driven you home myself, grabbed Lizard, and taken you both back here with me. But I didn't—and you didn't. I care for you very, very deeply, Emily—too much to do this."

"But I need you, Gene."

And then there was a long, deafening silence.

"I'm telling you what I know, Emily, about myself and you. We know the kinds of lives we had and liked. I can't give you that now."

"Then don't worry about my *life*, Gene. Let's just be together now, just once."

"It could never be once with you. Never. I wouldn't want it to be."

She didn't mean to sound desperate, but she couldn't stop the urgency in her voice. "Let's just meet for lunch then; let's at least talk about this. We'll pick a very public place, a place *teeming* with people."

"It wouldn't matter how public the place was—I'd drag you out of there in ten minutes. And then what? You want me, half in love with you? That's all you're willing to demand? I told you, I'm almost fifty, Emily. I'm not some twenty-year-old kid who needs to get his rocks off." Then he stopped talking; he lit a cigarette. She could hear him struggling with the matches. "Lady, when I call you and ask you this again, then you can tell me to go fuck myself."

"I would never say that to you."

"Well, maybe you should. I should have thought more."

"You should *stop* thinking, goddamn it. Just stop inventing more crises for us."

She kept him on the line, talking, plaintive as one of those blues singers, until their conversation disintegrated into a volley of disjointed phrases that led nowhere, that would not change their situation. Until finally he said, "I can't. Forgive me."

When the line went dead, she sat there with the phone in her hand before she could hang up, believing that his voice would materialize again, that he would recover from his bout of cold feet or moral superiority. When she realized that this was not going to happen, she replaced the phone in its cradle. She sat perfectly still at the kitchen table for the rest of the morning. She didn't smoke a cigarette; she didn't drink a cup of coffee; she didn't cry; it was possible that she didn't even blink. From the second she hung up the phone, something inside her snapped, as quickly, as cleanly as the cracking of a twig.

The following day was the worst. Since she had no reason to go to New York; there was no longer any reason to drive Lizzie to Philadelphia, where she would have stayed with Jane. Lizzie was disappointed; she had been looking forward to another ride in Jane's swivel chair, another try at the IBM Selectric.

"What are we going to do now?" she asked Emily.

Emily was still in her clothes from the day before—a black sweatshirt and jeans. She'd slept in them, or, rather, she had lain in them all night, awake on the couch, waiting for the phone to ring. It had rung at about eleven and when she answered there was no reply from the other end of the line. She said hello twice before the caller hung up. She couldn't explain it, but she knew it was Gene, calling to change his mind, then, having heard her voice, changing his mind back again. "Coward," she'd hissed when she hung up.

"Why do we have to do anything, Liz? I don't feel like doing anything. Really. Please, eat your cereal."

"It's too soggy," she said, dropping the spoon in the bowl.

Emily was cleaning out the junk drawer, making small piles of matchbooks, wrapping up stray rubber bands with one big rubber band, throwing out menus to pizza places and seafood take-out stores, throwing away bent staples and out-of-date coupons—anything to keep busy.

"Well, can we walk on the boards?"

"It's too cold to walk on the boards. Everything's closed."

"Well, can we go shopping at the Foodtown? You can buy me fish sticks."

Suddenly, Emily felt pain, a sharp pain, dead center, in her chest. She leaned over, holding the side of the drawer for support.

"What's wrong?"

"Nothing, Liz. It's just a pain. It's probably just gas or something. Eat your cereal."

"But it's mushy."

Emily straightened, slammed the drawer shut, and turned to look at Lizzie. "You eat three spoonfuls of that cereal right now, young lady. Do you hear me? I'm not in the mood for this whining about food today."

"But, Mom—"

Emily wagged her index finger at Lizzie. "No buts. Three," she said, holding up three fingers. "If you eat three we'll take a drive to Hoy's."

"Can I get something there?"

"Yes," Emily said. She took a washcloth from the sink and began wiping the table all around Lizzie's place setting.

Lizzie shoveled some cereal in her mouth. "What are you going to buy?"

Emily's hand was on her hip, the dishcloth balled up in her fist. "Ashtrays," she said.

There was nothing like a big five-and-dime for finding the odd, the unusual. When she was a kid, she used to save her allowance and then run right out, usually on a Friday afternoon, to the five-and-dime on Kings Highway, where she would buy all sorts of things she didn't need. She was fascinated by containers. The Noxema jar, for instance. There was something about the thick, cobalt blue jar holding all that white, menthol cream—like a secret potion. And she liked the travel-sized containers of toothpaste, mouthwash, baby powder.

"You're wasting your money buying those small tubes and jars of things, Em'ly. They cost almost as much as the regular size."

"I like them. I might need them someday."

She never used them, and as she got older she just moved them to the bottom drawer of her dresser with a heap of other things she no longer used or wanted. The day after her father left, after Francine refused to go looking for him in the snow, Emily remembered all those toothpastes and deodorants; she had collected enough to last her several months if she decided to run away from home and look for him herself. But she'd never been able to bring herself to go after him. She knew if she went, she might not ever find him, and by the time she returned home, her mother might have drunk herself to death.

While Lizzie stood transfixed in the aisle filled with toys and coloring books, Emily moved on to the household aisle. There were all sorts of ashtrays. Tacky ashtrays with pictures of the Music Pier on them for the tackier summer people who would bring souvenirs like those home to their aging aunts and uncles. There were disposable tin ashtrays, sprayed a greenish gold color, to be used for parties and then tossed away with the plastic spoons and paper plates. There were plain cut-glass ones and some of glazed ceramic. Emily bought one of each. Lizzie had chosen two Rainbow Brite coloring books, a new box of crayons, and a roll of Scotch tape, and laden with their treasures they approached the checkout.

From there they went to McDonald's, where Lizzie ordered her usual Happy Meal and Emily ordered one black cup of coffee. She lit a cigarette in the nonsmoking section and the woman behind her turned to reprimand her. "Can't you read the sign, miss? The place for you is over there," she said, pointing across the room.

Emily mumbled an "I'm sorry" and she and Lizzie moved. There didn't seem to be any *real* place for her, but if there had been, she couldn't have imagined anyplace more appropriate than the cloudy smoke-filled section of McDonald's.

"You having a good day now?" she asked Lizzie.

Lizzie shook her head no.

"Why not? I took you shopping, didn't I? I'm taking you out to lunch. What more do you want?"

"I want you to stop looking so mad."

Emily jabbed the cigarette out in the ashtray. It was one of those disposables like she'd just bought at Hoy's. She wondered if they supplied the McDonald's.

"I'm not mad, Lizzie. I just don't feel so hot today, okay?"

"Did something happen?"

Emily looked at her daughter's expectant eyes, how willing she seemed to hear the whole rotten thing, how anxious she seemed to tell Mommy that everything would be all right. "Nothing happened, Liz," she said. "Nothing."

She waited until ten after eleven to draw a bath that night just in case there was another call, just in case he had something to say this time. But there was nothing to disturb the stillness within the house, nothing but wind rapping against the windows, nothing but the occasional caw of a gull overhead.

In the bathroom she sat naked on the edge of the tub, her wrist under the water faucet checking the temperature. She wanted it hot, as hot as she could stand, so the bubbles from the bath crystals would last a long time, so her skin would be tinged pink, sore by the time she got out. She'd lit candles, several fat, scented votives, and positioned them on the inside edge of the tub, the sink, and on the windowsills. Then she turned out the lights. The white suds billowed up over the edge of the deep porcelain tub, and she stepped in, settled down into them, easing into the heart of wet clouds. She'd taken a large cut-glass ashtray and placed it on the outside edge of the tub, and there she stayed, shriveling up in the water, smoking one long cigarette after another.

During this bath Lizzie woke up, needing to pee, and before Emily could direct her to the powder room, she appeared in the doorway, rubbing her eyes. The steam and smoke hit her face all at once, startling her. Emily sat up quickly, splashing water onto the tile.

"Well, come in and go if you're going to go."

She padded into the room eyeing the burning cigarette suspiciously as she pulled her panties down and pushed herself onto the toilet seat. Her hair was wild, sticking up at all angles, but she was alert, fully awake, stunned. She rested her elbows on her knees, her chin in her hand, and swung her feet back and forth.

"I thought you had to pee, Liz."

"I'm trying," she said. "Why are the lights out?"

"Because I wanted candles, that's why."

"Can I have candles when I take a bath too?"

"No. It's dangerous."

She furrowed her brow, yawned. "But *you're* doing it."

"Elizabeth, pee and go back to bed. You have school tomorrow."

On command, she began to urinate.

"In school they told us that if you smoke your lungs will get black and you'll die. You're making your lungs black."

Emily took the washcloth, raised her knee, and squeezed, letting the water dribble over it. "I haven't been smoking long enough to have black lungs."

"How long does it take?" she asked, wiping herself and turning to flush the toilet.

"A long time."

She pulled her panties up, took a drink of water, and slipped the glass back in its holder. "They said my lungs can get black from other people's smoke."

"That will take even longer."

She paused, arms at her sides, and Emily could see her considering this information and its eventual impact on her well-being. "Can I have bubbles when I take a bath?"

"If I say yes, will you go back to bed?"

She nodded.

"Yes, you may have bubbles."

She leaned over then and kissed Emily on the cheek. Emily felt the tentativeness of the kiss, as if Lizzie wasn't sure this would be allowed anymore between them. The twinge of pain returned, bold and sharp, in her chest. "Go to sleep, kiddo. Go, go now," she said.

As she watched Lizzie leave the room, Emily was overwhelmed with the enormity of her responsibility. How could she protect Lizzie? she wondered. What kind of parent was she going to be now when she needed one herself?

EIGHTEEN

Some days Emily could feel the metal in her heart, a piece of shrapnel. She went to the doctor, describing her pain in amazing detail, opening the paper gown so that she could draw a diagram with her finger of its beginning, its travel across her chest. He claimed that everything sounded fine to him when he laid his icy stethoscope against her skin, but when he saw that she was not convinced, he agreed there should be tests. He recommended a cardiologist.

In the cardiologist's waiting room, she sat motionless, the only young person there. Across from her was a man, about eighty years old, well dressed, well groomed, sitting at military attention, one hand on his silver-headed walking stick. Sitting next to her were two women, also in their seventies or eighties, not as well kempt as the old man.

When the nurse came back to her desk, one of the women got up and pulled a bag of oranges from a canvas carryall. "Looky what I brought you today, Sandy," she said, holding the bag over the nurse's desk.

"Oh, Ida, I was wondering what you were going to give me today. Thanks," she said, taking the bag.

"Lucy's got something for you too," Ida said, turning to point to the other woman.

Lucy was bent over, rummaging through an identical carryall. "Ah, it's cookies. Chocolate chocolate chip. Half a dozen," she said. She got up too and laid them on the desk.

Sandy, the nurse, looked at Emily. "One of them brings me food for my health," she said, holding up the oranges, "and the other one brings me food for the soul."

Ida waved her hand. "She don't need food for the soul," she said to Emily. "She's getting married in a month. Right? A month?"

Sandy nodded vigorously, as if the very idea of marriage had left her speechless.

"Girls," she said then to Ida and Lucy, "this is Emily Hansen."

"She's pretty," Lucy said as if Emily were not in the room.

"Too young to be here," Ida said.

"We all know each other by first names in this office," Sandy explained to Emily. "That's Mr. Barker. David."

Barker tilted his head in Emily's direction. "You going to have *the* test?" he asked.

Emily assumed he meant a cardiogram; she nodded.

"It's not bad," he said. "I come once a month for mine."

Ida and Lucy had returned to their seats. Ida was the closest to Emily and she leaned against her; her breath smelled like spearmint. "We're sisters," she explained, "two sisters with bad tickers."

Emily smiled.

"This your first time here?" she asked.

"Uh, yes. Yes it is."

"You're awful young to be here. Isn't she awful young to be here, Luce?"

Lucy leaned around her sister, taking a good look at Emily.

"Are you Italian?" Lucy asked.

"Yes, I am. How did you know?"

"You live in south Philly as long as I have, you know."

"You're Italian too?" Emily asked.

Lucy waved her hand. "No. Jewish."

"Same thing," Ida said, shrugging. "Dr. Lutenberg's Jewish.

232 /

Great doctor, Emily. Whatever's wrong with you, he'll fix it. Guaranteed."

The sisters turned toward each other then and began talking about someone's uncle who had a bad heart doctor who botched his triple bypass, and they went on from there, tirelessly discussing the ailments and problems of relatives and friends. Every once in a while Emily stole a glance at Mr. Barker, who was eavesdropping on Ida and Lucy's conversation, shaking his head, mumbling a "that's too bad" at the mention of someone's diabetes.

The doctor saw Emily first. She lay quivering on the leather-covered table, the scratchy paper beneath her skin, while Sandy applied the jelly to her chest, then the small suction cups. The test took only a few minutes, and she was told to go into the doctor's consultation office.

"There is no irregularity on the cardiogram, Mrs. Hansen," he said, opening up a manila folder.

"But the pain, well, frankly, Doctor, sometimes it's very severe."

"Is there a history of heart disease in your family?" he asked.

"Depends upon your point of view," she wanted to say.

"No. None that I know of. Everyone—my grandparents, both sides—died of natural causes."

"Your parents?"

She shook her head. Then, "No, wait."

"Yes?"

"I forgot someone. I mean, my sister. She was profoundly re-tarded and there were other complications, but I remember that her heart was . . . not properly formed?"

He laid the folder down and folded his hands over it. "That's a frequent occurrence in the profoundly retarded. You said *was*, Mrs. Hansen. When did she die?"

Emily looked away. "In 1963. She was nine years old. She was in an institution at the time, and she contracted pneumonia. Conges-tive heart failure, they said."

When Emily looked back at him, she saw a puzzled look on his face. He brought one of his hands up to his cheek and rubbed it. He flipped the folder open again. He was shaking his head.

"Mrs. Hansen, it bothers me when a patient comes to me with the kind of pain you describe and I can't find a thing wrong. Now, I can order a phono and echo for you, but I'm telling you, they're extremely expensive. Not the kind of test one simply orders off the cuff. Have you had a stress test lately? Do you smoke?"

"I smoke."

"How much?"

"About a pack a day."

"Are you on birth control pills?"

"I'm a widow," she said.

Emily saw something light in his eyes.

"How long has your husband been dead?"

"It will be a year in January."

"I see."

He pushed the folder aside, excused himself, and left the office. Several minutes later, he returned with two coffees in foam cups. "How do you take yours?" he asked.

"Black. This is fine," she said.

He moved across the room to where there was a small table with miniature containers of milk on ice and sugar packets. He dumped two containers into his coffee, stirred it, and returned to his seat. He then proceeded to explain to her in a gentle voice that what she was experiencing might possibly be a reaction to stress. He had her tell him the nature of Peter's illness, what it was like taking care of him for that year. He wanted to know what kind of work she did, whether she had children, whether she had a fulfilling social life, friends, family.

"There's no one," she said. "Just my daughter."

He took out a prescription pad and dashed off a prescription for a weak sedative. "Just something to take the edge off," he said. "Then I want you to call me in a week and let me know if that pain has subsided any." He tore the slip of paper off and handed it to her. "I also suggest that you do something you enjoy."

234 /

He was standing now, had come out from behind his desk. She looked up. "Are you saying I'm imagining the pain?"

"Not at all. The pain is real, but your heart is perfect. And when that's the case, we have to look outside, at the externals of a patient's life, and see if we can't do something to change that so we can change the pattern of pain."

"I see," she said, standing.

"Don't forget now, call me in a week. Start taking those today."

In the hallway outside the office she took the prescription and ripped it up, tossing the flecks of paper into a wastebasket. Ida came around the corner. She touched Emily's hand with the disarming familiarity people dispense on the old and the pregnant, as if either state had no bounds.

"Did he fix you up?" she asked.

Emily didn't want to scare the old woman, nor did she want to disturb Ida's faith in her good doctor.

She smiled. "Sure. Guaranteed."

Ida nodded. "I told you. He's a good man, honey."

Emily waited until she saw Ida enter the examining room before she pulled on her coat. Oh, Ida, she thought, every good man I've known has been such a bastard too.

One morning when the pain woke her, she wished she'd not thrown the prescription away, but it had been too tempting, the idea of having pills like that. Like drinking whiskey. So while Lizzie dressed for school, she hunted down an old Ace bandage in the bathroom closet. Three inches wide, Peter had used it to wrap his weak knee when he was playing tennis, and even though it had been washed after its last use, it still held the odor of the gooey hot stuff he would rub into his skin before putting the bandage on.

She bound her chest with it, beginning just below her collarbone, covering the space between that and the bottom of her rib cage. It crushed her breasts flat, and when she stood back to look at herself in the mirror, Lizzie came into the bedroom. When she saw the incredible bandage, her tone was one of consternation but not shock; she had passed shock a few weeks ago.

"What is that now?" she asked.

She had already caught Emily staring off into space at nothing for hours on end; she'd caught her in the bathroom, lopping off inches of her long hair, making it blunt, hard edged, and she watched, mystified, as her mother's hair, clumps of it, swirled away in the toilet. She'd found Emily listening to the Helen Humes album over and over. The bandage then, that morning, must have become just one more incomprehensible thing to deal with.

"I have a pain, in my chest. It's stopping the pain.'"

"Are your bones broken?"

"Yes. Yes, my bones are broken," Emily told her, pulling her turtleneck down quickly. "Now let me finish getting dressed in peace, please."

But Lizzie didn't move. "What about my lunch for school?"

The pain always started at the center, at the hard nub where the ribs began, and worked its way across her chest like a razor. Emily gripped the dresser and squeezed. "I can't make your lunch today. Take it," she said, meaning money, "take it . . ." She waved at the brocade purse on the bed.

"Mom."

"Lizzie, take money to buy lunch. I can't make you lunch. Don't you understand how this hurts?"

Lizzie turned her eyes away when Emily lifted her head. "What's the matter, Liz? Why are you turning away like that?"

Emily could see that Lizzie was tenaciously clinging to her self-control, biting down on her trembling lower lip. "I want your bones to get better. When will they get better?"

Emily had to summon every ounce of strength within her to keep from saying it was going to be better, it was going to be fabulous. Gene loves us and he is going to be with us and all of us will be happy then. "By Thanksgiving," she said, "by then everything will be better than you can imagine."

"What about lunch?"

236 /

"You'll have to buy it at school. Mommy can't do it right now."

She shrugged, mumbling, "Okay."

Emily sat on the bed, beckoning Lizzie with a crooked finger. Lizzie's hair needed trimming and she needed some new clothes as well; she needed a mother whose mind was in the right place. Instead Emily held Lizzie's wrist, opened her hand, and laid two dollars on her tiny palm.

"Enough?"

"I only need one."

"Well, the other is just to have."

She took the money grudgingly for what it was—a payoff to be good, to leave Emily to her madness. Francine had done the same but with grander gestures and larger amounts, like the time she had tried to convince Emily to go on the junior class trip to Rome.

"And if I go, what are you going to do, Mother?"

"I'm going to redecorate the house, that's what. I'm going to hire people to paint and people to come in and lay new carpets. Then, Em'ly, when you return with your Italian leathers, you'll have a fresh-looking house to keep them in. That's what I'll do when you're in Rome."

If she could have believed her, Emily would have gone, but she knew better. She knew she would have come back to the same house with a mother who was more bloated, uglier, sadder. Francine would have cried that it was so terrible being alone, that she had needed just a few drinks to soften her, to calm her nerves, and she would have held Emily's hand so tightly in hers that it would have made Emily's eyes smart, her mouth water, and she would have promised, just like she always did, "I'm not taking another drink. Not a sip. This is not a good thing, this being drunk."

And so, she had never gone to Rome.

"Put the extra dollar in your bank," she told Lizzie.

The school bus honked outside and Lizzie let the dollar drift to the floor. Emily hurried her into her jacket, rushed her down the front walk, kissing her absently before she boarded the bus.

As she walked back to the house, she stopped midway up the

flagstone walk and took a good long look at it, feeling pleasure in the fact that it was well on its way to becoming a reflection of its owner. She had not bothered to winterize, so the combination of dense salt air and cold November wind had beaten the house mercilessly, chipping paint around the windows, making bubbles and buckles along the sides. The lawn, dead brown and frozen, would probably not yield anything green. The rosebushes and the azaleas that she'd not bothered to cover in burlap might not ever bloom again, but it just didn't matter to her now.

When Emily arrived at SPSC that morning, Jane jumped from her chair and came quickly toward her. She was holding one of those message slips in her hand.

"Wait till you see who this is from, Emily," she said.

Emily slipped her coat off and took her time hanging it on the brass coatrack in the corner. "Don't tell me, Jane, it's *Vogue* magazine and they want me for the Christmas cover."

Jane sighed. She held the slip of paper out. "No. Here. Look."

The message simply read "Have Emily call me," and there was a number with an area code she didn't recognize.

"I don't know this number, Jane."

"That's because its Nevada. Guess who's in Nevada?"

She would have liked for it to have been Gene who was in Nevada, who'd gone to Nevada to sit on a mountaintop and think things through yet again; Gene who had called here because he knew that's where he would find her on a Friday morning; Gene who wanted her to fly out there and live with him and Chris on his mountain. But she knew that couldn't be; whoever was in Nevada also knew Jane, or Jane wouldn't be so excited.

"Who?" Emily said, finally.

"Your mother. She called this morning, and we talked for about twenty minutes. I gave her an update of what's been happening here, and she said she never had a minute's doubt that you could handle everything."

"Did she say what the hell she's doing in Nevada?"

238 /

Jane was startled by Emily's anger. "She said it had to do with work, with the organization."

Emily was just nodding, not believing a word.

"And she said you should call because she thinks she's found something that will make you happy. That's what she said."

Emily stared at the number for several minutes. A few of the counselors had arrived during that time, saying good morning to her, and when they got no response, they hurried off to their own offices. Emily ran her tongue along the insides of her cheeks, felt the burning when her tongue touched one of the two ulcers in her mouth. Stress, Doctor Lutenberg would have said. Improper diet, the sisters with bad tickers might have concurred. She knew Jane was waiting for her to say something. She handed her the slip of paper. "Here, take it. I don't care what you do with it."

Jane shrugged. "Well, aren't you going to call her? She sounded so thrilled. She must have something very special for you."

Emily shoved her hands into the pockets of her blazer; she rocked back and forth on the toes of her pumps. "She's too late," she said. "Whatever it is, Jane, it's too late."

"Emily."

But Emily was already walking over to the desk, flipping through the appointment book. "Who've we got today, Jane? We have work to do here."

Jane came and stood by the desk. She picked up another message slip. "Lizzie's teacher called. Mrs. Akins. She said for you to drop by late this afternoon or give her a call."

"She say why?"

"No. Just that you should call her."

Emily could see that Jane was perturbed, and at first she was going to try and explain, but she decided against it. The Francine Perone that Jane knew was someone else—strong, in charge, quick as a whip—and she saw no reason to make her see Francine as anything else.

Emily picked up the message slip. "I'll be in my office if you need me, okay?"

Jane said nothing, just a simple nod as she sat down and swung her swivel chair away from Emily.

Twice during the course of the day, when Emily had free time and no new clients to see, she picked up the receiver to make a call. Once she only dialed the New York area code before she hung up, and the second time she dialed the entire number, but hung up before the phone could ring. Finally she made the call to Mrs. Akins.

Mrs. Akins explained that she thought "Elizabeth" might be having some troubles. She seemed reluctant to engage socially with the other children, seemed especially quiet, "almost withdrawn," she said. "I'd like to talk with you in person, Mrs. Hansen. Do you think we could speak today?"

"I can't be there before four. Is that all right?"

"Sure. I'll just make certain that Lizzie doesn't get on the bus. She can be teacher's after-school helper."

Lizzie's classroom was overflowing with Thanksgiving decorations, made by the students. Mrs. Akins, a willowy, soft-spoken woman with the perpetual smile allotted to all elementary school teachers, directed Lizzie to one of the desks in the front of the room and gave her some art supplies to play with. "Your Mom and I will be right outside in the hall, Lizzie."

Lizzie sniffed; she had just the beginnings of the change–of–season cold.

"Follow me," Mrs. Akins said.

Out in the long corridor, Mrs. Akins began to show Emily Lizzie's recent drawings. "I asked the children to draw a picture of how they see themselves in their families. This," she said, handing Emily a large, white sheet of paper, "is her drawing."

In the very center of the paper, no bigger than a pearl from a necklace, was a circle, colored in red, heavy red crayon.

"I thought at first that she was going to continue. You know, some children are very deliberate and take several days to complete their pictures. I thought this was just a part. But she was *very*

definite when I collected this. 'It's me,' she said. As you can see,"
Mrs. Akins continued, "the other children did work like this."

She then gave Emily a pile of papers, complicated drawings of
houses and yards, parents and siblings.

"If not for the withdrawn behavior, I wouldn't be so concerned.
We were all sorry to hear about Mr. Hansen last January—and I
know what a strain the upcoming holiday must be—but has anything else happened at home? Lizzie told me you were hurt. Something about your ribs. And she said she's not going to have a turkey
this year."

Emily pulled at the collar of her coat, pulled it close to her chest.
"I fell a while back and cracked two ribs. They're healing slowly."
She didn't think the story was convincing, but now that she'd
begun the lie she continued. "And as far as Thanksgiving goes,
well, I've been working very hard and I just haven't planned it out.
Of course, we'll have a turkey."

She returned the pictures to Mrs. Akins, who could not meet her
eyes when she said, "She's thrown her lunch away several times.
Monday she flushed it down the toilet, bag and all. We wouldn't
have known except that the toilet overflowed. That's when I decided I should probably speak to you. I thought it was entirely
possible that at home she was acting the same as always—to protect
you. Children do that. Well, you know," she said, "someone like
you who writes for children would notice if something were not
quite right. When I didn't hear anything from you, I figured she's
letting out the frustration here."

Emily was nodding while Mrs. Akins delivered her assessment of
Lizzie's behavior. "Yes, absolutely," she said, "I'm glad you called
me in. I wouldn't have known."

"Well, I feel better that you know now," she said. Emily was
having difficulty hearing Mrs. Akins's words, as if her voice were
coming in at low volume. "Her regular schoolwork is, amazingly,
excellent. Beyond that of the other children, actually."

Not so amazing, Emily thought. "You should have seen me as a
kid, Mrs. Akins," she wanted to say. "I could wipe the vomit from

my mother's mouth, undress her in ten minutes flat, get her into bed, and still pull an A on a math test. I flushed away peanut butter and jelly sandwiches regularly the year Maria died. Bag and all, just like Liz."

When Lizzie and Emily left the school building it was dark, and in the fall it always seemed darker in Ocean Gate at dinnertime than in any other place. There was no rush hour to speak of in a seaside town. Oh, in the neighboring towns of Parkside and Glenn Cove, life was more recognizably suburban, but in Ocean Gate there was only a sprinkling of stores and there were even fewer people who lived so close to the beach year-round like Emily. The quiet that was once so necessary to her as a writer seemed to have taken on its own violent powers; it bored away at her, it mocked her, it gave nothing back but the echo of her own voice.

She drove slowly down Atlantic Avenue wishing for lighted windows from the houses along the street. Here and there the faint glow from a kitchen light flickered, but most of the houses were dark, lying in wait until next summer.

"Are you mad at me?" Lizzie asked when they were stopped at the red light.

"No. I used to throw my lunch away too," she confessed.

The signal changed and Emily drove on.

"You did?"

"Yep. I would get an upset stomach just before lunch and while everyone else was trading sandwiches and cupcakes, I was thinking of a way to get to the bathroom with my paper bag and not get caught."

"I hid mine under my shirt," Lizzie said. She unsnapped her jacket to show Emily. "See, the sweatshirt's big. It's easy to stick it under."

Emily made the right turn onto her street and pulled into the driveway. She turned the engine off and twisted in the seat to face Lizzie. "You know, don't you, that you should have told me? Do you have an upset stomach every day?"

Lizzie wrinkled her nose, shook her head. "Not every day, but some days it feels like there's a tornado inside."

"A tornado?"

"Uh-huh."

"Because of me?"

Even in the shadows Emily could see Lizzie's eyes, see her wrestling with an answer that wouldn't be a lie and wouldn't offend her. "No," she said finally, "just because."

Emily drew her arms up around the steering wheel, she let her head rest on her hands, and she spoke, trying to keep her voice from breaking. "Lizzie, Mommy is trying to feel better, but sometimes it's hard, it's very hard."

"It's all right, Mom."

Emily sat up then. "No, it's not all right. And I'm going to be better, you'll see. Your stomach won't feel like a tornado anymore."

"It doesn't now," she said.

"Good."

NINETEEN

"Gin," Eva said. She slapped her cards down on the table.
"Hmm?"

"Gin. I have gin. I won, Fran—again."

Francine blinked and looked down at the table at Eva's winning hand spread out over her own cards. She was only half paying attention to their game because the other half of her attention was being spent on the view outside their hotel window, which looked out on a six-island Merit gas station with cash lanes, express lanes, credit/cash lanes, and self-serve lanes. There was even a minimart where travelers could buy anything from candy bars to cold medicines and toilet paper. In one afternoon Francine had counted seventeen gray Mercedes; the drivers always used the credit lane and the attendants always washed their windows with supreme care, never leaning on the hoods of the cars as they did with other customers. On the same block with the Merit station, wedged between two new granite-and-tinted-glass office buildings, was a thrift store she and Eva had visited on their fifth day in Vegas. Neither one of them had found anything interesting for themselves, but Francine bought a Deco pin with a square of black onyx in it for Emily and a Depression glass lamp with a rose-colored base for Lizzie.

"Eighteen," Francine said.

"What are you talking about?"

"There," Francine said, pointing down below, "that's the eighteenth gray Mercedes this afternoon."

Eva ignored her and began gathering up the cards, stacking them, then tapping them against the tabletop. "I think life on the road stinks," she said. "Look at us, reduced to counting cars and playing gin rummy."

Francine turned away from the window. "We don't have to stay in, you know. We can go out."

"To another casino? Lose more money than we already have? To hear Wayne Newton again maybe? Or see Tony Bennett for the one hundredth time?"

"You have a point," Francine said. "We can see what the boys are doing."

"We *know* what the boys are doing—sleeping. Sleep all day, up all night. A cockeyed way to live, if you ask me. Damn stupid."

"Did you and Benny have a fight?"

Eva shoved the cards at Francine, spilling the tight stack she'd just worked so hard at making. "Of course not. Benny's nothing to me. And anyway, I would never mean a thing to Benny. He told me all about the one woman he really loved. Doris, her name was. He met her when he was very young. They were engaged, and she wanted him to have a normal job—God only knows why. Who would want a home and a family when she could have all of this?" Eva said, smirking. "Anyway, he quit the band he was with. He tried a regular day job, playing music on the side, some nights, some weekends. He said it started to make him feel crazy. She couldn't bring herself to live *his* kind of life; he couldn't manage to live hers. She broke off the engagement, thus breaking his heart. A no-win situation."

"And you care for him a lot, don't you? Don't you, Eva?"

Eva shrugged; she was looking down into her lap. "No. Yes. I don't know. I miss Tony. And, and this traveling around—one week here, one week there—it's for the birds, Fran. I'm not cut out for this. I want to wake up in my own bed, go into my kitchen, yell at the neighbor's dog when I catch him in the backyard. I want

/245

to go to my Bingo games on Friday nights, and I want to go make my novenas on Tuesday nights, and I want to go to the cemetery twice a month and then go to Aunt Loretta's for her lousy, rock-hard meatballs and macaroni." She was crying now and looking around for her handkerchief. Francine handed her a tissue.

"It's just these delays that are getting to you, Eva, that's all. Look at all we've seen. We've been to the Grand Canyon, we've been in the museums in Chicago, we've been to the casinos."

Eva blew her nose, hard. "There are casinos in Atlantic City. We didn't have to come clear across the country to see them."

Francine had to give her that. She hated the casinos herself but had pretended otherwise for Eva's sake. Everything had taken much longer than they expected. On the way out to Vegas the bus broke down—transmission trouble—and they'd been forced to hole up in a Best Western in Utah for a week while it was being fixed. And then when they finally pulled into the neon town, they heard, through the grapevine, that the Jazz Lights were being held over a week at their previous engagement. Since it was her own and not Eva's pursuit, it was understandable to Francine that Eva was getting edgy; for those who weren't in the habit of making waiting and pursuing a way of life, frayed nerves were to be expected.

Francine got up and went to Eva, pulling her up from the chair. "Listen, I have a wonderful idea. Let's find a church. Would you feel any better if you could sit in a church for a while?"

"Not one of those ridiculous love chapels?"

"No. A real church."

"Catholic," Eva said.

"But absolutely," Francine told her.

They had to rent a car and drive far out of the town to find a house of worship that didn't have balloon hearts flying from the front door, Elvis impersonator ministers, or neon instead of stained glass in the windows. St. Calista's was a modest building, field-stone front, red brick sides, and slim modern stained glass windows—not the kind Eva was used to that usually detailed the Stations of the Cross, but they were pretty, even if they didn't represent anything.

"How's this?" Francine asked when they pulled into the asphalt parking lot adjacent to the church.

Eva nodded. "This is good. I feel better already."

Francine was hoping, as they climbed the double set of cement stairs to the door, that the church wasn't locked. When she and Eva were girls, a Catholic church was never locked. The nuns had taught them that that's where they should go if there was no place else to turn and they were stranded in the middle of the night. "Go to God's house," they said, "and He'll welcome you." But God's house held some very appealing objects for vandals and thieves—chalices of eighteen-carat gold, some with rubies and emeralds on them—and Francine knew that even God would not look kindly on being robbed.

She tugged once on the thick cast-iron handle and didn't feel it budge. But on the second pull the door opened. There was no one else inside, and Francine and Eva walked up the center aisle, Francine's pumps clacking against the marble floor. It was a simple altar ahead of her, rosewood, a rosewood cross hanging from invisible wire above it, a simple brushed-gold tabernacle. To the left was the statue of St. Joseph and to the right the statue of the Blessed Mother, dressed in a blue gown, looking down on the world under her feet and the snake she crushed between her toes.

"Let's sit there," Eva said, motioning to the first pew on the Blessed Mother side. Eva genuflected before sliding into the pew, and Francine followed behind her.

They sat for a while, just looking ahead, letting the scent of incense float around them, each of them with their private thoughts. Eva pulled rosary beads from her purse and she began them, her fingers rubbing each bead, her lips moving silently, saying Hail Marys.

Francine's eyes were fixed on the Blessed Mother statue. All young Catholic girls were taught to be devoted to the Virgin; she was to be their model for womanhood, for motherhood. Francine felt she had failed to aspire to this ideal even as a teenager, when she first began entertaining thoughts of those black musicians and musty supper clubs. She glanced out of the corner of her eye at Eva, now on her last row of Hail Marys, and she knew that Eva, however, had not fallen far from the ideal. Neither had Emily.

"She was the most remarkable child," she said aloud.

Eva made the sign of the cross, put her rosaries away. "Who?"

"My Em'ly. Did I tell you, Eva, that she once saved her allowance—she couldn't have been more than nine years old—and she went to the Woolworth's in town and bought beads. You know, those wooden beads, different colored ones that you put on a string?"

"For toddlers?"

"Yes, that's it. Well, every night before supper, she would disappear into the den with Maria. I was usually so busy getting things ready for dinner, I never paid much attention to what they were doing. I assumed she was watching television while Maria sat in the playpen. Then one evening, there was a phone call for Em'ly, one of the kids at school, something about a homework assignment. I called her and when she didn't come, I went in the den to find her." Francine paused, taking a deep breath. "She was in the playpen, Eva, with Maria and the beads. 'See the hole?' she was saying. 'You're gonna put the string in the hole. Do you hear? You're gonna do it.' Isn't that the most remarkable thing?"

Eva leaned toward Francine, their shoulders brushing each other. "I said this rosary praying that you'd just go home now, Fran."

Francine had considered this option once or twice herself. Give up, go home, be a mother, return to work.

"Too late to just turn around and go back, Eva. In just a few more days the Jazz Lights will be in town."

They were both looking at the Blessed Mother now. "Eva?"

"Yes?"

"Pray that it's him."

"All right. This is it. We've got the baby now," the doctor said.

Emily clenched Peter's hand in hers. "Where do I look?"

"You can look up here at the mirror or just look down, between your legs," the doctor said.

It had been a difficult and long labor during which they had strapped a fetal monitor around her hard belly. She had had to listen to the irregularity of the heartbeat and thought that her worst fears would be realized: she would give birth to a child like Maria.

She looked up. She couldn't see a thing over the round hump of her belly, only the metal ends of the forceps in the doctor's hands. This kid doesn't want to come out, she thought, doesn't want to be here.

"There," Peter said, breathing hard beside her, as involved in this labor as any husband could be.

"Oh," she gasped when she saw the tiny head. The face looked malformed. Where were the eyes? The lips? What had happened to her baby's face?

"All that trouble and she's out with the caul intact," the doctor said. He wiped the baby's face clean, lifted her high in the air, and placed her on Emily's chest. "Say hello to Mommy, little girl," he said.

Emily was crying; Peter was too, leaning over her and their daughter, who had come into the world with the veil. Emily remembered her father talking about it because his own mother had been born with it, and her great-grandmother as well. "It means she has the gift of vision," he'd explained. "Was I born with it?" she'd asked. "No, but don't feel badly. I'm not sure you'd really want to see the future. Wouldn't you rather be surprised?"

TWENTY

Emily wanted to make good on her promise to Lizzie that she wouldn't have to feel the tornado in her stomach anymore, so she asked Lizzie to have some friends over one day after school.

"Two friends?"

"Yes, two friends would be all right. They can come home with you on the bus, and I'll drive them home at dinnertime."

"Can we play in my room?"

"Yes," Emily said, "as long as you clean up afterward, and as long as no one touches the Madame Alexander dolls."

Lizzie had almost the entire collection of the famous dolls from foreign countries, from fairy tales and history. Peter had started the collection the day she was born, beginning with the bigger, more expensive dolls like Cinderella, Snow White, and Alice from *Alice in Wonderland*. He bought her a doll from a different country for each birthday and Easter, and another of the larger dolls for Christmas. Then last year there were rumors that the real Madame Alexander, designer of the dolls, had died, and suddenly it was next to impossible to find them, even in the stores that had always carried them. They doubled in price and therefore doubled in desirability, and because he wanted her to have all of them, he drove all the way to New Hope, Pennsylvania, to the doll shop that carried antique dolls, to buy them.

He didn't come home until after ten that night, a pile of the blue boxes with rosebuds on them in his arms.

"My God, Peter, there are eight dolls here."

He dropped the boxes on the sofa. "Em, you'll never believe it, I found the kid, the boy doll that goes with the *Little Women* set. Louie, Larry—"

"Laurie," she said.

"Yeah, that's the one." He bent over and opened the box, pulled the little boy dressed in a brown suit and hat from the box. "Here he is. Should have named him Louie. Who can remember a boy named Laurie?"

Peter was still able to go to work at that point, still had enough energy to putter in the yard on warm days, but Emily held the doll in her hands and she couldn't stop trembling. Peter was opening one box after another; he was so excited.

"And the lady at the store said this one is out. It was the last one any dealer of these dolls had in stock."

He lifted Juliet from the box, held her by her feet in his large hands. "She looks a little like you, Em," he said, holding the doll next to her face.

"Peter, stop."

He put the doll back in her blue box. "Stop what? Lizzie's going to go wild when she sees these."

He walked over to the end table with the drawer and opened it. He kept his cigarettes there, and a pack in the kitchen drawer, and a pack in the garage. He shook a cigarette out, brought it to his lips, lit it with the yellow Bic lighter he kept with him at all times.

Emily put the Laurie doll on the coffee table. "Why did you have to buy all of these now?"

He waved the cigarette. Emily thought it looked so out of character for him, an athlete puffing away like an eleven-year-old on a street corner. For some people a cigarette looked like a natural extension of their fingers; they were so smooth the way they handled it, sometimes you didn't even notice they were smoking. On Peter it just looked like a prop, something he could do, could use in order to seem unfamiliar to her, a gesture he could annoy her with so she wouldn't mind his not being around once the inevitable materialized.

"You know how hard they are to get. It's no big deal. Now you'll have them."

"Now I'll have them when, Peter? Say it, damn you! Say it! You never say the words. We never talk, we just pretend."

"Now you'll have them to give to her when I'm dead! There, is that better? Does that make you feel any better?"

She brought her hands up to cover her face. She was crying. "No, it doesn't," she mumbled. "No it doesn't and I'm sorry. I'm sorry I yelled. I don't want this to happen."

He was still holding the cigarette, drawing on it hard, making his cheeks gaunt. "I don't want it to happen either. You think it didn't rip me apart to buy these knowing I'm not going to see her face when she opens the boxes?"

Emily let her hands fall away. "I love you."

He sucked in once more on the cigarette, then stabbed it out in the ashtray.

"I love you too, Em. I love you to pieces."

Lizzie chose to invite Lynn Miller and Kathy Franks over for the afternoon. "I like Lynn better, but Kathy's having a birthday sleep-over next week and I'm invited."

"So you thought you'd make her feel liked, heh?"

"Yeah."

"Very diplomatic, Liz."

"What's that mean, that diplo word?"

"It means you handle people with grace, fairly, understand?"

Lizzie nodded yes. Emily wasn't sure how she felt about the idea of Lizzie's staying overnight at a girlfriend's house at such a young age. If they started having sleep-over parties at six, by the time they were fifteen their parents would have to send them on a cruise to Jamaica for amusement. But it was more than that. She would be completely alone in the house, and although she was trying her damnedest to hold on to what little controls she had left, she knew that without Lizzie there anything could happen. She was still wearing the bandage; the pain had not lessened any; in fact, it had grown stronger.

All through that morning and into the afternoon, waiting for the school bus to deposit the three girls out front, Emily tried to work. She sat at the typewriter for several hours, hoping to fill up the blank page, but nothing came. All she could hear was her own voice, the voice in her Maine story, the voice of "Real Love," and that was not the voice she wanted now. The only image in her mind was dust motes. If she pressed her eyes closed, she could see them in a stream of light, flying, but she couldn't get past the image, couldn't make it mean anything with words.

It must have been close to four thirty when the phone rang. In a half-hour she was going to drive the girls home and then she and Lizzie could have their dinner. She was proud of herself; she'd not snapped at the kids.

"Hello?"

The girls came running into the kitchen, Lizzie leading the pack. "We're just getting juice, Mom."

"Emily?"

There was so much giggling and movement in the kitchen, Emily was sure she heard the voice on the line wrong.

"Yes?" she said.

"Emily, it's Gene." When he said it, three words she could distinguish above the sound of the girls' chatter, she heard the congestion. He had a cold.

"You have a cold," she said, as if she talked to him every other day, as if absolutely nothing was wrong except for the fact that her chest hurt constantly and she was wearing an Ace bandage.

"Not serious," he said. "I get them when I smoke too much."

"Oh."

"I hear kids. Sounds like a party."

The girls left with their glasses of juice and the kitchen was quiet again. "No, no party. Lizzie just wanted some friends over."

/253

"Listen, the reason I called is—" She was thinking: Let the reason you called be that you're as miserable as I am.

"Is what?"

"I don't have a reason, except that I felt badly about everything, and it was getting close to Thanksgiving. I knew you'd have to face the first big holiday. I was thinking about you—I shouldn't have done this."

"How's Lottie?"

"It's not cancer. In fact, it was an allergist who finally figured out that she was having a reaction to the chemical they use in the hemodialysis unit at work. Very rare, but she got it. Causes loss of pigmentation. Until him it was very touch and go."

"How are *you* and Lottie?"

He paused then and Emily could see his face, as if he were standing right there in front of her, how tightly his lips would be drawn, his brow wrinkled as he thought his answer through. "We see each other. That's all."

That's all? That was a lot more of a chance than he'd given them.

"I miss you," Emily said.

"I miss you too."

"Then shouldn't we, shouldn't we do—"

"No. No, we shouldn't do anything, Emily. I just wanted you to know that I think about you, that you . . . that I think you are an admirable human being."

"There you go again, sounding like a jackass. What's so admirable about me, huh? That I didn't come on to you like some lovesick, horny widow? That, that I'm still this pure, untouched woman you fell in love with—I mean *half* in love with—from afar? Well, you came on to me and I am *real*, Gene. I'm not something you made up and wrote down, something you can pick up and read, who won't surprise you because you already know the ending."

She thought for a second that he had hung up, hung up halfway through her litany of his sins against her.

"I'm sorry."

"Don't tell me you're sorry. I don't want you to be sorry. I just want—I want to get off this phone. I can't talk now. I have to take the girls home. I have to feed Lizzie. I have to go."

"Okay," he said. "Okay. Please take care of yourself."

By midnight she had convinced herself that she shouldn't have gotten angry, that if she'd just kept her mouth shut, handled herself like an adult, they could have had a pleasant conversation, which could have been followed by more conversations that would have eventually led to what she wanted, what Chekhov called that "new, beautiful life" beginning. Instead she'd shouted, and even though her shouting had never ruffled him in the past, she was sure it had this time.

She felt she had taken one little step forward by having Lizzie's friends over, by acting like a normal mother, and that phone call had sent her back ten steps, back to the state of mind in which she could turn ordinary, fallible men into heroes.

On the night of Lizzie's first sleep-over party, Emily already knew what she was going to do. She'd called the infamous Madame Rosa and made an appointment; seeking the circumspect wisdom of a card reader was also something she'd never done in her life, and she figured she might learn something. She dropped Lizzie off at Kathy's house at six fifteen. Margie Franks was going to have a clown, who also doubled as a magician, deliver pizza at six thirty, thus providing food and entertainment in one shot. "Pick her up about ten in the morning," Margie said, "and go have some fun. Mom's night off."

Feeling sick, feeling her stomach turn like tumblers in a lock—metal grating on metal—she drove to Madame Rosa's. It was raining and twice the tires skidded against the blacktop. When she was about a hundred yards from the turn, Emily saw Madame Rosa's neon sign flashing out by the road. The letter *t* was burned out on the word *tarot*. She had to wait, stranded out in the middle of the Black Horse Pike, turn signal bleating impatiently as the cars sped by, before she could make the left turn into the drive. The house, sad and shapeless, was set far back off the highway, and she had to steer through the muddy road to the front door. When she turned the key to off, she sat in the car, immovable for a second. An ominous red light, like the light on top of a police car or an ambulance, twirled on a black stand in the front window, sending out ripe rays through the blurry night. She got out of the car and hurried up the lopsided steps to bang on the dirty maple door.

She was not greeted by Madame Rosa herself but by a boy she assumed was Madame Rosa's son. Emily couldn't figure his age; he was a tall, lummoxy type with a fixed vacancy in his eyes, but when he smiled he seemed to relax, and he waved her in, pointing to a gray sofa along the wall. "Mommy will be right out. She's got another person in with her right now. Would you like something? Some milk or water maybe?"

"Nothing. Thank you." Emily saw that he looked crestfallen by her refusal so she told him, "I'll have water."

"I can make coffee," he announced in a way that suggested he had just remembered this talent. "It'll be instant."

"Are you going to have some?"

He smiled. "We'll have coffee."

Waiting for him to return, Emily sat on the edge of the sofa, trying to stay her racing pulse, but the room didn't lend itself to comfort. Emily thought it austere and unhomey—no knickknacks, no pictures, no magazines or books, not even a television. The only furniture besides the couch was a maple table, an oval braided rug, a chair, and a floor lamp with a plastic cover over the shade. The spinning red light cast a fiery glow over the blandness, and she was beginning to think that Madame Rosa only rented the place and lived somewhere else when the boy returned, carrying a tray with two delicate china cups and a china pot clinking on top.

He set the tray down on the table. He had thought to include napkins, sugar cubes in a small glass bowl, spoons, cream in a white pitcher. He seemed so intent on serving her that he didn't take his eyes off the tray. He carefully poured the steaming water into the cups and left the stirring to her.

"She taught me how to do this when people have to wait," he said. "She says people should feel comfortable before she sees them." He straightened up then and put his hands on his hips. "Are you comfortable?"

"Yes, very," she said. And she sipped some of the coffee to convince him. Without knowing why exactly, she was beginning to feel terrified.

The boy flopped into the chair across from her. "You don't look it—comfortable, I mean."

"I am."

"Okay. Drink up then. She'll be out soon."

Emily felt compelled to drink the coffee as heartily as she could since he was just sitting there, not bothering to drink his. The rainfall outside sounded heavier, splattering against the windows. She drank the rest of the coffee, making quick smiles at the boy, who then finally drank some of his own. When she returned her cup to the tray, she told him it was very good.

"I like to make it for people, but I hardly ever drink it. You can have mine too." He leaned forward and pointed to his cup.

Although the offer of another cup of coffee did not constitute a threat to her safety, Emily was panicked. Her chest hurt. She glanced at her watch, saw that it was 7:00. Madame Rosa was already fifteen minutes late for their appointment, and with whom? Emily hadn't noticed any other cars in the drive.

The boy continued to sit quietly as if he were guarding her; she couldn't even manage to ask his name. The red light danced across his face, the shadows playing on his eyebrows.

She wanted out. She made some excuse about having left her wallet in the car and he stared at her, wordless, calm.

"I'm going out to get it, all right?"

"You don't look so hot," he said.

"I think it's this," she said, "this light."

"I think it's neat."

"Yes, yes it is, very neat. I'm going to get my wallet."

The five or so steps to the door seemed slower than any she'd ever taken. She was certain that at any moment she would feel his hand on her shoulder, hear him say, "Hey, lady, you're not going anywhere." But she made it to the door, turned the knob, and even turned back to look at him sitting in the chair.

"Bye," he said, smiling.

When she got into the car, turned the ignition, the car wouldn't start. She slapped at the steering wheel, pressed down on the accelerator. She was about to cry, murmuring "Please start," and when she turned the key, the engine roared. She couldn't tear out of the driveway the way she wanted to because of the mud. Until she reached the pike, she had the strong, very real sensation of sinking in quicksand, of being sucked into the earth forever.

With the engine idling at the lip of the driveway, she believed she had only two choices. She could go home, or she could make a left; she could drive to New York. As soon as the thought entered her mind, she recognized that coming here to Madame Rosa's was her way of stalling the inevitable. Both choices seemed equally reckless to her, but one of them, going to see Gene, was active. At home, she would only do what she'd been doing for ten months—smoking, swallowing her pain.

The car nosed out onto the pike; her right-turn signal was flashing, but she made the swift left. The window defoggers were working sluggishly, so she had to use the back of her hand to wipe the inside of the window, keeping her eyes peeled for the parkway entrance. Once she was on the parkway, she started to remember the oddest things: how much, for instance, she hated to see children playing hide-and-seek in the school yards, in parks. She could be moved to tears seeing the child who'd been dubbed "it" opening his eyes only to find that all the others had fled to impossible places. Whenever she heard the child cry out, "Ready or not, here I come," she always imagined the other children hiding together in one spot, snickering and exuberant.

The night he died, she had sat by Peter's bed, holding his hand. He was trying to entertain her by telling her stories of the worst tennis games he'd ever played. Emily knew the stories by heart and had even witnessed some of his worst defeats, but she loved hearing the stories again. When he told them, he brought it all to life. "You taught me that," he said. And as long as he was speaking it was possible for her to believe that he would get well. After talking, he complained that his throat was dry.

"What can I get you? What do you want?"

"What I want, I mean really want, Em, is vanilla ice cream. The good kind with the black flecks in it. I would love that right now."

She had no intention of leaving him to rush off for ice cream; she had no intention of denying him what he wanted either. She pressed the call button for the nurse, and when there was no response she got up, just to poke her head out the door and call to her. She was just outside, dispensing meds for the next room.

"When you can, he'd like some ice cream, please. Vanilla with black flecks."

The nurse nodded and said she'd have someone get it in a minute.

"They're getting it," Emily told him when she turned around. But Peter had left her when she wasn't looking, when she had so much more to tell him. A matter of seconds.

Emily had a brief respite from the rain as she drove into the Lincoln Tunnel, where for once traffic was not backed up for miles. She had never driven the streets of New York alone, but she was determined to do it now.

Gene's new apartment was on East Eighty-ninth, and after riding around in circles for close to twenty minutes, scanning for a space, she finally pulled into a parking garage. As she hurried down the block toward his building, it occurred to her that she'd given no thought to the possibility that he might not be home, so she started mentally listing places she might duck into for a cup of coffee until his return. What kept running through her mind, pushing her on in the rain, was what he'd said: "I don't care how public the place is, I'd drag you out of there in ten minutes." Then what she was doing now, this madness, this impulsive trek to his apartment, felt right:

confronted with her having come all this way in the rain, he would want her; if she could touch him, then he could be hers.

The building was directly across the street from a school. There was no doorman, but the outside glass doors were open. To gain entrance to the second set required that she use the lobby phone, punch in the numbers from the directory, and speak to him. She found the name Lisicky immediately, punched in the numbers, listening for the ring. The phone rang five or six times before it was picked up; she was ready to say his name.

"Hello, Lisicky," a woman's voice said.

Emily hung up, sure she'd gotten the wrong number, that she'd missed another Lisicky on the board, but when she checked again, she saw that there was only one G. Lisicky. She slumped to the floor, sitting crouched in the fluorescent lobby, her wet coat bunched up, hunting through her purse for her address book. Maybe she was in the wrong building, on the wrong street. But that was not the case. Shoring up her courage one last time, she pushed her wet hair off her face and punched in the numbers once again. The phone rang only one and a half times before the woman answered and said, "Yes, Lisicky. Who is it?"

Emily dropped the phone, backed away from it. It swung back and forth and for a second she could hear the warbled, "Who's there? Who is it?"

She didn't know what she expected to happen, but she didn't run out, not right away. The phone receiver hung from its cord; it had stopped swinging. The elevator light made its gentle ping, the doors opened, and he was there with Lottie, her fingers on his elbow. Emily's hand was on the steel latch to the door, her back against it. She was pushing, pushing to escape the look on his face. It was like looking through gauze in slow motion: Lottie's head tilting up toward him, concern and insecurity flashing in her eyes. Emily thought her ribs might burst when he didn't reach out to her to reel her in, when his hand went on Lottie's arm, holding her back, his only other movement, stepping slightly in front of his wife, shielding her from this scene. Then Emily felt the latch give way, finally, freeing her to run out into the night.

It took her a while to find the parking garage; she couldn't remember its exact location now. She walked into one garage and the attendant pointed her in the opposite direction. "Around the corner, lady. That way."

She would never remember how she managed to drive all the way home that night. It must have been the thought of Lizzie, who would expect her in the morning, that helped her steer herself back to Ocean Gate. If not for Lizzie, she believed she would have driven forever, until exhausted; she would have closed her eyes, given herself over to the endless black highway.

She had forgotten to leave the porch light on, and when she tried to put the key in the lock of her front door, she thought she was going blind; she couldn't *see* the hole, a hysterical blindness like her hysterical chest spasms—no physical causes, just the result of having seen the truth at a glance. It wasn't until the key finally engaged with the lock that she tasted the salt on her lips and knew that she was crying.

Emily closed the door and leaned up against it, still in her coat, staring down the dark hallway. There was a mirror to her right on the wall, but she was afraid to look into it, afraid to see what she had become. Instead she kept her gaze straight ahead.

The man in the bathrobe comes toward her, smiling, and takes her hand. She hears the music swelling all around him. It's as if he wants to dance with her, but no, he leads her to her bedroom, where he says, "Look. Please, look." Her eyes take in the bed. She sees herself with Peter making love; she sees them with Lizzie between them on a summer night, finding solace in the wedge between their bodies; she sees Peter alone, sitting on the edge of the bed, wearing only jockey shorts, his shoulders slumped, his face ashen, telling her it's time for him to go to the hospital; he knows it's time. She thought it so strange, how he knew his death was near in much the same way she knew, before Lizzie was born, that the cramps were the beginning of labor. "I don't want to look," she says. "I don't want to be in here." But she feels his hand on her shoulder, feels it push her down until she finds herself sitting on the bed. It feels hot, even through her winter coat. "It hurts," she says, "oh, it hurts." The man nods, the belt of his flannel robe brushing against her hand. He sits down with her, says, "Emily, rest now." And he is gone.

She sat there for the longest time, just feeling the tears on her face, feeling them drip down to her neck, still holding back until there was no reason to hold back any longer. The sound that came out of her was dark, the guttural "Aaahh" she heard from Margot, a sound so primitive it hurt her ears, hurt her throat to feel it. She shook off the coat, began pulling at her shirt until one button tore lose, and then she tugged at the bandage until it was off. She could see the red welts across her chest from having worn it so long. She rocked, sobbing, naked from the waist up, her arms covering her breasts. She knew that the man in the bathrobe would not come back, that this was what it felt like to let go of the dead and the missing, what it felt like to return to life again.

DREAMS, 1982

When the Jazz Lights' opening night finally arrived, Francine was lying on her bed in her hotel room, fully arrayed in her evening clothes and evening jewelry. She'd chosen something she believed Tom would expect to see her in at this point in her life—an unfussy black crepe de chine sheath, one long string of pearls with a diamond clasp, and a matching set of earrings. Despite the fact that she had spent well over an hour and a half scrupulously applying her makeup in the poorly lit bathroom, now she lay with a cold wet washcloth covering her forehead. All day her head had been throbbing, an ache that increased with each passing hour.

She was thinking about the night they'd met, how self-possessed she'd been at twenty, enough so that she had ignored the handsome stranger who glided up to her as if he had a right to, as if his taking her hand and pulling her with him to the center of the rink had been ordained. How appropriate that Harry James tune was, for he *had* made her love him, made her love him when love and marriage and children were still the furthest things from her mind.

And she wondered now if, when he left her, he was searching for a place where each breath would not be measured for its density, for the weight of its guilt or sadness. If he had found it, that place, she wanted to be there too.

There were two short knocks on the door, then Eva came in, flicking on the light switch.

"Off. Turn the lights off," Francine said, and she did.

"It's almost eight thirty, Fran. The show starts at nine."

"I know."

She pushed herself up against the headboard.

"Are you sick?" Eva asked.

"Just nervous, I think. You can turn the light on now."

Eva flicked the switch again, came fully into the room, closing the door behind her. She perched on the end of the bed, touched the toe of Francine's pump. "You look terrific," she said.

"Thanks."

Eva's bags were already packed, lined up near the dresser. "Well, Fran, I guess this is it. I think we should go, if you want to make the first set."

Francine swung her legs around, stood up, smoothing the front of her dress.

"Something's missing," Eva said. She got up and went to the dresser drawer Francine used. She opened it and pulled out a black-and-white silk scarf. "It wouldn't be you without this, would it?"

Francine took the scarf and stood before the mirror, adjusting it, wrapping it, so many twists and knots she could do blindfolded. She spoke to Eva's reflection behind her in the mirror. "Better?"

Eva made an okay sign with her fingers. "Perfect."

The Jazz Lights, seven men in navy blue jackets, white silk shirts, and skinny white ties, were tearing the lid off an old Tommy Dorsey tune when Francine and Eva sat down at a table. Francine remained with her elbows on the table, hands folded under her chin through the entire set, her eyes fixed on the clarinet player, Tom Riley.

Of all the bands she and Eva had heard over the past several months, the Jazz Lights were the best, even better than Benny T., and Benny T. was very good. Tom Riley was the right age, the right height and weight, the right hair—slightly receding and silvery. Even the set of his jaw, a bit slack, was how she had imagined it would be. As he played, swaying and tapping his left foot—which Tom had always done too—she permitted herself to believe it was him. They were together, a married couple of nearly thirty-five years. With their children leading full and happy lives, they had decided to sell the house. He left the firm and the two of them had taken to the road, rediscovering each other again. In her mind, Francine knew that this, this would be the part of their life together she liked best, watching him play, seeing him seduce strangers with his music, knowing that he loved her.

"You know you haven't said one word since we left the club, Fran."

Although it was Eva who unlocked the door, Francine entered the room first with Eva following behind her.

"I know how disappointed you must be. Fran? Come on, I'll help you pack. We've got an early plane tomorrow."

Francine was standing by the sliding glass doors, watching the shards of reflected light in the glass. She and Eva had decided that if Tom Riley was not her Tom they would both leave Vegas the following day; if it had been Tom, Eva would have gone home alone while Francine stayed behind to see how things worked out.

"I'm not going," Francine said.

She heard the keys being tossed on the bed, heard Eva sigh.

"What are you talking about now? There's no reason to stay here, Fran."

Francine turned around, reaching up to pull the scarf away from her neck. "I'm going to keep looking. Who knows? He may be in the deep South, he may be in L.A. There's plenty of places I haven't even begun to look."

She was folding the scarf into squares as she spoke. Eva hurried to her, snatched the scarf out of her hands. "You can't be serious. For crying out loud, Fran, he could be a farmer somewhere too, or, or he could be a lawyer at some firm in Seattle. He could even be *dead* for all you know! You did this because you wanted to bring something back to Emily, you—"

Francine saw the horrible thought click into place beyond Eva's eyes. She said nothing.

Eva rubbed her forehead, let the scarf fall to the floor. "I see. I see," she said, "I see what you're doing. When you couldn't deal with Maria, you drank, and when she died and he left, you drank some more, and when you couldn't do that anymore, you switched, right? SPSC for whiskey . . . and, and now this, this craziness for SPSC, for your own daughter."

Francine couldn't argue; she made no attempt to defend herself. She knew everything Eva was saying to her was true. She merely put up her hand, shook her head. "I can't stop, Eva."

"Hire investigators. Come home with me. Just leave here."

"I'm too tired. I don't want to go back and keep making it work—SPSC, lunch with Em'ly twice a year. I started out wanting to find him for her, you've got to believe that. But now I need to find him for me, for my own peace of mind. I want to keep going."

They stood in the center of the room and Francine believed that anyone who might have happened by, anyone who might have seen them, would recognize that they were women who knew each other and themselves well.

"I know which way my fabric's cut, that's what Mabel used to say whenever she wanted to make the point about who she was, what she could and couldn't do, Eva." Francine pointed to herself. "Surely not the best fabric, but I know it."

Francine picked up her purse, picked up the keys from the bed, squeezed them in her hand.

"Where are you going now?"

She smiled at Eva. "The night's still young."

"Another club," Eva said, her voice as dull as unpolished silver. "Absolutely."

It was easy to get a taxi outside the Holiday Inn, and although she wanted the second cab in line because the driver seemed much more alert to her than the other cabbie, she followed the protocol of hiring a cab and settled herself in the backseat of the first taxi in the lineup. She thought she caught a whiff of whiskey sailing off the driver's breath, but she was so acutely aware of that smell, she realized she could well have imagined it. They pulled away from the motel with a screech and a lurch, barreling down the four-lane strip, and by the time she was sure that it *was* alcohol on the driver's breath, before she could demand that the driver stop and let her out, the cab was already speeding through the red light, into the shiny black limousine that was making an illegal left turn.

PART FIVE

TWENTY-ONE

501 Fourth Street
Ocean Gate, NJ
February 20, 1983

Dear Eva,

When I looked at my calendar today I realized that it's
been nearly three months since my mother's death, since the
funeral, and that despite all of your help with the arrangements, all of the support you gave me, I never really thanked
you properly. I considered coming to Roxborough to see
you, and I still want to if you'll have us (me and Lizzie), but
I also wanted to say some things and I'm often better on
paper than in person. When I first started writing—God it
seems ages ago—my then-editor met with me for lunch.
She'd only seen one manuscript of a Flora Flamingo book,
and she was talking as if there would be hundreds of them
in the future. "I only have this one," I told her, "and you've
been talking as if you know there'll be more, that I can do
more. How do you know I'm any good?" I asked her. Well,
she smiled, very sly, a smile like my mother's could be
sometimes, and she said, "Because you can talk." I thought

I was being very clever when I said, "Just because I can talk doesn't mean I can write." Eva, this is my long-winded way of saying that in matters of the heart, for me at least, the reverse is true.

Where to begin? First to say how grateful I am that you stood by her, went with her on her search. I'm sure you probably thought she had a few screws loose, but I also know how convincing she could be when she put her mind to it. For years she tried to convince me that we could be happy, that she wasn't an alcoholic. She managed to convince me that she had been to the bottom of her despair and was on top of it at last.

I have cried myself to sleep nearly every night since November, wishing I'd been able to see through that hard edge she had, wishing I had known that for her the pain had never ended. All of the signs were there: she never dated any other man, never made a life for herself outside of her work, which when you think of it was just being on the other side of the desk, on the other side of the life she'd already lived, continued to live. Oh, she was a great one for dispensing advice. "You should learn to embrace the world a little more, Em'ly," she told me last summer at one of our famous luncheons, as if she were out there living it up, running from one party to another.

Eva, I think you were her only friend, real friend. I think, even though it hurts me to admit it, that she found with you what she could do best with another human being—be a friend. If I could have, I would have tried to be her friend, but it was impossible.

I know how angry you were with her; I was, *am*, angry too. I guess with me she was always going to need to pull away, like coming up for air, because, like it or not, I am my mother's daughter.

You said, that night at the house, the night of her funeral, that you felt responsible, that you felt you should have called me and told me what she was up to, that if you had she would still be alive now, that things could have been different. For a long while I thought that too and wondered why you didn't try to reach me, how you could have gone along with a plan that seemed so haphazard, so doomed to fail. What I didn't tell you then, and *should* have, was that she did finally try to reach me. It must have been just a few weeks before the accident. I never returned the call; she never tried again. When I think of it now, it's almost as if her leaving the way she did last summer was an omen; she'd left everything in my hands: her work, her grief and mine. What I'm trying to say is that I really don't believe your letting me know about her life on the road could have made any difference. She left with my father, wherever he went, nineteen years ago, and I don't think there was a way for her to come back once she *physically* started looking. So forgive me for not telling you then that I don't blame you, that I think you did what you felt you had to do.

Well, I see that I've gone on quite long here, but I didn't want you to think badly of her, not completely.

As far as SPSC goes, I'm still there on a part-time basis, but soon the organization will be turned over to Jane. I have a child to raise and my own work to do.

I don't know how you'll feel about this, but I haven't gone through her things yet. When I do, if you would, I'd like for you to do it with me. There may be something you want. I have the two mementos that are the most important to me, that meant everything to her: the purse and my father's bathrobe.

Again, thank you so much for being there in November.

Sincerely,
Emily Hansen

1120 Bella Vista St.
Roxborough, PA
March 2, 1983

Dear Emily,

It has taken me long to answer because, unlike you, I am not good with words. We would love to have you and Lizzie visit. You say the word and I will even make lasagna for you.

Thank you for asking me to look through your mother's things with you. I would like that, not because there's anything I want but because I would like spending that time with you. I've heard so much about you, and then being with you over those days of the wake and funeral, I feel I've known you a long time. I hope you don't think this is strange, but when I make my regular Tuesday night novenas now, I say prayers for my husband, for you, and for your daughter.

You know, she told me about the time you bought the beads for Maria, and she said, "She was a most remarkable child." Well, I want to say that after reading your letter, knowing what I know about your life, I think you are a most remarkable woman, but more important, and don't you ever forget it, your mother knew it too. I will call you soon to make a date for the lasagna.

Love,
Eva Mina

274 /

When Gene's play opened in New York in June, Emily and Lizzie were in Bangor, Maine. Barbara passed the newspaper to Emily at the breakfast table. It was after ten in the morning, a Sunday, and they were still in their pajamas, lazing about, drinking more coffee than was good for them, eating one too many bagels with far too much cream cheese.

Emily had arrived in Maine the night before, weary from the long drive but proud that she had packed herself and Lizzie up, closed up the house, and decided to spend the summer in a new place with the people who could share all of her memories and add a few of their own. With this history between them, the only living history she had left now, she found it easy to talk about Peter, easy to tell Lizzie the stories of the life she shared with her daddy.

"You've been immortalized," Barbara said when she slipped the paper into Emily's hands. By this time she had told Barbara everything that had and had not happened between them. Gene had called her the morning after her last trip to New York. He was worried, he'd said, seeing her like that. He had to be sure that she had gotten home safely. But she had just heard the news of her mother's death moments before his call, and when she told him, crying, what had happened, he said without a second's hesitation, "I'm coming. I'll be there." What amazed her was that she told him not to. "Why? Emily, you need someone there."

"And if you come, will you stay? I mean for good?"

"You know I can't, Emily."

Then that was exactly why, she explained, he shouldn't come. "You belong with Carlotta," she said. And she was relieved that he did not say that he loved her *and* Carlotta because she knew it, but she also knew that his love was one that was unfinished, one that needed to recede into a place where she would not be tempted to touch it.

Emily read the article carefully. The reviewer wrote that *Smoking in the Dark* was a fine portrait of post-Depression America as seen through the eyes of the character Hannah, a young widow, a singer at the crossroads of her career. "The play opens eerily, the curtain rising on the frail, darkened figure of Hannah smoking in the front yard, a recording of her own voice coming from behind her in the house. And from this moment on, Lisicky manages to make the stage sizzle, to scratch at the heart.''

"Are you going to see it?" Barbara asked, picking up another half of a bagel.

Emily put the paper down. There was a crease in the center of the paper, and she worked her fingers over it, smoothing it.

"I already know the story," she said.

Barbara licked some cream cheese from the side of her finger. "Well, that's true," she said.

Emily got up, ambled over to the sideboard to pour herself another cup of coffee. What was also true, she was thinking, was that sometimes relationships that didn't happen were *better* than those that did.

"Mom, when are we going to the beach? You said after breakfast." Lizzie came into the kitchen, dressed in her bathing suit, carrying her bucket and shovel, sunglasses pushed back on her head.

"We had a long breakfast," Barbara told her.

Fred junior came into the room just on Lizzie's heels.

"I'll say. You two have been eating all morning."

"Well, we were hungry," Emily said.

"We're going to miss the whole day, Mom. It's after ten now."

Just recently Lizzie had learned to tell time; she wasted no opportunity to inform Emily of the hour.

"All right, I'm coming. Just let me get changed and I'll meet you out front."

In her fictional version of Maine, Emily had not bothered to check the geography of Bangor, so she was disappointed to discover that the real Bangor rested on the banks of the Penobscot River. "I expected rocky beaches," she told Barbara, and Barbara explained that they'd have to drive to the coast for that. "Then let's do it," Emily said.

The Maine shoreline was more rugged than Ocean Gate's, more complex in its terrain, at some spots hilly, dune-covered, and at others smooth, the sand as cleanly white and fine as salt. Emily could not look either to her left or to her right without seeing the jetties, the extended formation of black-and-gray glistening rock that stretched seaward like strong, ominous arms. There was a high wind that day, battening the dune brush down, thrashing sand in their faces if they lay down on their blankets. They got chilly if they stayed in the water too long. Emily insisted that Lizzie put a T-shirt on over her suit; her lips were blue with cold. "Come on, we'll take a walk, kiddo."

She knew where she wanted to walk from the moment she first put her surf chair down in the sand. The slippery jetty was just a short way down the beach. She gripped Lizzie's hand tight when they started to climb it, when the sea spray, thick and white as fog, hit their faces on the ascent. She searched for the flat rocks, the safe planes on which they would not lose their balance. She wanted to get to the far end of the jetty, out to the sea, which today was the most magnificent shade of aqua.

"Okay, we can stop here," she told Lizzie when they were about three feet from the end of the jetty.

"Can we sit down?"

"Sure we can sit."

Emily did not let go of Lizzie's hand, even once they were sitting, even though Lizzie's small body was encircled by Emily's bare legs. Emily wanted to tell her daughter that in this life there weren't an allotted number of gains or losses parceled out to each person. No such thing as ten for one fellow and three for the other. She wanted her to know so she would be able to bear it that all of her sorrows had not been used up, that there would be more.

"Comfortable?" she asked Lizzie.

Lizzie nodded, pushed herself against Emily firmly, until Emily wrapped her arms around her.

But it was such an incredibly beautiful day, the sun burning strong on the surface of the water, that Emily said nothing. This child in her arms, who had been born with the gift of vision, could probably already see the imperfect future.

"Well, Liz, what do you think? What do you think of this?"

"I love it, Mom."

Emily pressed her face against Lizzie's cheek. "So do I."

ACKNOWLEDGMENTS

I would like to express my gratitude to the New Jersey Council on the Arts for its support in writing this book. Also, although the list is long, the project was long and would not have been completed without the emotional and financial support of the following people:

Thanks to my daughter, Austen Leigh, and to my husband, Bill, whose love brought sanity to the worst days. Special thanks and love to Paul Lisicky for his unflagging friendship and the countless times he listened to and read this book—in all of its incarnations. Thanks to my parents, Mary and Joseph Piccoli, for their devotion, and to Eileen and Mike DelViscio for their constant encouragement.

To everyone who read—Lisa Zeidner, David Bradley, Murl Barker, Betty Jones, Barbara Groark, and Joanne Gordin—thank you. Thanks to Jean Naggar and Barbara Grossman, who believed in the story before it was written. And to J., with my "old affection."

71 - tested new acquaintance for resilience.
Trying to find her father.

76 - 2 daughters.

79 - no one to turn to

84 - lose her when tell rest of story.

144 - what sort of qualifications.